WORTH the WEIGHT

Linda Wiges

Fallen Oak Publishing

"Wiges has an exceptional gift for writing dialogue and narrative. Worth the Weight is an amusing page turner with an ending you won't forget.
        --- Barbara Lounsberry, author,
            Becoming Virginia Woolf

ISBN-13: 978-0692385838 –Fallen Oak Publishing
ISBN-10: 0692385835

Cover Art by Andrew Bouska

DEDICATION

With much love to my first grandchild whose birth I was eagerly awaiting while I wrote the book. In a twist on the title, his arrival was *worth the wait.*

1
BEGUILED BY BEAUTY

"Come on, man! She's your mother!"

"I know, but I'm drying up, disappearing. All because of her."

"She can't help it. She's a sick woman."

"That's right. And killing her would put her out of her misery. It's my turn to live."

"But that's the trouble, man. Don't you know murder carries a life sentence? Would you be happier with that?"

"I'm already serving a life sentence with no hope of parole."

"People who weigh over five-hundred pounds have short life spans. She could go any day of natural causes. Then you'll really be free."

"My luck, she'll last until she's eighty. I'll be fifty-five by then. It'll be way too late for me and the lady from the library."

Donald Meester had been having such conversations with himself every day since he laid eyes on Amber McCall. Of course, he didn't know her name at first. But he did recognize a powerful attraction, and he knew from years of living with her that his mother would not approve. Some mothers longed to see their sons married, but not his. She knew Donald was her lifeline, and she wasn't about to let go.

Although he'd seen other women in their twenties who appealed to him in a mild way, they'd all been forgettable. It was easy to tell himself he couldn't date them because of responsibilities at home. The truth was, he may only have been using his mom as an excuse. But all that was before he was jolted to life by Amber.

Donald was starting his second week of work at the Markison Public Library. The job was one he considered an improvement over his previous position at Jackson's Mortuary. The library provided him hours that fit his personal schedule, and the building was close to his house. But it turned out he wasn't offered any more excitement or chances to make friends than he'd had at the funeral home. At least he hadn't thought so, until the Monday he spotted a mane of gorgeous red hair.

His initial impression was that the girl reading at one of the library tables had no face. Her head was bent so her features were hidden from view by her long fiery locks. Then, as if sensing his stares, she looked up. Taking hold of both sides of her shiny bangs, she pulled them away from her eyes. Her eyes. They were large and green. So green. He'd never seen a girl with green eyes. Of course, it was possible she was wearing tinted contacts, but still, they were breath-taking. And she looked straight at him. It was a quick glance, but he felt it all the way to his heart.

He noticed right away she was petite. Not skinny. He wouldn't like skinny. She definitely had curves in the right places, but you could just tell she'd never let herself get fat. Not like his mom. This girl's husband or son would never get a call at work to hurry home and help her get to the bathroom or to remake her bed because she was lying in her own waste. No, the object of his admiration was perfect as far as he could tell.

The pretty girl appeared at the library every day that week, always sitting in the same place. It was hard for Donald to get his assigned tasks done when she was around. His gaze kept finding its way to the table closest to the True Crime section. He was aware every time she turned a page or made an entry in her notebook. He would have given anything to be able to read the words penned by her graceful long fingers. Donald toyed with the idea of grabbing a dust cloth and cleaning her table, but he might get in trouble since cleaning wasn't in his job description. The thing was, he needed to keep his mind on business because he didn't want to find himself hunting for employment again. A year of his life had been used up by the last search.

He thought he'd be able to concentrate on work if he could talk to the amazing redhead just once. Finally, it happened when he was shelving returned library books. The lady had figured out he was an employee, and she asked him to direct her to the biographies. It was all he could do to answer, "The last row beside the window." His words sounded kind of croaky, because he hadn't talked to anyone all day, and it had been a very long time since he'd spoken to a person whose very appearance nearly made his throat close.

"Thanks," she'd said. Her voice was smooth and soft, an appropriate sound for a library. Another sign she was meant for him.

He'd watched her go out of sight into the stacks. Finally, she emerged carrying a book. Donald hurried to the front desk and hung around while she checked out. She didn't look at him, but he'd felt sure she wanted to. After she left, he asked his friend Charles, who'd just helped the girl, what her name was. "Oh, that's Amber. McCall. She comes here a lot. It seems like the library is her favorite spot to read." That was good news for Donald. It meant the Markison Public Library had lost its claim to being the dullest of all workplaces. Romance was in the air of the reading room.

The day Amber had asked the biography question would become known to Donald as the day of his epiphany. From that time forward, he began thinking of himself as a person, a person capable of deep feeling, a man with a future.

That evening after he helped his mother Margie get settled for the night, he went into the bathroom and took a good look in the mirror. What had Amber seen when she looked at him? Up to this point in his life, he'd never given a thought to his appearance. People were careful not to point it out, but he had the feeling he resembled his mother in some ways. Of course, he wasn't morbidly obese, but neither had she been at his age. Their faces were a lot alike, full and rosy-cheeked, but so far, Donald had only one chin. Both had light brown eyes with heavy lids and their lips looked like they were wearing lipstick, probably not a good thing for a man. Donald's arms were well developed, almost like a body builder, thanks to years of turning Margie and lifting her in and out of bed. His waistline was much less toned. To be honest, Donald had quite a spare tire for a thirty-year-old. His extra girth might have had something to do with the hot fudge sundae he had every night before bed. He knew, certainly, that it wasn't a good habit, but his mother seemed to enjoy eating with him so much he just couldn't refuse. At nine o'clock on the dot, she'd say, "Donnie, isn't it Sunday?" And Margie would giggle like it was the first time she'd ever said it.

At least Donald stopped after a single-dip, rather than the two triple-dips his mom usually had. He'd never understood how she could sleep after all that. The more he thought about Amber, the more he realized he might be required to forgo his own ice cream treats even if doing so broke his mother's heart. Girls usually like the guys with flat stomachs. He just had to watch that he didn't lose too much weight because Margie wasn't getting any smaller. Even though he was nearly six feet tall, he sometimes feared she'd fall on him, and he'd be flattened. He'd suffocate before anyone found them.

Occasionally, he considered the option of putting poison in her food. It was just a fleeting thought that didn't stick in his mind more than a second, and he always felt terrible afterward. She was completely at his mercy and totally trusted him not to give her anything harmful. It would be almost too easy. That was the trouble, and he knew it. Margie adored and depended on her son. He was her hero, so, even as he played with the idea of eliminating her from his life, he knew he never would. When he came to the part of his daydreams where'd he'd actually put a bag over her head or arsenic in her pudding, he forced his mind in a different direction. As long as Margie lived, Donald would keep on keeping on, bearing his cross, and wishing his life were different.

When Donald allowed himself to see his mother as other people did, he would get angry. It was hard to fathom how a human being could allow her body to become so disgusting. He'd been saying she weighed five hundred pounds, but he could be off by up to a hundred pounds. The last time she was weighed was five years ago when her brother got her onto a large scale at the grain elevator. She threatened to kill the next person who tried that. Her total then was five hundred forty-five pounds, but it had obviously climbed since. Unless she lost a bunch before then, Margie would go to her grave at an unknown weight. But after five hundred, the exact figures seemed irrelevant.

He usually blamed his mother for her own condition. Such morbidity was obviously pure lack of control on her part. But sometimes guilt would wiggle its way into Donald's consciousness. He understood, on an intellectual level, that he was part of the reason his mom was morbidly obese. He might even be the main reason. Every time someone asked the pointed question, "Where does she get all that food?" he had to admit it came from him. He bought the groceries, he did the cooking, and he served it. Often, he even offered encouragement by joining her at her feasts. Maybe you could say he'd already caused his mother's early death. A little poison might only be a formality.

Since Amber's first uttered word to him, she had occupied his daydreams almost constantly. A vague feeling hovered in his thoughts that he'd seen her before, or maybe a photo of her. He could account for that by reminding himself the beautiful creature had been the girl of his dreams long before she'd materialized. It was natural for him to recognize her.

After speaking with Charles, he was especially eager to see Amber McCall again. Finally, he'd be able to address her by name. They would no longer be strangers. As soon as he told her who he was, they would have taken a step toward courtship and marriage.

On Tuesday he got his big chance. He struggled to keep from running toward her when she came in the front door of the library.

Assuming she'd sit at the same table as the day before, Donald walked slowly in that direction.

"Hello, Amber!" The enthusiastic greeting left his lips as soon as she sat down. Perhaps he should have given her time to take out her book, but he'd been watching her empty chair for half a day already and had run out of patience.

The green eyes held suspicion. "How do you know my name?"

Donald saw no point in lying. "I work here, so I asked the desk clerk. You might want to know I'm Donald Meester."

"Oh. Pleased to meet you." She showed no further interest as she dug into her book bag.

Donald didn't move. He knew he wasn't supposed to chat with the visitors, but he felt his whole future might depend upon seizing this opportunity.

"We have some comfortable chairs in the other room if you'd like to be more . . . comfortable." What was he saying? He didn't really want her to go into another room.

"This is fine, thank you," she answered without looking at him.

"Great. Let me know if you need me. To find anything, I mean."

"I don't mind helping myself. I'm sure you have more important things to get done."

"No, I don't! Have more important things. I'm actually not that busy. And I know the location of any book you could possibly want."

"That's good to know." Their conversation was over, because as Amber began reading, the head librarian strolled past. Donald had to walk away. He felt pleased with himself, though. The short sentences were the most he'd ever strung together when speaking to a girl, at least to a girl he'd never met before.

The rest of the afternoon, Donald worked with one eye on what he was doing and the other on the object of his affection. He was afraid she'd leave, and he'd miss seeing her walk out. When she did gather up her purse and books, he impulsively dashed to her side. "Maybe we can go have … uh … coffee or something. Sometime."

At first Amber registered surprise and perhaps a little distaste, but then she smiled. It was almost too much for Donald. He couldn't remember the last time a pretty girl had smiled directly at him. It had to have been around first grade. "That might be nice . . . sometime," she said. And he watched her put her last book into the bag and walk out of the library, almost like she was eager to get away from him.

Donald was faced with the dilemma of what length of time qualified as *sometime*. One day? Two days? He should've just asked her to go to Starbucks that afternoon.

"You're such a weenie, Donnie."

"I know. I can't ever say what I want to. Maybe if I run, I can catch up with her!"

"You missed your chance for today. Chasing her down would be a dumb move. Girls don't like guys who seem desperate."

"You're right, but I want to talk to her some more. I'm going to go crazy until we finally get to have coffee."

"Yeah, man, but some women are worth the wait."

Donald managed to play it cool for a whole hour after Amber arrived on Wednesday. Then he figured out a reason to walk by her table. While doing so, he willed her to glance his way. A brief look from those green eyes should keep him going until the next day. But she did better than glance. She smiled. It was like she'd flipped the *on* switch. Words that had been resting on the tip of Donald's tongue for sixty minutes suddenly spilled out. "Wanna have coffee next door when I get off work tomorrow?"

"Well . . . I suppose I can. What time is that?"

"Three-thirty." As soon as the words left his mouth, he remembered Margie. He was off work at that time, but not free. Every day, without fail, he swung past McDonalds and picked up her afternoon snack, two big Macs, two super-sized orders of fries, and a giant coke. She was always waiting anxiously for him to appear with the two sacks, both of them for her. In fact, the fast-food store had gotten so they knew when to have the order ready.

What would happen if he didn't show up at home by three forty-five? That was also her bathroom time, so he would have to clean up a mess if she hadn't been able to hold it. And she might call The Pizza Joint and have them deliver a pizza or two to serve as her snack. She couldn't go to the door so they'd have to come into the house. That would make Margie uncomfortable. After all that, she might even call the police and report her son missing. The entire drama involved might not be worth a cup of coffee, even with the goddess of the library.

"Three-thirty is good. I'll get in quite a bit of reading before then," Amber replied.

Donald struggled to keep his voice down. "Great! See you tomorrow," he whispered, in spite of his internal misgivings.

2
FIRST FRAPPUCCINO

Amber was late arriving at the library on Thursday causing Donald to draw dire conclusions. *She decided I'm a psycho. Or a nerd. OR somebody told her I'm the son of the largest woman on the planet and likely going to turn out just like her.* She'd have had no way to learn his income, but the fact was that his library contract was for only fifteen thousand a year with no benefits. What girl would be attracted by that? It had been a blissful couple of days, having romantic hopes, but now he was back in the real world. Donald retreated to the storage room to do a little self-talk.

"What did you expect, man?"

"I don't know. A girlfriend, I guess. Mom always says there's someone in the world for everybody. I thought Amber was the one for me."

"No way, Donnie. You won't get anybody that special. Not unless you make big changes."

Donald was afraid to ask himself what changes he needed to make. He reluctantly went back into the stacks to face his faithful companions, boredom and disappointment.

Later, when he stepped back into the open reading area, he thought he was hallucinating. His eyes fell on Amber, reading as usual but at a different table.

"I was afraid you weren't coming." He was looking at her like she was a figment of his imagination.

"I had lunch with my . . . mom, and she did a lot of talking. Are we still on for coffee?"

Donald couldn't believe his ears. She remembered! "Yes," he said simply, trying not to reveal his eagerness. He didn't want it to be obvious he'd never taken a woman for coffee. Or tea. Or wine. And he was relieved to know she had a mom, too. A mom who ate. Would it be possible that her mom was obese like his? That was asking for too many miracles. He was satisfied that she wanted to go next door with him. He'd have to be careful not to expect too much.

He'd told Margie in the morning that he had to work late and he was sorry. He put in a DVD of *Julie and Julia*. He made sure she had a dry diaper for extra protection, then left a box of candy bars and some bottled water on her night stand. That should hold his mother until he fixed her an extra big supper. Donald's conscience was at ease when he and Amber met outside the library.

"It was nice of somebody to open a Starbucks so close by," she said cheerfully.

"Yes. It was." He had no experience at making small talk. The library didn't give him much help in that regard. People in there weren't supposed to visit, and if they did, it was in quiet tones so he couldn't learn from their conversations.

"You don't have to whisper, Donald. There aren't any noise rules out here on the street." Amber looked amused but not like she was ridiculing him.

"Sorry. Occupational hazard." He'd noticed himself doing that before. Store clerks often leaned forward to hear him better. No more. From now on he was going to speak up. He couldn't resist the impulse to shout to the next passers-by, "I'm Donald Meester, and I'm going to Starbucks with the lovely Amber McCall!" Let everybody eat their hearts out.

Amber didn't appear embarrassed. She just smiled and said, "Starbucks should pay you for the publicity."

Inside, they found a table in a corner. Fortunately, the next day was payday for Donald. By the end of the week, he usually had barely enough funds for McDonalds. His cash was easily spent satisfying his mom's appetite. But he'd been careful this week, cutting back on his own food so he'd have enough in case of a date.

Donald was grateful to see a large clock on the wall straight ahead of him. He'd be able to keep track of how close it was getting to five o'clock when he'd absolutely have to go home to his mother. He allowed Amber to order since this was his first visit to the popular coffee shop. He wouldn't remember what they had. He could've been drinking vinegar for all he tasted.

It was surprisingly effortless to talk to his new girlfriend. He'd been doing so in his imagination since he first saw her, so he already had topics and questions prepared. Sometimes he almost corrected her when she answered differently than she had in his daydreams.

Then Amber came up with a couple of questions of her own. They seemed to come right out of left field. "You aren't married are you? Or engaged?"

He had to pause before answering. Maybe they were trick questions. Why would he be having coffee alone with her if he were married? Maybe she'd been lied to once so now she was suspicious of all men.

"No. I'm single, very single." Donald had been sure it showed. "Like you." He was very observant. He'd noticed the absence of a diamond ring.

"Yes, I'm single now."

"Oh." She must have been married before. He'd never considered that possibility. He'd been sure she was as innocent and inexperienced as he was. "Do you have children?" He wasn't sure he wanted to hear the answer.

"No children. Thank goodness."

Donald was relieved on all counts. He would hate to be in love with a married woman, and he was pretty sure he wasn't ready to be a father.

"I'm actually free as a bird these days. Both men are deceased, so it's almost as if I were never married." She smiled brightly as if the dead husbands were good news.

"I guess you didn't have to tell me about them. But I'm glad you did." Unless her two marriages were very short ones, Amber must be older than she looked. That was no problem for him. Age was just a number when it came to true love.

"Yes, well, I have a feeling you and I could have a close friendship, so there can't be any secrets." She put her hand over his when she spoke. That gesture rendered him momentarily speechless.

Though her touch was beyond pleasant, her words frightened Donald. He kept secrets from everyone. He'd learned from experience that volunteering information was a bad idea. Especially information about his morbidly obese mom. Any mention of her caused people to judge him unfairly. He hadn't planned to bring up his mother to Amber until he'd already made an impression of his own. But since she was being honest with him, he felt he must do the same. He pushed away any thoughts of humiliation as he decided to open up to the beautiful creature across the table. He took a big gulp of his Frappuccino, hoping some caffeine would boost his courage.

"I told you I don't have a wife or kids." Donald looked at his cup. He couldn't make himself watch Amber's reaction. "But I do have a mother. I mean, most people have mothers … but mine is … unusual. She weighs more than five-hundred pounds and is pretty much confined to her bed. And I'm pretty much … confined to home and caring for her."

It was Amber's turn to be speechless. Finally, she replied. "I wondered why a good-looking man your age has never been married and doesn't seem to have a girlfriend. That's so sad."

He wasn't sure whether she meant sad as in too bad or sad as in pitiful and a total turnoff. "Yes. But there're people who have worse problems. I was never abused." He wanted to make that clear. Margie had doted on her only son. He'd always known he was loved.

"Donald, don't you know there are a lot of ways parents can abuse their children? Making them stay around out of obligation is one of them. It's actually one of the worst."

"Oh, she doesn't *make* me stay. I'm sure when I get married, she'll let me move to a different place." He was proud of himself for getting that into the conversation. In reality, he wasn't at all sure Margie would ever permit him to have his own house. But today, he didn't want Amber to be scared away by the prospect of moving in with him and his mother. "We just can't afford a companion for her right now, and I feel guilty about her condition."

"Guilty? Why should you feel guilty?" She was looking at him like he was deranged. He didn't like that look. He'd seen it before.

"She might have been different if I'd handled things better after my dad left us."

Amber did a double take but quickly recovered. "Oh! How long ago was that?"

"I was ten. Dad was a doctor. I don't think he even said good-bye when he went off to live with his nurse. It was too much for Mom. She turned to food. And as a kid, I just wanted her to have whatever would make her happy. When I'd find her crying, I'd go get her something sweet. I guess I never quit doing that."

"Well, you can't be blamed for having a kind heart. Don't you have any siblings or other relatives to help you?"

Donald could tell Amber was very interested in his situation. She was listening intently to his answers. No one else in his life was that enraptured by what he had to say.

"No. My uncle, her brother, used to help out, but he died a few years ago. I'm it now. Mom keeps telling me I'll be glad to be an only child when it comes time to collect her one-hundred-thousand-dollar life insurance. But I don't like to think about it."

Amber was quiet for a little while. Donald felt it was time to switch topics. No one enjoyed a date with a guy who talked only about himself.

"What do you do for a living?" he ventured. Maybe it was none of his business, but he couldn't keep from wondering how she had so much time to read at the library. Maybe her deceased husbands had willed her their fortunes. They could have left her set for life.

13

"At the moment, I'm not working anywhere. I'm on the lookout for just the right position. Something in . . . human services."

"I don't know of any of those kinds of jobs in town." He wasn't sure what human services involved, but as far as he'd found, there weren't a lot of any jobs in Markison.

"Well, I'm pretty good at sniffing them out if there are some."

"I sure don't want to do what *I'm* doing, but it's all I have time for."

"Donald, I think you're a saint, and you deserve better."

That second part was what he'd been telling himself for a long time, but it was nice to hear it from another person. He couldn't think of anything else to say on the subject. He had never been comfortable with self-pity.

Amber had an idea. "Do you think I could meet your mother sometime?"

Oh, why hadn't he filled the conversation gap with something about the weather?

"Well . . . I don't know. She almost never has company. It might scare her."

"I think I can win her over. And I won't stay long."

"Well, sure. I guess it'd be alright. Want to come over after work tomorrow?" What was that he'd just said? Again, his attraction to this girl was making him lose control of his tongue. It was too soon in their relationship for him to have to go through the stress of introducing his mother. And why would Amber insist he do so? Unless she could see Donald was the man she'd been waiting for and wanted to meet her future mother-in-law.

On the way home, Donald mentally found places to hide all the food in his mom's bedroom and decided to have her wear her pink dress. It wasn't exactly a dress but more of a hospital gown tied in back. And it made her look like a giant wad of bubblegum, but she loved it and would feel pretty. He wished the visit were over, but he knew that when it was, his budding relationship with Amber would be over as well.

3
TEA FOR THREE

Early Thursday morning, Margie still didn't know her son's new friend was coming to visit. Donald had kept the news to himself as he straightened the bedroom, vacuumed the carpet, and tucked away all signs of an overeater. His mother had been pleased with his sudden ambition, but she didn't understand it. "Donnie, you'd think the President of the United States was coming!" she exclaimed.

"You never know, Mom. It's an election year. It could happen."

"I hope not. I have to lose some weight before anybody important sees me."

"I'm *not* important. Is that what you're saying?" Donald knew Margie had been teasing, but in his heart, he questioned why she didn't care enough to make sure she would be around longer for him. Contestants on The Biggest Loser always used their loved ones for motivation.

"You know you're important to me, Donnie. Most people reject me as soon as they see me, but you'll always love me even though I'm large." Margie was just being honest.

Donald brought the commode over by the bed and helped his mother until she'd accomplished that chore. He rinsed and disinfected the bowl, put it away in the closet and washed his hands. Then he gave his mom a sponge bath and a box of breakfast bars to tide her over while he went to the kitchen to prepare her breakfast. Soon, she was contentedly munching on bacon strips and Sugar Pops, so he dared to bring up the coming visitor.

"I met this girl named Amber."

"Really? Where did you meet her?" She should know. There were very few places Donald got to go.

"At work, at the library. We talked, and I told her about you."

"Really? What kinds of things did you tell her?"

"That you're my whole family, and that you're the nicest mother in the world."

"Really? Well, that's sweet. My cereal needs more sugar, Donnie."

Donald grabbed a couple of sugar packets from her bedside table and dumped them into her bowl. "I think she's somebody you'd enjoy getting to know, so I invited her over here after work today."

"You what?" Her eyes grew very large, and she started smoothing back her hair as though it were the problem. "Donnie, tell her you changed your mind. You know I don't want to meet anybody the way I am. Why would you do that to me?"

"Trust me. You'll feel comfortable around her. I think you need somebody besides me to talk to. I'm sure she has other places to go, so she won't stay here more than a couple of minutes."

"I talk to the people at the shopping network for longer than that. But I have something to say to them."

"You could ask Amber about her family or her hobbies. That's a nice way to make conversation." He was a fine one to be giving advice on social skills, but he'd read self-improvement articles that talked about such things.

"It sounds like a waste of time." Like Margie never wasted time.

"I bet anything you'll have a great visit, and she'll love you." Donald was blowing hot air, hoping an appeal to his mother's vanity would do the trick.

Suddenly, Margie didn't think the stranger was worth the fight, especially when there were three slices of Danish waiting. "Well, okay. Only for you. I'll stand it for ten minutes." Donald relaxed. It had been easier to convince her than he'd expected. It must be a sign Amber would be a daughter-in-law his mother could tolerate.

"I suppose you've already decided what I should wear," she continued.

"Yes, I thought the pink dress would be the best. You look beautiful in that." Actually, there weren't many choices. Finding clothes to fit was impossible unless someone made them. And since his mom hadn't been out of the house in several years, Donald hadn't given her wardrobe much thought.

"If you say so. I hope it still fits." At least Margie didn't try to deny her size was increasing. She did cling to a few delusions, however. When describing her own figure at different times, Donald had heard her use the phrase *pleasantly plump*. His mom was a master of understatement.

Donny decided that if the dress was too small he would pull the bedspread up to her shoulders. "We'll get you changed and prettied up when I come home for lunch," he told her. "Maybe I'll have time to freshly braid your hair." His mother had worn a single long braid for the last ten years because it was something Donald had learned how to do. That style wasn't easily smashed by her head resting against pillows and would usually last more than one day.

"Think about what necklace you want to wear," he said in an attempt to get her personally connected to receiving a visitor. *And I'll spray some air freshener at the last minute. Lots of it.*

By early afternoon he knew preparations at his house were as complete as they were going to be. He supposed he should have been excited about introducing the two women in his life, but all he felt was apprehension. Donald hoped his date would stand him up. The get-together was sure to be a disaster. But then again, his poor mom would be sitting all afternoon in the pink dress trying not to get mussed. In spite of her protests, company was a treat for her once she'd resigned herself to it. He'd hate to see her let down. *And* he'd hate to hear her chastise him for lying to her.

Amber didn't come to the library to read. Taking advantage of her absence, Donald asked Charles at the desk what he knew about the redhead who was usually there. "I can't tell you much," Charles answered. "Just that I think she's a fanatic about crime. She reads about it here for hours and then checks out more books to take home. Not just novels, but nonfiction."

"Maybe she's studying to be a police woman or a lawyer."

"Maybe. Or maybe she just enjoys that stuff. I guess every reader has some subject they're passionate about. Hers just happens to be murder. I've wondered if she isn't planning to write a book herself."

"Maybe she is," replied Donald. "Maybe she'll be a famous mystery writer someday. Maybe she'll mention us on the acknowledgements page." But it worried him a little that she hadn't shared such an ambition when he'd asked about her work during their talk at Starbucks. She must not have thought he'd understand. Maybe that explained her interest in his obese mother. She wanted to write a murder mystery about her. He hadn't had time to do much reading. Maybe he should know Amber was a bestselling author and rich like J.K. Rowling. That could explain how she could get along without a job.

It didn't matter, he guessed, since she hadn't appeared yet. She'd probably decided that no one would want to read a book about a fat woman. He wondered if he should call his mom and tell her Amber was sick and wouldn't be coming. But just as he was reaching into his pocket for the cell phone, his favorite library patron walked in.

Donald's stomach did a little flip at the sight of her. Even though he'd just seen her the day before, he was again startled by Amber's beautiful eyes and complexion. Today she looked even more lovely than usual, because she was dressed up. A long flowing peasant skirt made her look charmingly Bohemian, and a green silky blouse complimented her coloring. Her spectacular auburn hair was pulled back in a low pony tail. He was immensely honored to know this classy lady and would be so very proud to introduce her to his mother. He wished he could call her his fiancé but knew that would be premature. He would stick with *my close friend*. That description shouldn't frighten Margie too badly.

The Meester's dark blue Ford Galaxy had seen better days. In fact, it had originally belonged to Margie's brother. Donald usually gave the vehicle no attention except to occasionally fill it with gas. However, when he opened the door for Amber to take her to his house, he fervently wished the Galaxy was a sleek, silver sports car.

When they stopped in front of his modest little dwelling, Amber pointed out hers. It was an ornate Victorian on the adjoining street, just a few yards from the Meesters' back door if a person cut across the grass. Donald was delighted but too preoccupied to comment on the happy coincidence. He was extremely nervous, wondering how the visit would go. Hopefully, Margie wouldn't mention food. Not that everybody doesn't talk about food at certain times, but she was as obsessive about that subject as Amber apparently was about crime. Margie would throw food into a conversation where it didn't have to be. The overweight woman was often judged harshly when people heard her say to a visitor she barely knew, "They say it's hot out today. I suppose you'll be stopping for ice cream on your way home." Or she might try, "Did you notice the clouds this morning? Sometimes they remind me of cotton candy. I wish we had some."

As they entered the front room, Donald called out, "Mom! We're here!"

"Good, Donnie! Did you remember my snack?" Couldn't she just forget about the fries for one day? Naturally, he hadn't stopped at McDonalds with Amber along. Didn't Margie understand he was capable of being embarrassed?

"Sorry, Mom. We didn't have time. I thought I'd make iced tea. Just a sec, Amber." He opened a drawer in a buffet in the living room and took out a bag of chips he'd stashed there for emergencies. He glanced around and was able to see the place as his girlfriend must. The room was dark and depressing. The furnishings were worn and outdated and nothing had been dusted lately. Fortunately, with the blinds drawn, that fact might be missed. The Meesters had little occasion to hang out in the front part of the house, so it didn't receive much attention on Donald's cleaning days.

Amber was looking around the room with interest. Maybe she actually liked antiques. He hoped so, because they had plenty of those, pieces that had been handed down from his great, great grandparents. Donald periodically had the urge to torch them all. He'd be happy with only vinyl and Formica which were easily cleaned. There wasn't room for nostalgia in his life.

He held his breath as they entered his mother's room. It, too, was dark. Nothing was different than usual, but he was seeing the gloom through Amber's eyes. The heavy drapes were pulled shut most of the time to keep the glare off the television. Immediately, Donald pulled the cord to open them and let in some light. He left the sheers closed to prevent the sun shining in their eyes. In spite of the spray he'd used, the air held a strong smell of urine. He desperately hoped his date didn't notice.

Donald and Amber stood at the foot of the bed where Margie was sprawled in what was meant to be a sitting position. Her pink dress looked a little silly, but Donald couldn't dwell on unimportant details.

"Mom, this is Amber, my very good friend. Amber, this is my mother, Margaret Meester." He'd always known how to make an introduction but couldn't remember ever before having the occasion to do it.

"How do you do, Mrs. Meester?" Amber asked pleasantly.

"Oh, don't call me Mrs. Meester. I'm Margie. What do you have in your hand, Donnie?"

"Just some chips for your snack. I'll get a soda to go with them." He was anxious to have that chore out of the way so they could visit. A small refrigerator on top of the dresser was full of Cokes so he grabbed one of those and popped it open. "Here you go."

"Aren't you going to offer Amber one?" Margie said in an uncharacteristic effort to be polite.

"Oh, sorry. Do you like Doritos and Coke?" he asked his guest without enthusiasm.

"No, thank you. I'm fine. I don't want to spoil my dinner," Amber said sweetly and, Donald thought, a little sarcastically.

"I can make tea. It'll only take a minute." Donald was trying to make up for his mother's offering of junk food. He started to leave for the kitchen.

"Don't go anywhere, Donnie. Why don't you kids sit down?" Margie sounded cheerful. Donald didn't hear that tone often, so he thought he'd better do as she said.

It was hard for him to see how the seating could work. The king-size hospital bed didn't leave room for much other furniture in the small bedroom. There was one oversized chair that Margie outgrew back when she was mobile. Its seat cushion sat at a strange angle because the springs were shot. Donald couldn't ask Amber to sit there. So he motioned for her to take the straight wooden chair he usually used, and he sat on the end of the bed. It was awkward but the best he could do.

"It's time for Ellen," Margie announced while crunching loudly on her Doritos.

"Forget it, Mom. It'll be a rerun anyway. We just want to talk. I want you to get to know Amber. I bet you two ladies have some interests in common." But he couldn't imagine what they'd be.

"This can't be the *we're-getting-married* conversation, can it? There's no way you can get married, Donnie. Not as long as I'm alive. I thought you knew that."

Again, Donald was humiliated. What must Amber think? "No, Mom. Nothing like that. It's just when two people are friends, they're interested in knowing the other one's family. Isn't that right, Amber?" He looked at her hopefully. Maybe she could rescue this nightmarish moment.

"That's right, Margie. Your son is such a good worker at the library and so friendly to the customers, I just had to know who'd raised him to be that way. I can see now where he gets his fine traits."

"Really?" Margie turned the color of her dress. "Well, I've done my best. And he's a good son. Except these Doritos he's given me are really stale. You're lucky you didn't take any." Still, she continued to stuff the chips into her mouth as though they were the best she'd ever had.

There it was. The food talk. How long before Donald could end this whole scene?

Amber seemed ready for his mother's comment. "You know, Margie, I like to read crime stories, and I remember one about chips that tasted funny. It turned out the woman's husband had put poison on them in order to murder her. Yours might be stale, but at least you don't have to worry about that." Amber smiled innocently like they were discussing the weather.

"Oh, my word!" Margie almost forgot to take another bite. "That sounds like a good book. Maybe you could show it to Donnie, and he could check it out for me."

"I'll be sure to do that. Now I really have to be going. Maybe we can talk longer the next time I come. It's been a pleasure, Margie." She was smooth. Donald was in awe. It seemed there was no time for tea. Amber was already standing up to leave. Nothing Donald's mother had said had seemed to ruffle her, but he noted she'd lasted less than five minutes.

"Thanks for coming." Margie had done pretty well at being civil. "Donnie, you can show her to the door, but first close the drapes and switch on Ellen. Have a good evening, Alice."

Donald sighed as he motioned for his guest to follow him. On their way through the living room, Amber stopped and looked around at the walls.

"Do you ever wonder how you'd get your mother out of here if there was a medical emergency or a fire?"

"I think about it all the time. If it were a medical emergency, we'd just have to hope there were some strong ambulance men on duty. Even then, I don't know if they'd get her through the front door. They might have to cut a hole in the side of the house. I've heard of that. In a fire it would all be up to me, at least until the firemen got here. I've been told it would be like trying to save a piano, except she'd be screaming and thrashing around. I just pray I won't have to find out."

"It all sounds so impossible," Amber said.

"I know. And I also get nervous when there're tornado warnings. We have a small basement, but there's no way I could get her down there."

"Maybe you could rig up a pulley system of some kind," Amber offered without much conviction.

Donald didn't like this discussion. People were always telling him how serious his mother's situation was, like they were informing him of something he didn't know. No one had any practical solutions. They just made him feel inadequate and scared. When he was younger, he'd dreamed of changing into Superman and being able to lift the house off of his mother to save her.

As they were getting into his car, he changed the subject. "I appreciate you coming to meet her. It means a lot to me that you were friendly and didn't act like you were horrified or something. She may seem kind of shallow and like she doesn't feel things, but she does. She can totally tell when she's being treated like a freak."

"I'm sure you're right. She must hate herself. I think most overeaters hate themselves."

Donald had never considered that. His mom always tried to pamper herself. Why would she do that if she hated Margie Meester?

"I don't see how you live there," she continued. "You're giving up your own life for that woman. I'd never do that. Not in a million."

Donald didn't respond to that statement. They rode the short distance to her house without speaking. He couldn't get over how forceful Amber's words had been. What she seemed to be telling him was, *"Not only would I not live there if she were my mother, I certainly wouldn't live there with your mother. Don't even think about marrying me and taking me home to Mamma. It will never happen."*

"Thanks again, Amber," he said when she opened the car door to get out in front of the pretty house, a pretty house to match the pretty girl.

"Good luck with your life, Donald," was her final word. At least it sounded final.

It was at times like those, when he resumed talking to himself.

"You're delusional if you think you have a future with that woman."

"Maybe. But if she doesn't like me a little, why did she bother going to meet my mother? Why would she even get in a car with me?"

"She pities you. Like an abused dog. Pat him on the head and say, 'Good boy', then leave him to his miserable existence. Plus, she was curious. She's undoubtedly heard about the fattest woman in the state. She wanted to see for herself."

"I guess I'll be able to tell how she feels about me when she comes into the library next time. I'll know the minute I see her if I still have a chance."

"Like I said, delusional."

With the visit over, Donald could reflect on the shocking fact that Amber was his neighbor. He couldn't believe he hadn't noticed her, even with the large tree that separated them. What other healthy young man would've been oblivious to a knockout like her being only a short walk away? He vowed to make up for lost time.

Margie didn't comment on the visit of Donald's friend. By the time he returned, she was concerned only about what she would have for dinner.

"Rachel Ray made beef kabobs with barbecue sauce on the grill this morning. That sounded good, Donnie. Can we have beef kabobs?"

"Sorry, Mom, but we don't have any skewers and, anyway, it would be too messy for you to eat in bed." He could just imagine trying to get the stains out and having to change the sheets an extra time. Once every two weeks was hard enough. "How did you like Amber? She's a beautiful lady, isn't she?"

"If you like red hair. I never trusted people with red hair. They always remind me of Aunt Ethel. She had such a temper. We always blamed it on her coloring."

"Well, I don't think you can judge all redheads by Ethel. Amber is actually a very nice person. Didn't you think she seemed nice?"

"She didn't stay long enough for me to tell. I'll never see her again, so it doesn't matter what I think of her. What have you planned for dinner, Donnie? I like to look forward to it."

"I don't know yet. Let's get you out of that dress." He might as well keep it clean for the next big occasion, which wouldn't come anytime soon if Margie had her way.

"You were right. Your mother is sabotaging your life. She's made up her mind that you'll never fall in love or get married. Margie may seem helpless, but she isn't. She's in control. You're just a puppet."

"She's frightened. She can't imagine how she'd survive without me. I can't either. If I could figure it out, I'd be gone tomorrow."

"You thought of a possible solution last week."

"I've put that out of my head. I can't even stand to kill a mouse."

4
PLOTTING OVER PIE

For two days, Donald watched the library door. No Amber. He told himself it was okay because she must be busy job hunting. That could easily mean she was out of town. If she found something, he'd have to act happy about it, but deep inside he'd be devastated. Even if she were to remain in Markison, she wouldn't have time to hang out at the library. Without that connection, he might never see her again. He found himself praying for just one more meeting, one more time to look at her.

By Friday afternoon, Donald was frustrated to realize the soonest he could hope to see Amber would be Monday. He couldn't imagine how he was going to survive until then. Weekends were always long for Donald, but this one was going to feel like an eternity. He played with the idea of stopping by her house. He wouldn't cut through the back way. That would make him seem like a prowler. He would go around the corner on the sidewalk and past her front porch. He'd pretend to be on a walk, and if he was lucky, she might be working in her yard. He would, of course, act surprised.

"Come on, Donnie. Are you in middle school, or what?"

"But I can't wait two more days to see her."

"Have a little willpower, man. Don't be so eager. She'll like you better if you don't follow her like a stray pup."

"Yeah. Maybe I can just call her."

"And say what? Ask her to go to a movie? Margie will throw a fit. Maybe you'd better just ease into this relationship. Let your mom get used to the idea before you start leaving her alone."

❖❖❖

Donald was still debating with himself midmorning on Saturday, when the phone on Margie's bedside table rang. He'd never given her a cell phone since he knew she'd only lay on it. As usual, she rolled toward her right and picked up.

"Meester residence. Margaret speaking." It always amazed Donald how sophisticated and businesslike she could sound when she wanted to. Then her voice dropped in disappointment. "Oh, hello, Amber. What can I do for you? Yes, I believe he's here somewhere." She shoved the receiver at her son who was standing about a foot away.

"Amber?" He couldn't believe it. She was calling him! It was a miracle!

"I'm in a cooking mood. I wonder if you'd like to come over for a meal today. Either lunch or dinner. I have something to talk to you about."

"Sure!" Oops. He'd better think this over. "Except first I'll have to take care of Mom's food . . ."

"Of course you will. You name the time. I can work it out."

"Well, how about … uh … one o'clock? We should be done here, and she should be ready for a nap."

"Perfect. I'll see you soon."

Donald's expression was euphoric as he lowered the receiver.

"Oh, my gosh. She invited me for lunch."

"Is that what they call it now-a-days?" His mother could be good at sarcasm.

"I don't know what you mean. It's just a simple meal with a lady."

"So I'm *not* a lady. Is that what you're saying?"

"I'm not saying anything like that. Just let me have a sandwich with a neighbor, okay?"

"Well, if you think you have to. I was looking forward to the two of us watching golf. But I guess I can just lay here and cheer for Jordan with no one to hear me."

"I won't be gone all afternoon. You can catch me up on what I miss." He wasn't going to fall for her poor-me act. He wanted this too much.

Donald drank tea while his mother ate a pan of macaroni and cheese and four peanut butter sandwiches. He considered those items a dry combination so he tried to give her some canned pears on the side. As usual, she wasn't interested in fruit. "That stuff isn't worth the chewing. It does nothing to fill me up!" was her usual complaint.

Donald was hungry himself, but he wanted to stay that way so he could appreciate whatever Amber fixed for him. Even if she served a lettuce salad, he knew it would taste better than anything he'd have at home.

Dressed in khakis and a blue polo, he felt he looked as good as possible when he rang her doorbell. Amber was wearing white short shorts and a tight blue tank top. Lovely as her face was, he knew he was going to have trouble keeping his eyes focused there.

"Come in, Donald. I'm just finishing up. Have a seat. Make yourself at home."

"I'd be glad to help. I cook all the time. Such as it is."

"No, you're my guest. It'll just be a minute." She disappeared then, and he was free to look around.

Donald was immediately struck by the pleasant aromas. There were food smells, appetizing ones. And a clean air scent that didn't make him want to run back outside.

The house wasn't huge, but it showed signs of recent restoration. Donald was pleasantly surprised at the interior. For years the residence had been visible through his kitchen window when the trees were bare. It had never been of any interest to him. He'd always suspected it was dark and drafty inside, and occupied by elderly people who never went out. The Victorian seemed to be just another old building that would eventually be torn down.

Though the McCall house must have dated back to the 1800's, the furnishings looked as though they'd just been purchased. In Donald's opinion, Amber was a fabulous decorator. The front room was light and inviting, so different from his own. She possessed antique objects like his mother did, but Amber's managed to look expensive and homey rather than dusty and depressing. The most modern pieces were two leather recliners facing the television.

The room as a whole looked like heaven to Donald. All its surfaces gleamed, offering the idea she'd cleaned especially for him. He felt sure his visit was important to Amber, that she wanted him to be favorably impressed and eager to return.

His eyes kept going back to the identical armchairs. That aspect of the picture was a little puzzling. Why did she need those? It looked like a couple lived in the house. The chairs could be from when she was married before. He was jealous of the man who had sat next to her. It ought to have been him. He and Amber should have been sharing couple-things like the evening paper, a big bowl of popcorn, a dog or a cat, and maybe even a child. In the short time he was left alone, Donald invented an entire married life for them.

Suddenly, the house was filled with soft music. Romantic violins. He was mesmerized. Where was the sound coming from? Were the angels playing a concert in their honor?

Amber appeared at the door of the front room. She looked very domestic yet sexy in a plaid apron that hugged all her curves. The short shorts didn't show beneath the apron, so her long, lovely legs were very noticeable. And Donald noticed.

"I hope you like the music. I thought our lunch would be more enjoyable if we have a little something to set the mood."

It had never occurred to Donald that eating required special music. Regardless of the background noise, his mother was always in the mood to eat. "It's nice," he said and meant it. Anything would taste wonderful with Amber's company and the exotic atmosphere.

Her green eyes held his for a moment, and then she announced, "Lunch is ready. Come on in the dining room." A dining room. It

29

sounded so much better than eating off a TV tray in his mother's bedroom.

"I'm coming, De…" He'd almost said *Dear*.

Slow down, Donald. You're going to blow any chance you have if you come on too strong.

Donald did his best to be mature and casual as he partook of the grilled salmon and salad Amber had prepared. The table had been carefully set as though for an evening dinner party, not an ordinary Saturday lunch. She'd even gone so far as to produce fresh flowers for a centerpiece.

The meal was very tasty, and the conversation was easy. Later, when he'd go over every minute of the visit in his mind, he'd realize he hadn't learned a single new tidbit about Amber. She, on the other hand, had found out all about him and his mother.

"Has your mom always been grossly overweight? Have you known her any other way?"

Donald thought of the woman in the picture on his bookcase. She had been only twenty-five when it was taken. He wished he could remember those days better. He knew she'd been much prettier than the mothers of his classmates in elementary school. "Yes. She had a good figure when I was little."

"Her life now seems to be a true waste. Have you thought about getting her gastric bypass surgery? It'd be expensive but would change her whole future. And yours."

"We talked about it before Uncle James passed, but Mom wouldn't even consider the idea. She's scared to death of having an operation. And I'm sure it would be really risky at her weight."

"I suppose. But just living's a risk for her. She must have all kinds of health problems."

"But she doesn't. She's healthy as a horse. It's been a few years, but the last time I had a doctor examine her, all readings were within normal range. Blood pressure, heart rate, cholesterol. There weren't any alarming side effects of all the weight. So she reminds me of that when I bring up the bypass idea."

"Hmm. Amazing. That she's so healthy. What about you, Donald? Are you healthy? I know you're in good physical shape, but inside you must be dying. What are your dreams? What would you be doing if your mother didn't need you so badly?"

That was a good question. With many answers. In the years since he'd graduated from high school, it had become his favorite pastime, imagining himself in a different life. He'd have enjoyed going into medicine like his dad, but it was too late for that. He'd considered vet school, seminary, and accounting. Any job, except an orderly in a nursing home, seemed better than playing nursemaid to someone who had no desire to improve her life. He even envied guys standing in the hot sun working street repair.

"I'm not sure, but I know I'd have gone to college or to some sort of trade school."

"You could've done that online."

"I know. I almost did, but it would've cost too much. And I was afraid I couldn't keep up with the studying as long as I had to go to work and take care of Mom at the same time. I keep telling myself I'll still do it."

"Well, I think you should. It isn't fair you have to give up your own ambitions. Maybe with a degree you could get a good paying job and hire a companion for Margie."

"That's a good idea, but when I bring it up to her, she gets really agitated. She says no one but me can take care of her. I think she's afraid nobody else would let her eat what she wants."

"It sounds like you let your mom control your dreams." Amber refilled his water. She did so with her right hand, her left arm was draped across his back, her hand resting on his shoulder. That position allowed her thick, silky hair to brush against his face. As she leaned across him, Donald could smell her intoxicating perfume. The resulting sensations made it hard for him to concentrate on what she was saying. "Have you ever wondered whether you'd be better off if she…wasn't around anymore?" She left briefly then and came right back with dessert.

Donald wasn't sure he'd heard her correctly. When she reappeared, he tried to clarify her words. "You mean if Mom were to go away for a while? Travel wouldn't work for her. We've thought about it before. There are just too many obstacles. She always says she'll go when she loses some weight."

"I'm not talking about a trip, dear. I'm referring to her going away . . . permanently."

She'd called him *dear,* but Donald could tell it wasn't an affectionate term. And he told himself he was misunderstanding the meaning of her suggestion. "You mean . . . if mom . . . were dead?" The words were almost impossible for him to utter aloud.

"That's right. Just thinking hypothetically." She was looking at him very intently. Like his face were a crystal ball.

Did she somehow know his darkest thoughts? Had his other self ratted on him? "I . . . I guess I'd be better off, but I don't want her to die." Daydreaming about it was one thing, but he didn't like talking about it with a real person. Especially not with Amber. He didn't want her to think he was some maniac. He thumped his index finger up and down on the table cloth and tried to think of a way to change the direction of the conversation. Maybe it was time to discuss her hobbies. Or the weather.

"You can be honest, Donald. Many people have had those thoughts with far less reason than you have. Sometimes it's just fun to play *what if?* Amber talked while she cut a pie into equal pieces. She might have been chatting about a new recipe. "There's no harm imagining. Nobody can read your mind. Just think, you'd be free to marry if you were on your own. Don't you ever wish you could do that, Donnie?" She sat a slice of peach pie in front of him.

Did Amber mean he'd be free to marry *her*? His heart was beating fast. This lunch was turning out to be a more momentous occasion than he'd expected. How could he eat pie? He wished she'd come right out and say what she seemed to be hinting. He looked around. Maybe he'd be able to leave his dark little house and move in here. A life of bliss suddenly seemed within reach.

"Calling Donnie! She's talking about killing your mother. Don't listen. You wouldn't want to marry a woman who'd even think of that. Even if she's just having fun with you. That's weird, man."

Donald could feel his cheeks burning. The conversation with his date had become a very personal one. He wasn't used to having those with anyone, let alone a female. "I suppose I could marry if my mother were gone. It'll happen naturally someday. I just have to be patient." It was the sad truth. He'd have to be patient until he was old and gray. No woman of child-bearing age would be interested by then.

"It isn't like Margie would have a productive, enjoyable life cut short. What would she be cheated out of? More food? More TV?"

She was trying to be patient with him, he could tell. But he picked up a hint of irritation in her voice. That frightened Donald because all he wanted from her were loving feelings and admiration. He had to admit Amber made sense. He'd thought of it all before, but she was making it sound like there was some action he should take. She must have seen he was weakening, beginning to see things her way, or she would've dropped the subject right away.

"Donald, I just want you to know that if you're serious about changing your life, I'd be willing to help. That's sort of a hobby of mine, making dreams come true. And I'm good at it. In fact, I'd take care of all the details. You wouldn't have to do a thing. Provided we could come up with a suitable financial agreement."

Donnie's hand began shaking so hard he couldn't bring the pie to his mouth. "I … uh … don't have the money. Just mother's disability and my flimsy salary from the library. I'm sorry. I really have to get back home." He abandoned the dessert and found his way to the front door. Suddenly, the walls of this previously comfortable home were closing in around Donald.

Amber caught up with him and put a hand on his arm. Gently turning him to face her, she spoke tenderly and confidentially. "Before you discard the idea completely, just think it over. I know what I'm suggesting is shocking, but the risks would be almost nonexistent, and the rewards would be fantastic."

It was then Amber did something meant to seal the deal. She kissed Donald on the lips. It wasn't a passionate act, but it was definitely a kiss, not a peck. Then, her green-eyes forcing him to return her gaze, she closed with, "We can talk about my idea in more depth when you've had a chance to mull things over. No pressure. Only if it's right for you."

"Okay," he managed to say. "Thanks for lunch." And he was out the door, walking through a fog away from the love of his life and back to his prison.

"You can't be considering her proposition. She must be criminally insane. My gosh, she could still be married. That's why she has matching recliners! She's probably trying to get your mom's insurance for her and her husband."

"But I don't know that. She could also be trying to find a way for us to be alone together. I have to give the whole thing some thought before I say no."

"You'll do that alright. You won't sleep a wink until it's settled. Not after that kiss. And how are you going to look your mom in the eye?"

It wasn't necessary to look at his mother right away. She was watching the golf tournament or rather Jordan Spieth. As soon as she heard the door, she greeted him in the usual way. "Donnie! I was afraid you were going to forget my snack! I'm starving."

He was almost relieved to hear her whiny voice, to see her messy room. It made his life feel familiar.

The least I could've done was bring her a piece of peach pie.

.

5
SINFUL SIGNING

Two o'clock in the morning was a time when most residents of Markison were safe in their beds. If Donald and Amber were married, they'd most likely be sleeping soundly, snuggled together after making love. As it was, he was sitting on his front porch swatting bugs and trying to figure out what to do about Margie. Currently, she was listening to all-night talk radio and had the volume so high Donald could barely hear himself think. He had left his room with its thin walls and come outdoors where the fresh air would clear his head.

"There's no way to make sense out of this dilemma. You can sit out here all night, and you won't know any more when it turns daylight."

"Sure I will. I can weigh the pros and cons and arrive at the best answer."

"There are too many unknowns. What is a suitable financial agreement? What kind of a killing is Amber thinking of?"

"We'll pin those things down if I agree to move forward. I understand that."

"I don't think your conscience will let you get by with a thing like this. You'll spend the rest of your life regretting it. You might even end up in a psych ward."

"You're wrong. I'd have Amber to keep me sane."

"Also, old boy, there's the matter of Hell. That's where murderers go when they die."

"You can go to Hell for your thoughts, too. Even if I don't do it, I'll be wanting to, so what's the difference?"

"It sounds to me like you've made up your mind. If you can ignore Hell, then you're hopeless."

Donald served his mother her breakfast still clad in his clothes from the evening before. He hoped she wouldn't notice.

"Goodness, Donnie, did you sleep in your clothes?"

"Yeah, Mom. I was so tired I fell asleep before I even had a chance to shower." If only that had been the truth. He felt like a sleep walker after the night of arguing with himself. At dawn, he'd actually resorted to prayer. That was useless, he realized. God wasn't likely to answer back, "Go ahead and have your mother killed." No, he was pretty much on his own with this decision, and he felt like he had to make it that day. Delay wouldn't change anything, and Amber might give up on him. She would think he was immature, wishy-washy, and therefore, not good husband material.

Bath time and toilet time were two of Donald's biggest challenges. They were lengthy and disgusting processes, but he had no choice. Forcing Margie to take care of her own personal hygiene would be asking for trouble. The bathing was a serious matter and couldn't be rushed. The large folds of skin rubbing together were prone to create sores and lesions. A person had to take special care to see that all the sweat was washed away with soap, rinsed, and powdered with a paste of corn starch. Those folds were the reason Donald sometimes had to put up with air conditioning even in the winter. Perspiration was not only smelly but dangerous to Margie's wellbeing. Donald was used to wearing a jacket in the house almost all through the year. It was a nuisance but saved him treating the sores. Sometimes he was in a hurry to get to work or was just plain tired from being awake all night. At those times, he was tempted to skip the bath, but knew he'd pay the price.

The parts of their routine producing the worst odors were, of course, the toilet parts. There was really no way Donnie could have described the messes he'd been forced to clean up. Most of the time he was able to get her to the bathroom in time. But when she'd been holding it all through the day, it was often impossible. The bed pan was hard for her to use and often resulted in a mess in the bed or on her clothes. Because of her lack of exercise, Margie was generally constipated. That condition called for laxatives, and they would produce runny, splattery stools. Due to the excessive amounts of food and drink the woman consumed, there was a lot of waste to be dealt with. Donald's hands were continuously red from all the washing, and he still felt perpetually dirty. The only blessing was that two years ago, Margie quit menstruating. That was a cleanup job he was happy to see go.

He'd endured all the work and unpleasantness for a long time and had much more to look forward to—at least he did if he ignored Amber's proposal.

The first years he took care of her, Donald would tell himself the job was no worse than caring for a newborn. However, babies were only helpless for a short time. Lately, he'd been longing for an odor-free, manageable existence, one suitable for sharing with a wife. He doubted he was going to marry a nurse's aide, the only female who might accept such conditions. He was more than certain from what he'd heard from her so far, Amber wouldn't go near a bedpan or near a man who did.

Even while he resented the things he was forced to do for his mother, he knew it couldn't be easy for her either. She must still have a little pride. She dealt with it by pretending.

"When I'm myself again, I'll be sure you have clean clothes laid out for you every day. I know it's been hard since I haven't been able to do my motherly duties." She said this as though it had been a few days since she did the washing, rather than twenty years.

Too late, Mom. I need a wife now. Not a mother.

"It's okay, Mom. I don't mind washing the clothes. And I have plenty to choose from. I just fell asleep in what I was wearing." He'd been forced not only to lie but to repeat the lie.

"Donnie, I was watching the Home Shopping Network yesterday."

"I thought you quit that habit." He'd had the credit card cancelled to prevent her obsessive buying. They had jewelry in every drawer in the house. Each time she ordered a piece, she'd be hopeful it would fit her neck, wrist, or fingers. They never did. Amber was going to inherit a lot of costly trinkets someday.

"Oh, I did quit. But I like to watch sometimes just to see what they're offering. Yesterday they were selling a double strand of pearls just like the one Danny gave me."

Danny was her late husband. Donald remembered her throwing the pearls across the front room when his dad left. Who knew where they ended up. "I haven't seen those for a long time. You didn't give them to that redhead, did you? I couldn't bear to see her wear them. It would almost be as bad as giving them to Danny's nurse!"

"No, Mom. I wouldn't do that. Aren't you going to finish those eggs?"

Donald was more impatient than usual with her accusations and with her confusion about time. He'd read where obesity increases a person's chances of getting Alzheimer's. Maybe it was happening to Margie. Yet another reason to consider stopping her decline.

❖❖❖❖

Late morning on Sunday, the day following Amber's diabolical proposal, Donald looked out the front door to see a young man approaching the house. *An odd time for a social call.* Donald opened the door a crack, prepared to send a Jehovah's Witness on his way. Those people always upset his mom and were hard to get rid of. Usually they traveled in pairs, though. Sometimes they even brought a child along. Donald recited his standard statement.

"We already have a church home so we don't need any brochures," he told the man who was smiling pleasantly and didn't appear to be carrying any pamphlets, only flowers.

"I know you do, Donald. The same church home as me." He reached out his hand and shook Donald's. "I'm Pastor Guthrie. I just started at Church of Hope, and I'm trying to make sure I meet all my parishioners. I thought maybe you and your mother might enjoy these. They were on the altar this morning." He handed over a vase of roses.

The man didn't look over thirty, so Donald was immediately uncomfortable. How was he supposed to call somebody his own age *Pastor*? Knowing Margie wasn't prepared for company, Donald gently guided the young man toward the edge of the porch away from the door. "I'm sorry we haven't been to church lately. It's hard for my mom to go anywhere, and I hate to go without her."

"I'm sorry about that. I know you'd both get encouragement from our services."

Donald wanted to ask what kind of encouragement he was offering but decided it didn't matter. His life was rapidly moving beyond any potential for spiritual help. "Thanks. We might come sometime if it works out."

"Donny!" came from inside the house. "Do we have company? Tell them I'm indisposed right now."

"It's ok, Mom. It's nobody." Donald gave the minister an apologetic look. That comment had sounded insulting. "Sorry."

Pastor Guthrie was undeterred. "We have a handicap-accessible van with a lift that would work for your mother. And we can send people to help load her on and off." Someone had obviously described Margie's weight problem to him but must have over-simplified it, leaving out her contrary temperament. To Donald it all sounded far from simple. He was afraid he was burned out, not willing to make the effort anymore. He managed to dismiss the reverend with, "We appreciate the offer. I'll call if we decide to use the van." And he turned and carried the roses inside.

Was a church van the best future he could hope for? Was his choice always to be loading and unloading Margie or staying home? Amber's plan was looking more practical than the one offered by the Church of Hope.

❖❖❖❖

For the first time, Donald dreaded seeing Amber. He knew one look at her would weaken him even further. When he was around her, it was hard to think rationally, and he wanted his decision to be an objective one, based on logic and not emotion.

When he entered the library office on Monday, he was still in a quandary. He chastised himself for being so indecisive, but what kind of a man would he be if he could make such a call easily? Perhaps he should rely on his instincts and wait to see what words came from his mouth when he was forced to tell Amber his answer.

She was later than expected, but finally arrived at the library looking cool and confident. In her stylish green skirt and white top she looked like your average respectable business woman, except more beautiful than any Donald had seen. And only he knew that her *business* wasn't average at all. She immediately went to the stacks and removed a copy of Mystery of the Tainted Chips and brought it to him. "I didn't forget. Let Margie enjoy herself." Then she handed him a manila envelope and left to sit at her usual table.

Donald took the book to the backroom and put it where he'd remember to take it home. His mom was a slow reader so she might not have enough hours left to get it read. It occurred to Donald that Amber could kill his mother with poisoned chips and the book, if found in the house at the end, might serve to implicate him.

No one was around so he made himself examine the contents of the envelope. The paper he took out was typed and looked very official. Amber was extremely organized. He was sure she'd thought of every needed detail. So confident was he in her intelligence, he saw little reason to examine the document. Having no legal experience, Donald was hardly in a position to critique Amber's words. Besides that, the part he did read made his hands shake.

40

CONTRACT

On the 6ᵗʰ day of June two thousand and fifteen, Amber Louise McCall and Donald Lee Meester enter into the following agreement:

Amber Louise McCall will provide services desired by Donald Lee Meester in regard to his mother Margaret Ann Meester. There is no deadline for the completion of said services. When services have been rendered, Amber Louise McCall will be paid a sum equal to exactly half of Margaret Meester's $100,000 life insurance policy.

No conditions may be put on the manner in which the work is completed. Amber Louise McCall and Donald Lee Meester will not speak of the matter from the signing of this contract until payment is made. Both parties are bound to this contract in spite of future changes of heart.

There were places for two signatures at the bottom of the page. Donald stared at the document. The words turned to a blur. He tried to gather his wits and assess what he was being asked to sign. He knew it would be helpful to have an attorney go over the wording, but he knew no attorneys, certainly none who'd want to be party to a contract killing.

At first glance, it seemed like a very straightforward agreement. Fair to both people. Official. Clean. It sounded like a normal transaction. He knew nothing of the law regarding the wording or handling of such a contract, but Amber seemed to be calm and well informed, as if she did this sort of thing every day. He wondered why she was in such a hurry. Shouldn't he be taking a respectable length of time before signing away his mother's life? On the other hand, such a delay would only drag out the agony.

He glanced at the door of the office where Amber stood, as exquisite as a model. She was, by far, the most perfect female he'd ever seen, except for stars on TV. "I'll sign first if you want me to," she declared without bothering to ask whether or not he was on board for this criminal agreement.

"Okay," he managed to whisper. He wasn't thinking at all. Donald was still mesmerized by the stunning green-eyed stare and her charming attitude of impatience. This was the woman who, if he played his cards right, could someday be Mrs. Donald Meester.

"But first we need another copy," she was saying. "We'll sign them both, and then you and I will each have an original."

Another example of her efficiency. He'd never have thought of double signatures. It made him feel secure, knowing she wouldn't let anything go wrong. It was like having a caring family attorney and a lover all in one fabulous package. He didn't find it at all difficult to put out of his mind the lethal intent of the contract.

Donald pointed to the library copier. Amber made one more contract to go with the first. She signed and dated both then handed them to Donald. When he hesitated, she placed the paper directly under his hand and gently placed the pen between his fingers. For a fleeting second she rested her hand on his in an intimate show of support. Just as he started to sign, an unexpected thought entered his numbed mind, "*$50,000. I'm giving her $50,000. If I did* the *deed myself, I'd have $100,000. Enough to fix up the house.* But it seemed too late to tell Amber he wouldn't hire her. At any rate, he could never do the killing himself, so it was a moot point.

Amber saw he needed another nudge. "I could ask for more of the insurance, but since you are so special to me, I don't want to leave you with nothing." She really did have feelings for him in spite of the grim nature of what they were about to do.

He also realized that if the two of them got married in the future, the whole sum would be kept in the family. That made the decision much easier. Donald finished his signatures.

"Keep yours in a secure place," she was telling him. "Maybe a lock box at the bank." She took two more sheets of paper from her tote bag. "I need a little information from you, Donald. Things about your house and your mother's habits."

That request came as a surprise. It was one thing to sign his name but another to write out facts about his mother. It seemed like an invasion of her privacy. But he supposed Amber knew it was necessary and would keep the information to herself. He glanced over the papers that looked much like the tests he'd taken in school. There were questions about the entrances to their house, even a chart for him to sketch in the furniture. There were blanks for the names of anyone who came and went from the outside. That wouldn't take long. Most disturbing were the inquiries about Margie's bedtime, favorite foods, and her medications. It was hard to understand why Amber would want to know so much about the person she was going to kill. If he were the outsider doing the deed, he'd rather know as little as possible so he wouldn't feel personally connected.

"I need to get back to work," he told her honestly. "Can I get these to you later, after my break?"

Amber looked annoyed that he wouldn't drop his work duties to write his mother's death warrant. "I suppose I can stay and read that long. But don't forget. Keep them in the envelope and give it to me when I check my books out at the circulation desk. Don't ask me any questions." She paused to stare into his eyes. "Do you understand how important it is we not appear to be acquainted?"

Donald nodded reluctantly. He wondered if it was as hard for her as for him to pretend to be strangers.

"By the way," she continued in the same business-like tone she'd been using, "I need a house key. Get one made if you have to and drop it into the mailbox by my front door. As soon as you possibly can. It could be months before I get to concentrate on Margie. I have other projects that have to take priority. But I do need to be able to get in when I find a free hour. To look around."

"Uh, I have an extra key you can have." His stomach felt uneasy as he told her that. He understood why she needed to have access to the house, but, still, handing over a key didn't seem like a smart thing to do. He felt they should discuss this part of the deal, but she'd ask him why, and he didn't have a reason. Just a feeling.

"Don't even think about keeping the money from me. If you break the contract, you'll suffer the same fate as your mother. If you tell the police about me, I will show them your signature and you'll go to jail the same as I will." She was speaking matter-of-factly, almost as though the instructions were ones she recited often. "Now I have to emphasize again that we don't talk after today. We can never be linked in the minds of any of the people of Markison. I won't even be coming into the library to read while you're working. The next time you and I connect will be after you've collected the insurance and paid me half. I'll want a cashier's check."

"But how will I know when it's going to happen?"

"You won't." Amber smiled sweetly and walked back to the reading room to sit with her back to him.

Donald felt empty, lost. The biggest event in his life, and he couldn't confide in anyone. Not even his true love. The reality of this project wasn't anything like his imagination. He'd pictured himself and Amber conferring about the killing, discussing the details, spending many hours together. Nothing like that was going to take place. It was disappointing from a romantic standpoint, but it sounded easy from a guilt perspective. As soon as he completed the nasty questionnaire, it would essentially be out of his hands. Except for the contract, which he wouldn't think about, he could go about daily living as though Margie had the same chance of passing away as everyone else. He needn't concern himself about his mother's coming demise. It was considerate of Amber to take that burden from him.

It had been during the lowest points in his life when Donald had previously harbored homicidal feelings about his mom. He had never felt very guilty about those because he convinced himself many children felt that way at certain times. The thoughts had usually come when he was especially frustrated with his situation and had nowhere else to go but to the fantasy game of *wouldn't it be nice if . . . ?*

He'd often imagined having a sibling to share the burden of Margie's care. They could've helped each other and eased the responsibility. Of course, with his luck, the brother or sister would say "I'm outta here!" and Donald would be in the same place he was now.

It wasn't long after his high school graduation when Margie became dependent on her son for her everyday existence. Since then, Donald had been aware he could eliminate her just by not helping her live. When the idea first occurred to him, he reasoned it would not be the same as murder. Even now, that method seemed a lot less evil than giving her life insurance to someone for putting her to death. One might think he had no feelings at all, but Donald wasn't your average cold-blooded mother killer. He actually loved her very much.

"You just love yourself a little bit more," his other self accused. *"Don't try to rationalize things. You aren't any better than the Menendez brothers."*

During his mid-morning break, Donald took the questionnaire with him to the lounge just off the office. Normally, he'd have a soda or a cup of coffee at this time, but doing that today would imply he was making a party out of spilling all his mother's secrets. If he'd known he'd be required to reveal so much personal information, he might not have gone through with the plan.

He glanced at the first question. *Describe Margaret's daily routine: eating times, TV watching, nap times, etc.* Answering was pretty easy. Margie's actions were very predictable. Amber could watch her for one day and figure that out for herself. Donald was reluctant, however, to offer anything that would make his mom look foolish or strange. The fact that she spent most nights watching TV and listening to talk radio made her sound frivolous. And if he told that she slept off and on all through the day, she'd sound old. So he wrote that she slept from 11:00 p.m. until 8:00 a.m. every night. What difference would it make?

Describing the people who came and went in the house was a snap. No visitors came around. It was just Margie and her son with the neighbor lady, Amelia, stopping in occasionally to be sure they were still alive. Others in the neighborhood stayed away. Donald was aware that made Margie seem like a very easy person to attack. After all, she was alone in her room for several hours a day while he was at work and throughout the night. And she had no way to defend herself.

Naming his mother's favorite foods was pretty easy, too. She liked and consumed anything edible at any hour. The trouble was that he ate pretty much the same fare, just less of it. How could Amber poison Margie's food without risking that Donald would ingest it as well? Surely, she'd never risk bringing harm to him. And she must realize that he had to stay alive to inherit the money she was wanting him to share.

Drawing the diagrams of their furniture was the most time-consuming requirement. He toyed with whether to do it wrong, put pieces in the wrong places, but remembered that Amber had been inside the house when she came to meet Margie. He was sure she was observant enough to have taken a mental photograph. The only thing he dared change was to place Margie's bed further away from the window than it actually was. He didn't want Amber realizing it would be possible to just raise the sash, reach in, and stab her victim. The mental picture that scenario brought to mind was unbearable.

He was just putting the finishing touches on the diagram when his supervisor, Sadie, came in. "You seemed deep in thought, Donald. Do you have something heavy on your mind?" She was a good person, so he knew she wasn't just being nosey.

"No, I was making out an order for some new furniture for the house. I was trying to remember some measurements I took last night. I guess my memory isn't so good. It would've helped if I'd written them down." Donald was not prone to long answers, but he felt the need to over-explain his lie. He was afraid Sadie might somehow have seen what was on those papers in front of him. Like that sweet woman would recognize the kind of questionnaire even if she'd gotten a good look.

"I do that, too— make something complicated that should've been simple."

Simple was a word that was becoming more and more foreign to Donald.

❖❖❖❖

Handing over the folder of damning facts had been a disturbing act. Especially, since Amber just shoved it into her bag like it was some trivial data, not worth any remorse. Those answers in his own handwriting made it look like Donald had actually participated in planning the murder. He almost chased Amber down before she got to her car to demand she give back the questionnaire. But he didn't.

"You've done it now, my boy—made things easy for Amber. She's hardly going to have to earn her fifty thou."

"I didn't help that much. I slipped in an answer or two that wasn't true. There were a couple of things I just couldn't bring myself to be honest about."

In commemoration of the signing, he stopped at Starbucks to buy a large caramel latte with a piece of double chocolate cake and a brownie. They were new treats for his mother. Donald was determined to make her last days or weeks as pleasant as he could. He resolved that if her life was going to be cut short, it would be twice as pleasurable as it would've been if Amber hadn't entered the picture.

Margie's eyes lit up when she saw the Starbucks sack. "Oh, Donnie! What a lovely surprise! You're such a loving son. I'm sorry I was cranky this morning about the stupid pearls. I guess I wasn't wide awake yet. I know you'd never do anything to hurt me."

Donald wished she hadn't said that.

6
REVEALING RESEARCH

Donald was able to sleep that night, simply because he hadn't had any rest since Amber's business proposal. By four o'clock, however, he was awake and sweating profusely. Memories of his nightmares were vivid. They lingered most of the morning, making him wonder how many of his sleep experiences were premonitions of events to come. He'd dreamed of Amber setting fire to the house. All was lost except for Margie. Amid the blackened, burned-out rooms, the fat woman and her king-sized hospital bed were untouched. She was eating a sundae and laughing. "Donnie, dearest, you know I'm too big to melt!"

Donald was afraid his nights—and days—were apt to be filled with just such disturbing visions until the ordeal was over. Amber must have hundreds of murder methods in her repertoire after reading so many crime novels. He knew he was going to be going over and over the possibilities up until the moment he found Margie dead. Even though he was a conspirator in the plan to eliminate her, he felt like the hunted one. It was a foregone conclusion that he was going to be looking over his shoulder, consulting fortune tellers, hearing noises. Why couldn't Amber just let him know when she was going to do it? And how. The suspense could make *his* heart stop before Margie's did.

Contrary to his answer on the questionnaire, Donald was well aware his mother didn't sleep soundly. Her size prevented her from changing positions, so, though she didn't mention it, he knew she had aches and pains. She spent many nighttime hours with the lamp on, listening to the radio or reading. It was going to be hard for Amber if she planned to attack Margie in her sleep. Besides the lie about her sleeping through the night, Donald had omitted some other facts that could've helped his fiancé (as he liked to refer to her in his thoughts). He deliberately didn't write down that Margie called for the bathroom at two o'clock every morning. He'd thought he was helping his mom by not revealing all her habits, but he may have just made it likely her attacker was going to show up while she was awake. Murder wouldn't even be necessary. His mother would die of fright.

Donald scolded himself. Amber had taken the pressure off by saying she'd do the deed. Now here he was, worrying about things he didn't have to worry about. In theory, he should be as relaxed as a baby. But then, babies don't arrange to murder their mothers.

❖❖❖❖

Donald had been walking to work since he didn't have to hit McDonalds afterward. Margie had become a Starbucks fan, and that shop was on his route. Today he went a little out of his way to go past Amber's house. As he'd been directed, he dropped his extra house key into her mailbox. He had the feeling she was watching from a window, but if she was, she stayed out of sight.

The afternoon brought no sign of Donald's love at the library either. She'd told him she wouldn't come during his shift, but he'd dared to hope. Apparently, she was serious about staying away from him.

Charles noticed her absence, too. "Wonder what happened to your cute little redhead? Hope she isn't out committing one of those crimes she reads about!" He laughed at his own joke. Donald didn't find it funny.

When leaving work for the day, he saw his reflection in the glass doors at the front of the library. Donald was surprised he recognized the man in the khaki pants and blue shirt. The image looked identical to the one he caught sight of every day at the end of his shift. How could a person sign a contract to have his mom killed and look just the same afterward? Of course, he couldn't see his eyes clearly in the reflection. They must certainly give away the dark soul lurking inside. He walked onto the street, sure passersby would notice the change, but as they did every day, the citizens of Markison ignored him. Donald concluded that a criminal mind is surprisingly easy to hide.

❖❖❖❖

Two full days passed. No Amber. Donald couldn't stand it. Between sleepless nights and uneasy days, he was becoming extremely downcast. Even his mother could sense his depression.

"You don't seem yourself, Donnie. I think giving up ice cream has been bad for you."

"No, Mom. I've just been having trouble with my boss." That was a strange excuse to come up with. His boss, Sadie Harms, was the most nurturing woman a person could work for. He'd often thought he'd have liked her for a mother.

"Well, I don't want you to be unhappy. You may have to quit that job."

"No! I mean, we got it all worked out today."

"Well, good. That calls for a celebration. Why don't you order a cake from the bakery?"

"Yeah, Mom. Good idea." Why fight it? She wasn't going to get that many more cakes.

❖❖❖❖

By Friday Donald had decided to take things in hand and go over to Amber's house. He wasn't sure what he was going to say, but he had to see her. They wouldn't have to talk about Margie. They could just chat about subjects other couples enjoyed. He would take a detour past his neighbor Amelia's peony bushes. She'd told him to help himself. Any girl would open the door to a guy with flowers.

A large white van was in the driveway, so Amber must be at home. He'd never seen her car and had pictured something smaller, but he was still learning about her. He held onto the peonies proudly as he pressed the doorbell.

An unshaven, muscular man in a sleeveless undershirt opened the door. In spite of his redneck appearance, Donald thought he saw a little facial resemblance. He told himself the man was Amber's brother. "Hello, I'm Donald Meester. I wonder if I could talk to Amber."

"Well, I'll be dammed. Ole' Donald is bringing the lady posies. Sorry. Amber isn't receiving today. Come back next year." And he let out a raucous laugh as he closed the door.

For a minute, Donald stood frozen to the spot. Then he threw the flowers off the side of the porch, went around the house and ran across the grass to his own back door.

"Uh-oh my boy. You have been had. Me thinks your lady already has a boyfriend. Or a husband. Didn't you already suspect that?"

"Not really. Deep down I didn't believe it was possible. Maybe he's just her younger brother playing tricks on her."

"He didn't look younger. I think you'd better stay away from that house. You know what she said about not being linked. Don't go back unless she invites you."

"But having her so close is killing me. I feel like I'm wasting precious nights by not being with her."

"Get over it, man. Take a hint. She's a business partner. Nothing more. At least not until that contract is fulfilled."

❖❖❖❖

That night Donald made use of his sleepless hours by doing an internet search. He wasn't clear about the exact nature of the information he was looking for, but he knew he had to find out more about his girl. He'd prefer to learn things directly from her, but since she was so modest about discussing herself, there was always People Finder. She couldn't shut him out of that route. He typed in Amber McCall. Over fifty records appeared for the United States. He was almost afraid to open any of them. He narrowed his search to *Iowa.*

Scanning the headings, he realized that even in just one state, Amber McCall was a very common name. It was funny that ever since he met her, he'd felt she was unique. One of a kind. Of course, she still could be. Of all the individuals his computer named, there could only be one woman with the amazing qualities of his Amber.

He read about Amber McCall the pet groomer, Amber McCall the makeup artist, Amber McCall the college student. All of the women sounded like exceptional people, but they didn't seem to be the lady he was searching for. He was sure he'd sense something when he read *the one*. He was disappointed he couldn't locate her on Facebook or any social websites. Those spots would've made it easier to get to know more about her personality. The only source left to try was the newspaper archives.

At 2:30 a.m. he ran across a recent article from the Chicago Tribune. *"McCall Questioned in Murder Case"*. How many people with her name are implicated in a murder? Donald read on without exhaling.

A new suspect has emerged in the murder of Emily Wooten, the bedridden woman living with her son Edwin in a Chicago suburb. From the start, Edwin Wooten has been considered a prime suspect. Authorities now have reason to believe Edwin's girlfriend, Amber McCall, may have been his killer-for-hire. She was questioned for two hours Wednesday, but no arrest has been made.

Donald was in shock. The few facts of that story bore an eerie similarity to his own situation. Alarms were going off in his head. As much as he didn't want to know any more bad news, he couldn't stop himself from going on to another item that also looked like something he needed to know. The article was eight years old.

After repeated questioning by authorities, Amber McCall, wife of the late Dr. Barry McCall, was released. Though she has been considered by many to be a person of interest in her late husband's suspicious death, police were not able to obtain evidence to further hold Ms. McCall.

"Oh, man. Oh, man. Oh, man."

"I know it sounds bad, but what kind of sweetheart am I if I believe things on the internet without even being sure it's my Amber I'm reading about?"

"You know it's her. And you shouldn't be surprised. Amber is taking your money to kill your mother. It isn't like she pretended to be Mother Theresa."

"No, but I thought Mom would be her first. That her attraction to me was making her do something out of character."

"If you still believe that, I've got a bridge I'll sell you.'

Donald was all out of responses. The internet searching had told him a lot about the lady he'd chosen as his future life partner. If the articles were to be believed, other men had thought they had the same chance with her he did. According to what police seemed to suspect, Amber was a professional, a killer for hire. Donald hadn't believed until lately such people existed outside movies and TV. As a child, did she aspire to make her living that way when she grew up? Did people go to school for training in the art of murder? He couldn't imagine how anyone would automatically know how to do it without getting caught. Maybe Amber was a natural. He'd heard of natural-born killers. The thought was too creepy for late night contemplation.

Donald had been attracted to Amber at their first meeting and thought she'd felt the same way. But if she were anything like the person described in the articles, she didn't love him any more than she had Edwin. What were the signs she had looked for that let her know Donald would make a good client? He was sure he'd never said he hated his mother. He'd never say it because it wasn't true. Maybe she saw something in his eyes when she'd been at his house getting acquainted with Margie. No, she'd seemed to make her decision the day he had lunch at her place. That was the day he'd mentioned his mom's life insurance. He thought back to the conversation he'd already replayed in his mind many times. Yes, he'd even mentioned the amount, $100,000. If only he hadn't shared that personal information with her. He wondered if Amber limited her projects to guys who could pay $50,000. Not a lot of young men were only children and in line for such a large inheritance. The more he allowed himself to wonder about Amber's true colors, the more determined he was to find out what kind of people became hired assassins. He really wasn't trying to learn bad things about her. His hope was to read that sometimes a very loving, gentle soul took a wrong path because of something bad that happened in her life. Perhaps he'd be the one to restore her goodness.

Surprisingly, there were articles to be found on the topic of personality traits of hired killers. He wondered if he were the only person in the world who was reading them. His hopes about loving souls were immediately dashed when he spotted phrases like "compartmentalizes emotions" and "detachment necessary to view a human being as a target." He was comforted by "low or non-existent violence threshold." There was also a mention of "ability to melt into the background." Blending with the background would be hard for Amber with that flaming red hair. He imagined her having a closet full of brown wigs.

One characteristic struck him as being totally on point – "Has a strong desire for material wealth." He was pretty sure after his research that Amber didn't care about helping him achieve a better life. And she had no personal connection to Margie so no reason to want her dead. She didn't even have uncontrollable homicidal urges like a serial killer. Her whole motivation was money. His mom's insurance money.

Since he was getting more world-wise by the minute, it became clear he should've researched the cost of putting a contract out on someone. He did that now. The answers he found made him feel like the sucker of the year. The average payout for such a job was estimated at around $23,000, far under the amount he was giving Amber. He hadn't even thought to question the dollars involved. To his thinking, killing a human being was such a huge thing to do for someone, no amount of money could adequately pay for the service. He'd never given any thought to his mom's death benefits so the money had never before seemed real to him. And he'd certainly had no experience with employing a hit woman.

Donald could hear the radio from the next room, but he was reasonably sure his mother was dozing by now, oblivious to the disturbing things he was learning about the woman he'd introduced as his good friend. His last thought before the sun came up was, *I gave her a key to this house.*

7
MIRACULOUS MAIL

Through the eyes of any casual observer, Saturday was dawning beautifully. A clear sky and mild temperatures followed a peaceful night. Nothing appeared amiss. But Donald knew differently. Because of his own naiveté and self-centered desires, he had made a disaster out of an otherwise tolerable existence. Nothing short of a miracle would save him from the damage he'd done to his life.

Going by what was happening to poor Edwin Wooten, Donald would eventually end up in prison. Staying away from Amber was preventing her from becoming a suspect, but why wouldn't authorities look at the son, the only person in the house with Margie? The single item of proof he would have that someone else committed the murder was the document he'd signed. If he showed that to police, he'd be proving his part in a conspiracy. His only hope was if his mother died soon of natural causes or if somehow he could stop Amber. He found himself wishing the Chicago police would hurry up and learn she was the hit woman for Mrs. Wooten. It felt wrong to hope his former love would get convicted, but he had to admit if she were in prison, he'd be able to breathe again.

Usually checking the mail was a highlight of the day although Donald rarely received anything. The usual assortment of catalogues and magazines appeared for Margie to enjoy. They would keep her entertained since her daytime shows weren't on during the weekend. Donald was surprised to see a letter addressed to him, Donald L. Meester. He was used to opening only pieces that said *Resident*.

He took the envelope into his bedroom and prepared to read it word for word. Even if it were a summons to jury duty, it was still personal mail. The possibility crossed his mind that perhaps it was someone set to blackmail him over the agreement he'd just entered into. But he quickly discarded that idea. It was too soon to expect a note that said, "*I KNOW WHAT YOU DID,*" so he read on:

Dear Mr. Meester:

My name is Lauren Hunt. I am a graduate student in Health and Physiology at the University of Iowa in Iowa City. Currently, I'm working on my master's thesis, The Role of Emotional Psychology in Weight Loss of the Morbidly Obese. In order to prove my theories, I am going to need a subject. I am intrigued by your mother's story and feel sure she and I could have a mutually beneficial arrangement. A woman in our department used to know Margaret when they were young, and she explained that Margie, as I believe she's called now, has become morbidly obese and is homebound. I hope you don't mind that I obtained your address from the Internet. Maybe I should've called first, but this way you will have a chance to consider my proposal before we talk. It is my belief, if I were allowed to work with your mom for a period of up to three months, I could change her attitude, teach her about diet, and make a difference in her quality of life.

I'm offering, free of charge, to befriend Margie, explore her habits, and initiate changes that will put her on the road to a more healthy future. From what I know of your circumstances, I'm guessing my help might be welcome. My work on your mother's behalf would free you to be away from the house more than you are presently able to be. When it works with your schedule, you and I would need to collaborate on Margie's care.

Enclosed are my references and my contact information. I will be happy to send any other documents that will help you decide whether to accept my proposition.

Thank you for your consideration. Providing you agree to the plan, the sooner I can start, the more benefit to Mrs. Meester. I've only allowed until the middle of August for the on-site phase of my experiment. I look forward to hearing from you.
Sincerely,
Lauren Hunt

Donald was sure the letter had been dropped from the sky. No one but God knew how badly he needed help. Lauren Hunt must be the name of his guardian angel. He read the contents over and over, trying to figure out if it could be a scam or a mistake. The references were from professors who made glowing remarks about their student. Of course, those letters could be forged, but they were on the letterhead of their individual departments at the University, and each invited him to call to confirm the information.

It was clear he needed to consult someone else about the arrangement Ms. Hill was proposing. Goodness knew, he'd already jumped the gun with one female promising him assistance. Ironically, he didn't want to enter into something that would ultimately endanger his mother. One saw so many shows on TV about con artists, it made a person cautious. This didn't seem like a con, though, because no money was involved.

Who should he talk to about it? Margie would throw a fit. Just the thought of being the subject of a fat study would make her as angry as a redhead. And she would hate the idea some stranger was going to take away her favorite foods. It actually did seem a cruel thing to do, but Donald knew enough to know a menu change was needed.

"Don't get too excited. This student hasn't met Margie yet. Your mom may be a bigger challenge than she's looking for."

"Right. But it still feels like hope. I need that."

"Maybe. But the final outcome for your mother is going to be the same either way. Do you want somebody to starve her and make her exercise, for nothing? She's going to be checking out any day."

Donald wondered if anybody's head ever exploded from the turmoil going on inside it. Then he wondered what Amber would think if another woman moved in. Would Lauren be in the way? Would she be in danger from Amber? If Amber had killed before, what would the death of one graduate student matter? Or . . . maybe it would be easy to frame Lauren for his mother's death. It occurred to Donald he was thinking more and more like a criminal. That wasn't who he wanted to be. More turmoil.

❖❖❖❖

The rest of the weekend was spent vacillating between inviting Lauren to start immediately and playing it safe by refusing her offer.

He knew his mom would be distressed over another woman coming into her home, which wasn't as tidy and attractive as it was years ago when she was in her prime. You'd think she'd be used to their life by now, but she held on to some remnants of her past as though they'd only recently changed. "When I lose some weight, I'll get back to my cleaning routine. I know I've let things go lately." Donald didn't take offense. He admitted he wasn't the world's best housekeeper, but he believed he was doing more than most sons did. There were only so many hours in a day.

One thing for sure, he intended to do some inquiries on Monday. There'd be no need to get his mother all excited unless he learned for sure Lauren was who she said she was and the arrangement might work out.

❖❖❖❖

During his morning break at the library, Donald phoned two of the professors Lauren had given as references. He was very ill at ease making the calls because he had no confidence when it came to speaking with such educated people. He was sure he sounded like a country bumpkin, halting and ignorant. But he managed to ask each man two questions, "Is Lauren a kind and honest person?" and "Is she qualified to handle a woman with Margaret's special needs?" Donald believed if the men were honest, those answers should tell him what he needed to know. Luckily, the professors were very enthusiastic and offered more information than he requested. Nothing he heard gave him any cause to hesitate.

Still, he felt he should run the proposal by someone. He wished his uncle were still alive. It really sucked to be Margie's only family. It was too much responsibility for someone like himself who'd already proved he had remarkably bad judgment.

When Sadie Harms in her green pant suit walked through the door of the break room, he couldn't wait to get her opinion. The woman always affected him that way. She existed in his life as a voice of sanity.

"Sadie, a lady wrote to me and said she wants to use my mother as her subject for a study about obesity. She'd come live with us for a couple of months. Do you think I should look into that idea at all? I mean, I don't want to force Mom into something she'll hate, but if it'll help somehow, it seems like –"

"Oh, hon. That woman sounds like exactly what Margie needs. And what *you* need. You can't keep living the way you do forever. Something's got to give. Maybe this is your big chance to change your lives."

"Yeah. Or maybe it's too good to be true." *There might be a catch."*

"There is, Donnie. You're the catch. You're the snag in the fishing line, the fly in the ointment, the stumbling block in the—"

"Okay, okay. I get it. But I think I'll go for Lauren Hunt's plan anyway. Maybe I'll be doing something right for once. At least until Amber puts a stop to it."

8
HESITANT HOPE

By afternoon, Donald's intentions were firm. However, the thought of calling a woman made him very nervous. *I just have to focus on her and not on myself.* No matter how tongue-tied he was asking his questions, he'd likely be able to decide if the woman was someone his mother might be able to tolerate. It was a lot to expect from a phone interview, but he was willing to give it a try. To get a little privacy, he used the landline in the library office.

"Hello." She had a nice hello. Not too forceful, not too timid.

"Hello. This is Donald Meester. You sent me a letter about working with my mother."

"Oh, yes! Thanks for calling so soon. Are you interested?" She sounded eager. She wasn't the kind of person who tried to be coy. She seemed very genuine. It would be hard to disappoint her.

"Yes, I'm interested. That's why I called. I just wanted to say that. I called your references. They were really good. Before I can accept, though, I'll have to see what my mother thinks of the idea."

"I completely understand. Just do your best. If you'd like me to be present when you tell her, I'd be happy to. Her feelings about the arrangement might depend on whether we hit it off or not."

Donald thought of Margie's unkind comments about Amber. There was almost no chance she'd like this woman any better. But there was nothing to do but find out. "I'm sure you're right, but I should prepare her a little. I'll try to do that tonight. I'll call you tomorrow to set up a time if she doesn't absolutely forbid it."

"Wonderful. And, Donald, please keep in mind you'll be doing this to help your mom. She probably won't understand that right away, so you might just have to insist."

He thought about how unsuccessful he'd always been at going against Margie's wishes. But he presumed this Lauren girl knew what she was talking about. "I'll try," he assured her.

"One other thing that might make a difference . . . I have a five-year-old son named Grady who'll have to be with me part of the time when I'm with Margie. He's a very good boy, but he isn't always quiet. If she likes children, it could help the cause, but if she doesn't, I suppose we shouldn't force it."

"Oh. I don't know what to say. I don't remember ever seeing Mom around a child. I have no idea how she'd react."

"You can use your own judgment, but I suggest I bring Grady with me when I first meet her. Who knows? She might like him better than me."

Donald, himself, found the idea of a young boy in the house to be a very intriguing one. He wouldn't know how to talk to him, but someday he hoped to be a father, so there was probably no better time to practice.

❖❖❖❖

Timing was everything when it came to dealing with Margie. When Donald was about to try talking her into something he was sure would be poorly received, his only chance was to do it after she'd eaten and had a little snooze. There was a small window of time when, if one of her favorite shows wasn't coming on, she might become engaged in meaningful conversation. If she showed signs of being restless, he'd bring out the nachos to keep her hands and mouth busy. Crunching had become the usual accompaniment to their conversations.

"Mom," he started, not really knowing how he was going to approach the subject of Lauren and Grady. "I got a pretty interesting letter today."

"Well, Donnie, any letter would be interesting to you. You never get them."

"I know. But this one will interest you, too. Do you want me to summarize it or read it word for word?" He was proud of himself for not giving her the choice of ignoring it.

"How long is this letter? I might need something to keep me hydrated. Give Mama a Coke."

Donald wished he'd thought of it before. He pulled two from her fridge before he proceeded. He read Lauren's letter in its entirety, glancing up often to gauge his mother's reaction. Her facial expression didn't change. When he finished, he waited for her to start yelling.

"I don't get it," she said calmly. "What does this woman want again?"

Donald sighed. Patience. He hoped Lauren had a lot. "She's a graduate student at the University. She's studying Health and Nutrition and needs a thesis project. She's hoping she can visit you now and then and help you . . . with your health."

"What could she do about that? I bet I'm as healthy as she is. She wants to put me on some diet, doesn't she? Lettuce and lemon water. No thanks."

"I don't think that's what she's talking about, Mom. Don't you just want to meet her? She sounded real nice on the phone. It's time you had another woman to visit with."

"You just brought me a woman last week. I must've made a bad impression because she hasn't been back. I was going to tell her how much I liked the murder mystery she found for me, but I didn't get the chance. You said *she* was nice, too. I have you for company, Donnie. You're all I need."

"It isn't the same, Mom. You need a female. Somebody who can talk about your shows and who can do your hair better than I can. Doesn't that sound fun?"

"I'm not asking for fun. That's pretty much in the past for me. Do you remember, Donnie, how much fun you and I had when you were young? I was a good mother. I took you to the swimming pool, and to a farm to go horseback riding." Margie sometimes had a better memory than Donald did. *Horseback riding? What farm?* He'd had an outstanding childhood—in her dreams.

"Yeah, Mom. You were the best. But let's settle this about Lauren. I want her to come here for just a few minutes to see if you can picture having her around more. If you don't like her, I'll send her away. No problem." He was pretty sure he wasn't using the firm approach Lauren had suggested, but he was a creature of habit. Maybe Lauren would want to make *him* her project.

The debate ended without being resolved. But Margie hadn't absolutely refused to have another visitor so Donald took that as a victory. He'd see if Lauren could come the next afternoon before his mother had time to reconsider. He felt a little guilty about deliberately not mentioning the child, but maybe Grady could plead his own case.

"What are you doing now, man? Something else crazy? Whatever happened to the nice boring library guy?"

"I don't think I even know him anymore. It seems like my life is spiraling out of control. But it's better than not having a life."

"If you bring in a kid, you're going to regret it."

"I know. But this is a good chance for Mom, and I have to give it to her if she'll let me."

"Or if she has enough time left."

In the middle of another sleepless night, Donald returned to a previous thought still nagging his subconscious. He was convinced Lauren's proposition was well worth serious consideration, maybe even some risk. After all, she was willing to help Margie without pay. But she had a son. That meant two extra lives might be in jeopardy. What if they wanted to live in the same house with Donald and his mom? Lauren hadn't mentioned such an arrangement, but she may have thought it was understood. What if Amber settled on fire as her homicidal method of choice? She would think Margie was alone in the house when she wasn't. He was going to have to write

Amber a note. Of course, she might throw it away without reading it. She'd been so emphatic about the fact they couldn't communicate with each other. Donald would have to think of some way of forcing her to read his message. Right after he made arrangements with his angel.

❖❖❖❖

"Lauren? This is Donald Meester. I'm calling to set a time for us to get together and discuss your proposal." He'd rehearsed that line in the early hours of the morning after he'd forced himself to quit stressing about her safety.

"I can't wait to meet Margie. Just tell me the day and time. Grady and I'll be there."

"How about this afternoon around four thirty?" He'd calculated he could have his mother's after-work rituals done by then and have an hour before she'd be ready to eat again. Maybe only forty-five minutes before she became restless and demanding. He'd have to watch the clock.

"Is it okay if I bring Grady with me? I haven't found child care yet."

"Uh . . . I don't mind. I can't promise anything about Mom though. She might say most anything. I never know what to expect."

"Don't worry about it. Grady's a pretty tough little guy. And I'll try to prepare him for a woman who doesn't know many children. We'll see you later!"

Donald wasn't sure if he should look forward to their arrival. Most things he attempted didn't turn out well. Why should this be different?

❖❖❖❖

"Okay, Mom. Remember, I said a lady named Lauren is coming today to meet you?"

"You told me, but I don't understand why. Do you want me to wear the pink dress?

65

Donald didn't want to put on airs for this visitor. Lauren might as well get the true picture before she signed on. His mother's dingy white gown would have to do.

"No, Mom. Amber, the lady who came before, was more of a girlfriend. Lauren is different. You don't have to impress her. But I hope you'll be civil."

"Aren't I always? You say that like I'm a little kid who doesn't know how to behave."

Margie was more perceptive than she knew.

"I'm sorry." Donald was always apologizing for something she misinterpreted. "I know you know how to behave. You just don't always want to. You need to keep in mind Lauren only wants to help."

"I don't need help. Do you?"

"Well, in a way. I could use a couple of extra hands to take care of you."

"Don't be insulting, Donnie. I realize I'm heavy."

"I'm sorry. I wasn't talking about lifting you. I need help in general. Lauren will explain."

"Well, she'd better not start in on me about how I'm too sedentary and should start exercising. That isn't going to happen."

Donald prayed Lauren wouldn't mention the word *exercise* right away. That would cause a scene. There was no doubt about it.

❖ ❖ ❖ ❖

At work, Donald kept a pad of paper close by to jot down notes as they came to him. So much depended on Lauren's getting off on the right foot with Margie. He wanted to do his part by giving her heads up on a few things.

"You'd think you were actually trying to prolong your mother's life, Donnie! Wasn't it less than two weeks ago you signed a contract to have her killed?"

"Don't remind me. But I'm hoping it will be months before Amber fulfills that contract. In the meantime, maybe Mom can have a fuller life."

"Margie's weight didn't come on overnight and it won't go away overnight. It could take a year to make any noticeable difference. Amber won't wait that long to make a move. She wants her money."

"I know. But Mom might have time to lose just enough so she can fit into some kind of casket or box. She deserves a dignified burial."

"If the poor woman only knew. She's going to be starving and suffering through exercise just so somebody can put her in the ground."

"Shut up."

❖❖❖❖

Before he left the house that morning, Donald had used the dust cloth and vacuumed the center of the front room carpet. He wasn't really trying to make an impression, but he hated to think Lauren would decide he and his mother lived like pigs.

As usual, while he was doing household chores, Donald fantasized about having his own place with a wife. Keeping things nice would be much more of a pleasure then. He pictured a perfect little cottage with lots of light, fresh flowers all over the room, and a sofa just big enough for two people to cuddle after supper. He couldn't lose sight of that dream, even though it meant his mother's demise. She'd had her chance for married bliss. It was his turn.

Now, as he awaited his guests, he looked around at the dark furniture, the worn rug and the heavy lined drapes and wondered if Lauren's little boy would think he'd come to a haunted house.

Donald had no idea what horrors Amber might have in store for them all. Hopefully, she'd choose her method for his mother carefully, making sure it was quick, painless and appeared to be a natural cause of death. He also had to hope she'd be careful not to take out any innocent bystanders. He had to admit he didn't know Amber well enough to predict her behavior. This graduate student and her son could be walking into something very hazardous. Much as he needed their assistance, he knew he should cancel the meeting.

9

ARRIVING ANGELS

Lauren gazed at the small house with the flaking white paint. The yard hadn't been mowed for a while, and there were no shrubs or flowers to be seen. The porch had narrow pillars and one very short step. It would be accessible by wheelchair if someone were pushing it. The picture was neither strongly unappealing nor inviting. Like its inhabitants, the property seemed to be getting by, but needing attention.

Before Lauren let Grady hop out of their aged Ford Tempo in front of the Meester property, she gave him last-minute instructions. "Remember, don't use the word *fat*. That word can make people feel bad, and we don't want to do that."

"Okay, Mom. I won't. But if she's fat, she might have candy for me!" Grady already had one foot out the car door.

"Well, don't ask her for any. That wouldn't be polite." Lauren could tell she was in for a challenge. Grady had the softest heart of anybody she knew, but she couldn't expect tact from a five-year-old. She had to hope Margie had a sense of humor. Lauren knew "fat and jolly" was hardly ever a reality, but she and her son might get lucky.

The front door opened before she pressed the doorbell.

"It doesn't work," said the tall man in front of her. "I'm Donald Meester. You must be Lauren Hunt." He sounded slightly mechanical and awkward, as though he'd memorized his lines.

"Yes, I'm Lauren. I'm so glad to meet you. And this is my son Grady."

Grady stuck out a small hand. Donald hesitated but finally bent down and shook it.

There was silence then, while Lauren wondered what Donald was waiting for. Surely, he didn't plan to interview her on the porch. Still, she was pleased to have a minute to take in the appearance of the man she'd talked to on the phone. Very dark eyes and hair. *I've seen a lot worse. I've **dated** a lot worse.* The man in front of her was actually quite nice looking. He was muscular and only a few pounds overweight around the middle. The trainer in her assessed him as "easily fixed". The disconcerting aspect of his looks was the fear in his eyes. Perhaps she'd find out soon what that was all about.

"Uh . . . do you want to come inside?" Apparently, he hadn't learned any dialogue past his opening sentence.

"We'd love to. We can't wait to meet your mother."

"Yes, well, uh . . . she's looking forward to meeting you also. I hope." Lauren couldn't help feeling sorry for the young man. He continued to appear unsure of himself and almost apologetic. Maybe there was more than one person in this family who could use some counseling.

The front room was obviously unused. She felt like she was walking through a museum. It was a relief to step into what must be Margie's room. Even though she'd been researching morbid obesity, Lauren found herself stifling a gasp at the first sight of Margaret Meester. Her massive body covered the entire width of the king-sized hospital bed. She was propped up with pillows and appeared to be awaiting the worst.

The bulky, wide-eyed woman actually had a pretty face. Lauren knew that was cliché, but it was the truth. For a person fifty-two years old, Margie had remarkably smooth, creamy skin, a naturally rosy mouth, dark snappy eyes, and very white teeth. Lauren tried to picture what she'd look like at a normal weight. She'd probably be a beauty.

Donald simply stood watching the scene, forgetting to make an introduction. He seemed to expect his mother to do something embarrassing.

Lauren decided to take the initiative. "How do you do, Mrs. Meester? I'm Lauren Hunt." And she offered her hand.

"Pleased to make your acquaintance," answered Margie, accepting the hand shake with little enthusiasm. "Who's the boy?"

Apparently, Donald hadn't told his mom to expect a child. "This is my son, Grady. He's five. He's been looking forward to meeting you."

Grady marched closer to Margie and held out his hand for a shake. Margie just looked at him, so he gave up and laid the hand on her quilt. He was staring at her in amazement. "You're really fat!" he announced loudly.

Lauren cringed. Grady looked at his mom with horror. As soon as the words were out, he knew he'd said a bad thing.

Margie turned pink, but only replied, "It's because of my thyroid." Lauren supposed that must have been her standard explanation. Not that she should have to explain her size, but Lauren could imagine Margie often saw the same comment she'd heard from Grady in the eyes of adults she met for the first time.

The boy had no idea what a thyroid was. "Don't feel bad. My cat was fat, too. She died."

Lauren didn't wait for Margie's response. "Anyway, I'll be looking for daycare for Grady. Maybe you can tell me who to call about that."

Margie showed her usual tact. "Are you married? I mean, does the boy have a legitimate father?"

Grady didn't know what legitimate meant, but he cheerfully piped in. "My dad was named Grady Hunt, too. He was a soldier."

Margie was paying enough attention to catch the past tense. She looked at Lauren. "Did he pass away?"

"Yes. He was killed in Afghanistan while I was pregnant with Grady. My husband never met his son."

The room was quiet. Even Margie was rendered speechless for a moment. Then she surprised everyone. "Well, if you want to bring him with you when you come, I don't mind. I haven't been around a child in a long time."

Lauren watched Donald relax. He must not have anticipated his mom's acceptance. Maybe there was a chance for this venture after all.

Everybody seemed in a good mood, so Grady dared to bring up the other forbidden topic. "I'm kinda hungry."

Before Lauren could silence him, Margie broke into a smile. "Me, too! I usually have a snack about this time of the day. Donnie, find Grady and me some candy bars."

Donald immediately left the room to fetch some food. Grady was showing Margie the cartoon station on TV. Lauren could see trouble ahead. *I'd better find daycare before Grady sabotages this whole project and learns some awful eating habits.*

It seemed the most that could be expected from the first meeting in her subject's bedroom was that everybody would like everybody and be receptive to Lauren's continued visits. After Margie and Grady had consumed candy bars, Donald showed his guests to the front door and followed them to the porch. It was a relief to get outside and away from the unpleasant odor that prevailed in the large woman's room. Lauren was sure Donald tried to keep his mom clean, but with so many folds and creases to wash, it must be an ongoing and impossible task. He was, no doubt, blessedly immune to the smell by now, but it would be surprising if many people voluntarily came to visit. She was surprised Grady hadn't commented. One of his future statements was sure to be, "You stink!"

Lauren had the feeling her host had something grave on his mind so she lingered to give him a chance to articulate what was bothering him.

"You probably aren't as interested now that you've met Mom." He must be speaking from past experience.

"Oh, I like her fine and so does Grady. Anyway, it isn't necessary for me to like her. She qualifies perfectly for my purposes." *If Donald can put up with her for thirty years, I should be able to last a couple of months.*

Donald looked at Grady and back at Lauren, then tried again. "But this house . . . it isn't a good place for a child. I'd be afraid for him."

Lauren didn't quite understand what he was trying to say, but assumed it had something to do with Margie being a bad influence on her son. "Don't worry. I won't bring Grady along that often, and I'm very strict about his eating habits. Today was an exception. There's no way I'll let him use your mom as a role model."

Grady was getting restless and running toward the car, so Donald let Lauren go. "I wish you luck finding child care and a place to stay."

"Thanks!" she called back. "I'll try to call you tomorrow."

As she drove away Lauren looked back at the forlorn figure on the porch. He'd been polite, but he must be worried she and Grady were going to invade his safe, routine existence. Donald didn't understand yet that Lauren had come to save Margie's life—and maybe even his.

10
RISKY RENTAL

Lauren's first visit with the Meesters had been successful in terms of establishing rapport but a miserable failure in terms of laying out a plan for a working relationship. It had become clear to her a couple of huge obstacles needed to be removed before she could start improving Margie's—and Donald's—lifestyles.

For sure, she had to arrange daycare for Grady so she'd have Margie's attention while she tried to assess and modify her habits. It seemed obvious the woman was taken with her son, so Lauren would need to use that attachment to enhance Margie's experience rather than allow it to be a distraction. That balance was going to be tricky.

Donald was another kind of challenge. In spite of his concern and devotion to his mother, he was obviously not helping her in the ways she needed him to. If Lauren were to make any progress, she'd have to educate that man.

❖❖❖❖

Mother and son spent the night in the one motel in town. It was barely adequate, not a place she'd want to make her home for more than one or two nights. She decided to ask the elderly desk clerk if he knew of any rental properties.

"I can't really think of any. Do you need a whole house or just a couple of rooms?"

"I can't really afford a house, and I'm only in town temporarily. An apartment or a few rooms would do. Where I won't have to sign a lease."

"Can't come up with anything off the top of my head, but I'll think on it. There're a lot of big old houses in Markison. It's just a matter of asking the right person."

Lauren thought of Donald and Margie's tiny home. It didn't seem right the town's biggest person had one of the smallest houses. But even if they'd had room for Grady and her, she didn't think she could bring herself to live there twenty-four seven. A gloom hung over those dark rooms making her anxious to seek the light of the outside. She was going to need a sanctuary between sessions.

While she was pondering her next move, a red-haired young woman, who had appeared to be waiting for someone, stepped closer. "I'm sorry to eavesdrop, but I overheard you say you need a temporary place to rent. I think I might have just the answer."

"Really? Do you own an apartment?"

"If you don't mind being in the basement. My partner and I live on McKinley Street. The downstairs is completely finished, with a fully functioning kitchen and bath. We've never rented it out before, but we've talked about it."

Lauren couldn't believe her luck. "I don't mind the basement if it has a private entrance." Having to walk through this woman's living quarters would be a definite deal breaker.

"Oh, yes. It has that. Are you looking just for yourself or for more than one person?"

"Just me and my young son. He and I could share a bedroom. It'll just be until school starts back home."

"That would be perfect. We plan to be away quite a bit this summer, and it would be great to have someone in the house. There's a tiny room a child might like. And we could lower the rent if you end up watering plants or something."

The women introduced themselves and arranged for Lauren to come to McKinley Street late that afternoon.

❖❖❖❖

Lauren immediately liked the house. It was a mid-sized Victorian with flowers lining the sidewalk to the porch. The place was exactly the type of family property she wanted to own someday. The lady named Amber was outside talking to a tall muscular fellow who must have been her partner, but she didn't introduce him. She walked away from the man and led her prospective renters around back and through the basement door. Lauren recognized the steep stairs as a possible problem. Grady was already bounding down them at a dangerous speed.

"I love it Mom!" he declared. He had a similar reaction when Amber showed them the little room she'd spoken of. "This is mine!"

It didn't take long to decide the apartment they were looking at was better than the motel, and Lauren was eager to get the housing settled. They came to an agreement on cost, and since Lauren's length of stay would be short, Amber bypassed a lease.

Exiting the basement into the back yard, she saw the place she was moving to was directly behind the Meester's. "I can't believe it. I'll only have to walk a few steps to work!"

Lauren expected Amber to share her pleasure at the discovery, but the redhead registered what looked at first like dismay. "You mean you're working for Margie and Donald Meester?" she asked. "What on earth are you doing?"

"I'm actually a volunteer hoping to teach them about nutrition. I won't be there all the time. Just in and out."

"In and out," Amber murmured to herself. "I'm surprised Margie would allow such a thing."

"Well, I'm cautiously optimistic. She might change her mind, but I think my son has won her interest." Grady was running laps around the back yard. It had been a while since he'd had any space for play.

"Amazing." After that assessment, Amber seemed finished with their conversation. She promised to have the downstairs rooms cleaned by the time her renter returned the next day. Without saying thank-you or good-bye, she hurried through her own back door.

As they walked to their car, Grady screwed his face into a sour expression. "Mom, I like the house, but not the lady."

She was surprised at that remark. "The lady" was very pretty. Lauren would have predicted her son would be smitten. She decided it was a good thing she hadn't chosen to pursue child psychology.

When they arrived at their apartment, the landlords didn't appear to be at home but had left the key in the lock of the basement door. Small town trust. Lauren had grown up on a farm and didn't remember her family ever locking their doors. But in an unfamiliar town and with Grady in the picture, she was going to be glad for the security. Lauren supposed she was lucky the woman could even find the key since they'd never rented the apartment before.

Fortunately, there were no furniture pieces to deal with because the Tempo didn't have enough space for anything large, and a five-year-old wouldn't have been able to hold up his end of the lifting. It turned out not to be necessary to seek Donald's assistance. Mother and son got a workout going up and down the twelve basement steps. An example of old-home architecture, the stairs continued to be of grave concern to Lauren. They were simply boards with nothing behind them. There were gaps between steps which a child's foot could slip into, and it would be easy for Lauren to catch her heel on the back edge of one of them. There wasn't even a railing to prevent a small person from falling over the side. She made a mental note to mention those obvious dangers to her landlady.

Lauren was grateful the rooms were furnished. The items Amber had provided weren't her style but would do for as long as they'd be there. After several years in college housing, the arrangement didn't look half bad. The couch appeared to be firm and comfortable and was, hopefully, free of dog and cat hair. An old trunk served as an end table that held a TV she hoped worked. Grady would be delighted to find it had a DVD player. The kitchen had basic utensils and dishes. There were TV trays to eat on or they could use the living room coffee table. The bathroom had the essentials, including a shower. Floors and countertops appeared clean, and the area didn't smell like a basement. She would be happier here than at Donald's house.

It was fun for Grady to personalize his small room. It contained only a twin bed and a homemade bookcase. He quickly put his toys on the shelves, most likely the only time they'd be there. His sleeping bag would be serving as bedding for a few days. The boy's main task was to use his crayons to make a sign for the door that announced it was GRADY RUM.

Lauren was pleased her son so highly approved of his new quarters, temporary as they were. Grady had been moved about a lot in his short life. This was the first time he'd had his own *rum.* Sadly, he'd have to leave it behind in only a few weeks. With any luck she'd have found a more permanent home by then, one that would last throughout her boy's school years.

11
INTERESTING INSIGHTS

Summer housing taken care of, Lauren was ready to give serious attention to the Meesters. If it'd been winter, trudging with Grady through the snowy backyards to Margie's house might have been difficult. But on a beautiful June day, it was a quick walk, even though they were both loaded down with toys. Donald had promised he could get a day off from work, and she found herself looking forward to seeing him.

"Will the fat lady have Snickers again?"

Lauren realized the question had been inevitable. "I hope not. We want to teach Margie there are better snacks."

"I think Snickers are the *best*!"

"Well, please don't tell her that. Anyway, we may not see her today. I'm just going to talk to her son Donald."

"Donald doesn't like to talk."

But Donald met them at the door and seemed determined to be a good host. He directed Lauren to sit in the one plastic chair on the porch and brought out a folding one for himself.

Grady tried to make things easy for the man who seemed to have forgotten to provide for him. "I don't sit in a chair when I'm outside." He plunked himself down on the porch floor and dug into his suitcase. Out came toy cars that were immediately accompanied by his loud sound effects.

Lauren motioned for him to hush. She was eager to get started.

Donald seemed to want to delay the interview. "What do you like to drink? We have Coke, Pepsi, lemonade, or Kool Aid."

Lauren was poised with pen and legal pad to record the session. The smallest item might be significant when she analyzing Margie's weight problem. She noted the only liquids Donald offered were sugary ones. "Water would be fine for me, thanks."

"Water? Okay. If you're sure …"

"I'm sure. Water is my favorite drink. Grady's too."

Donald seemed puzzled by such a tasteless choice but went to get it. When he returned, Lauren was trying to find a quieter activity for her son. Fortunately, she'd brought a coloring book and crayons.

"Okay, Donald – is that what you want me to call you? I notice your mom uses *Donnie.*"

"I've never liked Donnie," he said quickly. "I'd sort of like to go by Don, but no one calls me that. You can call me anything you want to."

"Don is a good name. Grady and I will use it. And your mom likes Margie instead of Margaret?"

"I guess. Dad called her Marge and later it turned into Margie."

Lauren proceeded to ask Donald about his father's years of cheating and the man's ultimate departure. Hoping it wouldn't stifle their dialogue, she continued her note-taking. She was interested in the family on a personal level, but also needed the documentation for her paper. Finally, she got around to the effects on Donald. "Do you ever see him?"

"I used to. He'd come and take me places. Mom hated that because she'd be left alone for the weekend. It made me feel guilty the whole time we were gone. Dad only lived four more years after the divorce. He was killed in a car accident."

"From what you've told me, Margie loved him a lot. How did his death affect her?"

"She's never wanted to talk about it. She wouldn't even let me go to the funeral. It was soon after that she started gaining weight. She told everybody it was her thyroid gland causing her to get big. She still says that."

"Has she ever been diagnosed as having a faulty thyroid?"

"No, but she hasn't seen a doctor in a long time."

"Why do *you* think she got heavy?"

"She always had that tendency. But when she was younger, she watched what she ate because she wanted to look nice for Dad. He was handsome, and she knew lots of women liked him. After he left her, I think she told herself he'd come back sooner or later so she kept taking care of herself. When he died, she must have decided there was no reason to diet anymore. Plus, she was really depressed. She didn't take any nerve medicine, but the worse she felt, the more she ate." Donald looked across the yard as he relived the early years with his mom. "I was just fourteen, and I didn't know how to stop her. I knew she'd be awful to live with if I hid her sweets."

Lauren suspected that speech was a very long one for Don. It might have been the first time he'd had the chance to tell his mother's story to anyone. Maybe no one had ever asked.

"And you didn't get out on your own before her weight became a serious issue?"

"No. She was getting pretty huge by the time I graduated from high school. She came to the ceremony, but that's the last place I remember her going. After that, she stayed in the house. She was too embarrassed to be seen." There was a short pause while Donald considered the situation. "For over ten years I've been her errand boy and her only friend."

"You never attended college?"

"I almost enrolled in the community college here in town, but decided it would be too hard to do that and keep up with mom's demands. She'd taken to her bed by then. I couldn't see any career in my future so there didn't seem to be much use for education."

"Did your mother forbid you to move on?"

"Uh … not in so many words, but I knew she'd probably have a breakdown if I left. Guess I sort of felt like one man in her life had deserted, so it was up to me to stand by her."

Lauren was tempted to lecture Donald. Why couldn't he have shown some backbone? Why couldn't he see he was hurting his mother more than helping her? What a sad life he'd had, just because of his dysfunctional parents and his own misplaced sense of duty. Her resolve to help this family was growing stronger. Maybe it was her destiny to give this man/boy a life.

She looked over at her son who was bent over, coloring. How was she going to explain to him that the people living here weren't the kind of adults he should look up to? These were adults to pity.

"You don't seem particularly unhappy with your life here. Lots of young men would resent being tied to their mothers for so long."

She thought she saw a flash of feeling cross his face, but Donald recovered and replied, "I just look at it as the cards I've been dealt, I guess. Mom doesn't have it easy either."

"Donnie! I need you!" came floating outside, breaking up Lauren's comfortable exchange with Donald. She hoped he wouldn't end up feeling guilty about talking to her and clam up the next time she asked a question.

"Don, just sit here a minute. If you hop up the second she calls, she'll never want to get out of that bed and do anything for herself."

"I know. But . . , she's not apt to change now. I should've made her wait a long time ago." And, like a robot, he rose from his chair and went inside.

Lauren marveled at the wisdom of his last words.

While Donald was seeing to his mother, Lauren waited patiently. She could've gone in to help, but her instincts said there was no emergency, and she wouldn't be welcome.

The floor under her seemed about to give way when she shifted her weight to look over at Grady. On closer inspection she could see the whole porch was rickety, maybe even unsafe. And a good coat of paint was needed on every surface. She was surprised Grady hadn't yet discovered the popular past time of peeling paint. It was all so loose she was almost tempted to help it along herself. The house could have been a cute one. Probably had been at one time. Today it was an example of extreme neglect. She wondered if Donald was incapable of simple maintenance work. Or maybe he wasn't able to take on a big project because it would mean time away from his mom. It would be a slow process to paint a house with your mother calling you inside every few minutes. Also, she felt sure, Don must have let the property deteriorate along with his spirits. The place had become his prison. Why would he care to make it look nice?

The sound of running footsteps on the grass drew her attention. Thinking it must be Donald, Lauren got up and looked around the end of the porch to catch sight of a man hurrying away from the Meester house. Her impression was that he'd come from the back door. It wasn't odd that someone from the neighborhood was accustomed to using the back entrance when he came over. The surprise was that it was Amber's housemate (boyfriend? husband?). He was hurrying back to the Victorian where she and Grady now lived. Had he been talking to Margie while Donald was on the porch? She almost called to the man, meaning to tell him they had friends in common. Then she realized she didn't know his name. For some reason, the seemingly unimportant incident made Lauren uneasy.

"Can we go now, Mom? I want to go home and watch Sesame Street!"

"In just a couple of minutes, honey. We want to tell Don 'bye." And she wanted to ask about the visitor. An amusing thought made her smile. *Maybe Margie is having an affair with the neighbor guy. Unlikely.*

Donald came out of the front door. His expression told her he was upset. Margie must have scolded him about having a porch conversation she couldn't hear. "I'm sorry," Donald said, "but I have to do something now. Can we finish our talk tomorrow?"

Lauren was disappointed at not getting to ask her question about the neighbor, but it was probably for the best. Whoever came and went at the Meester's was none of her business. At least not unless he was someone who would interfere with her mission.

12
NECESSARY NOTE

Margie was crying hysterically when Donald entered her room. A few minutes of talking softly seemed to calm her down. He considered using a package of cookies for comfort as he often had in the past but, after a hesitation, decided against it.

It had been necessary to get rid of Lauren and Grady before he questioned his mother about what had her in such a state. He'd hated to send his new friends away. It had been very pleasant sitting on the front porch chatting like a regular person.

"Donnie, you just can't imagine how scared I was," Margie lamented. "If you'd been here, that man couldn't have gotten in!"

"I was here, Mom. Just not in this room. I can't always be in this room with you."

"If somebody attacks me or robs us, you'll have it on your conscience."

Donald was both irritated and afraid. He was more irritated than usual by his mother's constant neediness and her tendency to blame him for any mishap. He was afraid because he knew whatever Margie had seen was the beginning of the homicide he'd set in motion.

"Slow down, Mom. No one is here now except you and me. Just tell me what you saw." Margie was shaking. Donald had never seen her do that.

"I was lying here watching the shopping network, and I dozed off. You hadn't turned on any lights, and the curtains were closed so it was kind of like night. Something woke me up so I looked to see what had made a noise, and there was a man beside my bed! It looked like he was rolling up a tape measure. I hope he hadn't been measuring *me*!"

"Are you sure it was a male? Was he man-sized?" Amber could have pulled a hood up over her head.

"Donnie, I can tell the difference between a man and a woman. And this man was big—a giant!" He always had to allow for his mom's exaggerations.

The intruder must not have been petite little Amber. But it could've been her muscle-bound friend. He'd look like a giant to Margie.

"He must've thought I was asleep because he didn't seem to be in a hurry. Maybe I should've screamed, but I couldn't make a sound!"

"You don't think he was stealing anything?" Donald knew the answer to that one. What would he steal in Margie's bedroom?

"No. If he'd have opened the drawer of my nightstand, I'd have bit his hand off. Nobody steals my jewelry. But he just took a second to look around and then crept out through the kitchen. I couldn't see if he was carrying anything. As soon as I heard the back door close, I hollered at you!"

"Well . . . that's . . . uh . . . really strange. You're sure you didn't recognize the man?"

"He was nobody I've seen before. Definitely, a stranger." Since she never went out, all the men in town were strangers to Margie—except the pizza delivery boy.

"Oh, Donnie, I could've been murdered in my bed! Or raped! Why don't you lock the doors? You have to start locking the doors!"

"Yeah, but it's daytime. It doesn't seem necessary in broad daylight."

He was going to have to tell Amber her work had to be done at night. It was the only way to be sure she didn't run into Lauren and Grady.

Margie resumed her list of reasons for being afraid so Donald interrupted, "I'll lock them, though, if it'll make you feel safer."

"It will. It's so scary not being able to run away. I just have to take anything somebody wants to do to me."

Donald saw an opportunity for an educational moment. "The thing we need to do is help you lose weight so you aren't trapped in this bed. That's why you need Lauren."

"Now don't try to trick me into going on a diet, Donnie. I'm not going to blame myself for what happened here today." She paused for thought. "You know, we ought to call the police. That man had to be a criminal of some kind. And I bet he left behind some DNA and fingerprints." Margie sometimes watched Law and Order.

His own involvement in the goings on in his mother's bedroom prevented Donald from wanting to call in law enforcement. "Nobody tried to hurt you. The police would just tell us to lock our doors."

Donald was saved more explanation when Margie remembered her stomach. "I've been so shaken from all this, I forgot my afternoon snack! How could I do that?"

"It just goes to show, Mom. When you have other things to think about, you forget to be hungry."

"Well, I hope you're not suggesting I live in fear for my life so I can get skinny."

Donald's head was thumping again. He felt the whole plan was getting beyond his control. First of all, he'd thought the agreement about the killing had been with Amber, not some male friend of hers. The fact that a man was in on it made the whole thing seem more sinister. Before, it was only Donald and his future lover trying desperately to be together. He hadn't said she could allow other people access to his house. It was becoming increasingly likely that Donald himself wasn't even safe anymore.

"We aren't out of chips are we, Donnie? There should be another bag around here somewhere. I think some of those would help my nerves."

Realizing Lauren would be unhappy with him but afraid to refuse his mom, he handed her a bag of Cheetos from a box of snacks on top of the refrigerator. That box was sure to be taken away in the near future. To Donald it seemed cruel to subject Margie to so much trauma and then turn around and deny her the only thing that could make her forget it.

"Oh, man, you are a real screw up. What are you going to do to keep those people out? They have a key. And they have to get to know the lay of the land, so to speak, before they actually commit the crime. So they'll be back."

"I'm going to have to get the locks changed. And I think that's expensive."

"If you do that, and they can't get inside, they'll only have one way to kill Margie. Set fire to the house. That would be a terrible way for her to go, trapped in an inferno. Is that what you want?"

"Of course, it isn't! I was hoping for something painless like sleeping pills."

"You should've done the job yourself."

As usual, things became clearer after Donald had the talk with himself. If he hadn't been so in love, if he hadn't been such a coward, he would've chosen a humane way to free himself from his mother and done it with compassion. Like having a beloved pet put to sleep.

This wasn't the first time the idea of death by fire had surfaced. How was he ever going to live any kind of life with the picture of a burning Margie in his head? He had to abandon any idea of changing the locks. Doing that would make Amber very angry. Chances were good she'd incinerate the house with both him and his mom inside.

His inner self had one more comment on the subject, *"Man, whatever made you think you loved a woman like Amber?"*

Donald couldn't think of an answer just then. Green eyes no longer seemed like enough.

❖❖❖❖

Donald's bedroom reflected the same lack of appeal as the rest of the house. The striped curtains he'd had as a teen hung limp and faded on the two small windows. He used to wash them occasionally, but it had been years since the last time. The only items of furniture were a small chair and a desk that held a computer and small printer, a bookcase the contents of which he had no memory, a small television that needed repair, and a single iron bed with a mattress that could be more aptly called a mat. A rag rug in the center of the floor had added coziness at one time, but when the threads started to give way, and it fell apart, Donald took it to the basement. Currently, the pine floor boards were dull and splintery. The only lights were a study lamp and a dim overhead bulb.

The mother of his childhood would never have stood for such a dreary room. She'd have been all about colorful curtains and bedspread, cashmere rug and cute little pictures on the wall. Since she hadn't seen his bedroom for years, those things hadn't even been considered.

The appearance of the room didn't really bother Donald. He was in it only during sleeping hours, and they had been rare lately. Every night had become a lengthy battle to fight off anxiety as he tried to solve unsolvable problems. Donald lay in the dark afraid to turn on a light for fear it would disturb his mother. He never closed his door all the way so he could hear her if she called to him.

Twenty-four hours had passed, and he was still wrestling with the question of how to protect Lauren and Grady. He'd promised himself he'd let Amber know of their existence, but he still hadn't figured out how to do that. Though he'd looked out the window countless times a day trying to see if she were at home, there'd never been a sign of her presence. He remembered her saying she had *other projects*. Those could be in another town, maybe another state. He refused to ponder what kind of projects she was talking about. She was able to leave town knowing her goon was busy laying the groundwork for the Meester mission. Things should be all set by the time she returned.

Since meeting Lauren, hearing her plan, and learning what kind of woman she was, Donald could see there was hope for his mother. Wonder of wonders, a Mary Poppins had landed to bring order to the lives in this house. If only she'd come a week sooner. He'd never have signed that agreement—kiss or no kiss. You'd think he'd have only to go to Amber, who was supposed to want his happiness, and tell her things had changed, that he no longer had reason to have his mother killed. But Donald couldn't forget the clause in the contract, "in spite of future changes of heart." His so-called girlfriend had anticipated his coming to his senses. The best he could do now was to make sure she harmed *only* Margie.

Donald got out of bed and went to the kitchen for the phone book. He looked up *McCall.* The town had recently stopped printing addresses in the book along with the names. There were three listings. One was A. McCall. If it were Amber, she wouldn't pick up. He knew that for sure. But he could leave a message.

There were things wrong with the message plan. Number one: A. McCall could be Andrew, or Adrian. He'd have to be lucky— and he wasn't—for the listing to be Amber. Number two: She would probably be just plain mad that he was trying to tell her what to do and wasn't following her no-contact order. And another sure outcome would be his agonizing for days over whether she actually had listened to the message. He'd end up going to her house to find out, and he could just imagine her fury if he did that.

"Donnie! Is that you in the kitchen?"

"Yeah, Mom! Just getting a glass of milk."

"You scared me. I'm too afraid to sleep. Is that your problem, too?"

"Nope. I'm not scared. The doors are locked."

"Did you double check?"

"Yeah, Mom. I double checked. Good night."

He expected this same dialogue would be going on every night. But not forever. Soon it would all stop.

"Can I have some milk?"

"Sorry, Mom. I just drained the jug. Go to sleep." He wasn't going to let her start midnight eating demands. It was the one area where he'd managed to get his way so far. There were usually candy bars and drinks within her reach, but he didn't have to fetch them.

Before he drifted into a fitful sleep, Donald wrote a note that he planned to slide under Amber's door after work the next day.

Dear Amber,   I want to let you know we have visitors in the house. A woman and her young son. They'll be here a lot for the rest of the summer. Please take care not to harm them or be seen by them. I'm sure you understand. With love, Donald.

He'd debated with himself about how to sign the note, but decided it was best to go with the feelings he'd had when they first met. The words might serve him well. How could she refuse the request of a man who declared his love for her?

13
WICKED WIDOW

Two important matters of business awaited Lauren on Friday morning. Her destination was the County Health Department on the edge of town. The people there would likely be able to give her the name of a daycare where Grady could spend his afternoons. And she hoped they could give her the name of a nurse or physician's assistant who'd be willing to go to Margie's house and give her a basic exam, including a blood test, to determine whether she actually had a thyroid problem.

Lauren needed to protect herself in case her subject had some adverse physical reaction to exertion. Her heart would need to be very strong. Also, in case the woman had a medical condition, such as the thyroid one, Lauren would want to see she got the needed medication.

The middle-aged woman who greeted her wore a tag showing her name to be Marilyn Connor. Lauren hoped Marilyn had children of her own so that she'd take the request seriously. "I'm new in town, and I'm looking for childcare for my five-year-old son. Do you know of any place that might have an opening?"

Marilyn smiled and answered without hesitation. "You're in luck. My son's daycare just lost a child. The little girl moved, and I don't believe they've filled her spot. I'll call and find out for you. Can you give me your contact information?"

Lauren was only too happy to leave her name and number. We're living on McKinley Street. In the McCall house," she added.

"Interesting. Have you met the owner?"

"Yes. Amber's her name."

"Hmm. I guess I thought she'd probably sold the place by now. She isn't back in town to stay, is she?"

"She seems to be. She's living in the main part of the house."

"Amazing. Didn't think we'd ever see her around here again." The receptionist's tone indicated her low opinion of the woman in question. Lauren was anxious to know why. Maybe she hadn't made the best choice of landladies after all.

"Did Amber leave town on a bad note?"

"You could say that. She was tried for the murder of her second husband after being a suspect in her first husband's death. People around here call Amber the Red Widow."

"Why?" Lauren hated to be slow, but she didn't understand the title. Judging from Marilyn's comments, it wasn't complimentary.

"Well, her hair is kind of distinctive. She doesn't look like a Black Widow Spider. The Red Widow is showy but just as deadly."

"She wasn't convicted of anything, was she?" Lauren asked. Surely her landlady wasn't an escaped prisoner.

"She was investigated both times, but no, she wasn't convicted. They couldn't find enough evidence to prove foul play in either case, but once the idea has been brought up, people form their opinions."

"It doesn't seem right to treat her like a murderer when all the evidence is circumstantial. If she were guilty, I doubt she'd have come near Markison again."

"You'd think. But who knows what goes on in a mind like hers. People here just assume she got away with murder at least twice, and the last one was our well-loved vet. Of course, small towns are always looking for something to talk about, and her being pretty made it all juicier. I shouldn't be worrying you. She's never killed a *woman*. That we know of."

"Well, that's a relief," Lauren said with a nervous laugh. She was already wishing the summer were over. "I'll wait to hear from you about the daycare," she said as she steered Grady from the building.

Out on the street, it dawned on her that she'd arrived with two questions for Health Services. Since one was still unasked, she'd have to go back inside. Grady was getting impatient, but she had no choice. Marilyn had left the desk, no doubt, to tell her coworkers about the woman living in the same house as the town murderess. A young nurse was getting off the phone, so Lauren spoke before the woman could walk away. "Excuse me. I need some advice. Who would I talk to about getting a physician's approval to start an exercise program?"

"Maybe I can help. Are you asking for yourself or someone else?" Lauren was trim and fit, so the nurse was probably having trouble sensing the problem.

"I'm a trainer and am about to start working with an obese woman. She hasn't seen a doctor lately, and I don't think we can get her to an office. At this point, she's practically immobile."

"You must be talking about Margie Meester."

Lauren should've expected the Health Department to know which obese woman she'd been referring to. There couldn't be that many people in Markison too heavy to leave the house.

"Yes, I'm going to work with her to see if I can help her lose some weight."

"Good luck. I don't mean to be disrespectful, but I've heard she's a pretty bull-headed woman. I understand a couple of our nurses offered to work with her about five years ago, and she threw them out on their ears. Maybe she'll like you better."

"We'll see, I guess. I'm wondering if you know of a physician in town who would cooperate by signing a permission slip for Margie."

"Actually, I'm sure I can help. I do home nursing care. I can give a basic exam and draw some blood. Then I can take it to Dr. Anderson. Unless a problem shows up, he'll probably sign off without seeing Margie. He's known of her for years, and I'm sure he'll want to encourage her. He might even be willing to stop by her house if you're sure she doesn't own a gun."

"I can't guarantee anything. So far, she hasn't personally given me permission to help. I'll have to get back to you." Lauren had to be careful not to charge ahead without having Margie on board.

"Okay. I hope to hear from you. My name's Kerry. Why don't you leave your name and number just in case?"

Lauren wrote her information on the nurse's pad, careful not to include her address. She didn't feel up to hearing again how dangerous her landlady was.

"Is Margie sick?" Grady asked after trying to make sense of the conversation he'd just heard.

"I don't think so. Sometimes it's hard for very big people to do exercises, so we can only let her if a doctor says it's okay."

"I can help her, can't I? I could move her arms up and down. That's how I do jumping jacks!"

His mother had taught Grady that callisthenic two years ago. She believed it's never too soon to begin exercising.

"You never know. Maybe you can be my assistant coach."

Grady had high hopes. "I'll help her run laps around the yard!"

"Good luck with that," Lauren laughed. She knew the chances for success with Margie were slim. It was going to take a village to persuade Donald's mother to get active.

❖❖❖❖

By a fluke of timing, Lauren drove into the driveway of their new apartment right behind the landlady. After the creepy things she'd learned that afternoon, Lauren was not eager to face the woman. She'd hoped their connection would be one from afar, a check in the mailbox from Lauren, absence from Amber. That was apparently too much to hope for.

"Hello there." Lauren decided it couldn't hurt to be civil. The Red Widow hadn't yet threatened her or her boy. The poor woman could be the victim of small-town gossips who didn't have enough real excitement to talk about.

"Hello," the landlady responded sullenly. She was hurrying to get her bags out of the car so she could escape conversation.

"I think Grady and I are going to be really comfortable in your basement. You'll have to tell me if the TV gets too loud or anything."

Amber looked Lauren in the eyes but didn't honor her with a smile. "It won't. I'm not home much."

"We won't be either. We'll be at the Meester's most of the time. Do you know Margie?"

"I met her once," Amber answered crisply. And with that, she and her packages disappeared into the house.

It hadn't been the warmest of exchanges, but it hadn't been totally hostile. Amber had made it clear she wasn't interested in playing neighbors with anybody, but that was okay. She didn't seem like the type of person Lauren would want for a friend anyway.

Grady was helping unload the groceries. Again, he'd been unimpressed by the pretty redhead. "She's growly. And she doesn't like little boys."

Lauren took the jug of milk from him and walked to their entrance. "I don't know how you can tell that. It's only the second time you've been near her."

Grady regarded his mother with long-suffering patience. "She won't look at me. She doesn't want me to live here."

"I think you're reading too much into her face. She's probably just had a busy day and is too tired to chit chat. I feel like that sometimes."

"I bet she's *always* like that. Her eyes don't smile at me like Margie's do."

Grady had a point. The green eyes were startling and lovely, but not the least bit friendly. It could have been Lauren's imagination that the widow's glare held a threat.

14

MARGIE MANAGES

The note to Amber resided in Donald's pocket all day at work. Periodically, he'd take it out to read and revise. After several tries, he finally recopied the final version just before his shift was over. He'd held out hope all day that Amber would reappear to do her research. He'd have either slid the note across her table or found a way to talk to her. Her books had to come due eventually, but the library stayed open until 7:00 p.m., so he knew she'd wait until he'd gone home to make her returns. If she were even in town.

Donald decided to walk over to Amber's and leave his message under her back door. It would be easy to scurry home from there. He should be able to do his errand in broad daylight without being seen. If he went over after dark, his mom would have a million questions.

Like most old houses, this one had cracks around the openings. Delivering his note was a cinch. He shoved it into the gap beneath the screen, out of sight. As he turned to go home, the basement door opened. Donald's heart stopped. His instincts told him he was in big trouble if he ran into Amber at that moment. He received an even bigger scare when the person who stepped onto the lawn was Lauren. Both of them uttered startled yelps.

Lauren recovered first. "I'm surprised to see you here, Don. I don't remember telling you where we're living." Then the truth seemed to dawn on her. "You didn't know we were here, did you?"

"Uh . . . no. I had no idea. I still don't get it. Do you know Amber?" How awkward could things get?

"We just met her Friday. At the motel. She told me she had a room for rent. Pretty convenient, huh?"

They had to get away from Amber's house. It wasn't possible for Donald to carry on a conversation in her back yard. He wasn't sure what he anticipated happening, but he knew it wouldn't be good. "Do you and Grady want to go for a walk?" It was a beautiful summer evening, and walking with a pretty woman and her child would mimic Donald's daydreams—almost. In his dreams, he was smiling.

"Love to," Lauren responded. "We were just starting to do that. Grady's getting Dino the Dinosaur. He'll want to go with us."

As if on cue, Grady popped out of the door with a large stuffed animal under his arm. "Hi!" he greeted them. "Dino wants to walk ten miles!"

"Well, your mother doesn't want to go that far. Which way, Don?"

He pointed to the right, the direction of the town park. They walked in silence for a few minutes while Donald struggled with his inner voice.

"What exactly are you going to tell Lauren? It seems like she and Grady have found the perfect place to stay."

"Yes, but what if she and Amber talk? What if Amber tells her the plan? I don't think she'd do that but, even worse, what if Amber decides to get rid of Lauren? She'll only have to walk downstairs to get it done."

"Oh, man. You're a worry wart. What if we get attacked by giant turtles? What if the world ends tonight?"

"That'd be good. Then I'd never have to know what happens."

Grady walked ahead, softly talking to his stuffed pal. It sounded like he was giving the dinosaur a guided tour. Listening to the innocent chatter of the small, blonde boy, Donald felt like the most despicable of people.

Lauren didn't appear to be thinking badly of him—yet "I'm sorry I went ahead and arranged to rent an apartment without consulting you. I could've used your advice, but I was in such a hurry. The motel was pretty expensive and didn't seem very clean."

"But you're in a basement. It must be dark and damp." Donald was thinking it would be like his own, the place he referred to as *the dungeon* in his thoughts. He agreed with Lauren that she shouldn't have jumped the gun.

"It's really pretty comfortable. And it's furnished, and close to your house, and Grady has his own room."

How could Donald argue? He could see why the new digs would appeal to her.

"Do you know Amber pretty well? I mean, you were going into her house when I came outside."

Donald had been wondering how to explain that. "I only know her to say hi. She invited us to a neighborhood picnic, and Mom wanted me to tell her we can't come because we have something else scheduled. I'm sure we won't be missed." As always, Donald used the most words when he was lying.

"Amber doesn't seem like she'd be that friendly a neighbor." Lauren was very perceptive.

"She usually isn't. I hope she'll be nice to you and Grady though. And that you'll like the apartment." If it was anything like the upper part of the house, it should be great. Maybe Lauren and her son would get the benefit of the piped-in music.

Lauren's face clouded. "The apartment will be fine. But today I learned something that has me worried."

Donald couldn't even respond. Many things had *him* worried. He held his breath. There might be an additional something to be worried about that he hadn't even considered.

"We were at the County Health Department, and I told the receptionist where we're living. She seemed pretty appalled and told me Amber is known as the Red Widow around Markison. Did you know that?"

97

"No." Donald had always known he was ignorant about what was going on in town, but never more than now. "What does that name mean?"

"She's as dangerous as a poisonous spider who kills its mate. Amber is lethal. Or at least folks in town think she is. She was a suspect in the death of her first husband and stood trial for the murder of her second one. They couldn't prove anything either time, but most people think she's guilty of causing both deaths."

Donald's headache was blurring his vision. The woman he'd loved was a killer. And a con artist, apparently. He had to be the most naive person in Markison.

"You're more gullible than that five-year-old in front of you."

"Love does that to you."

"If you really loved Amber, you'd have faith in her. She wasn't found guilty. Why do you have to believe the worst?"

Suddenly, Donald was ashamed of himself. He'd turned on Amber so easily. Was it because he'd always suspected deep down something was fishy about the dead husbands she was so eager to forget? Lauren was looking at him for some wise words. All he could say was the same thing he was telling himself, "Maybe people are just jealous of Amber because she's pretty and kinda rich. They may like to think something's wrong with her."

Lauren looked doubtful.

Grady temporarily stopped the scary speculations. "It's a park! Can we play on the merry-go-round? Please, Mom, please!"

Lauren didn't say no. Her boy had been very patient with his two dreary companions. For several minutes the little group took a break from stress. Don and Lauren took turns pushing Grady and Dino on the merry-go-round. Then they each made a couple of trips down the slide. The monkey bars were the boy's favorite. His daycare activities had left him with plenty of leftover energy. When he climbed to the top of the bars, Grady could see the city swimming pool over a rise just a few yards away. The three had no suits with them, so in spite of the boy's pleas, they could only watch. Lauren promised her son they'd come back soon when they could go in the water.

Donald lived just three blocks from all this recreation, but he hadn't been near the park since he was in elementary school. Some things just weren't appealing when you were by yourself.

"We're having fun, aren't we, Don?" Grady called from the bench of a picnic table where he stood to look over the fence at the pool.

"Get down, honey. We need to go back and fix some supper." Lauren called.

Donald looked stricken. "I forgot about Mom! She'll be starving. She's alone and wondering what happened to me!"

"I'm sure she's fine. It's only five o'clock. And being hungry for a few minutes isn't going to hurt her."

"She really hates that. I've got to go. Will you forgive me if I run home now?"

"Of course." But Lauren didn't look happy. He'd have to deal with that later.

Residents of McKinley Street must have wondered if Donald Meester's house was on fire. He ran so fast, he didn't even glance toward Amber's place on his way past it.

❖❖❖❖

Donald wasn't sure what he feared, but he was shaking when he opened the back door. Sounds from Margie's TV blared through the house, as usual. He peeked into her bedroom. There she lay, looking abandoned. The give-away that this wasn't just any day was her facial expression. Instead, of the usual delight at his arrival, she was glaring at her son. Donald noticed her flesh was dotted with perspiration.

"If looks could kill, you'd be a goner."

"I deserve it. I forgot all about her."

"Imagine what it'll be like not to have to hurry home. You'll be able to eat out if you want, ask a girl to dinner if you want."

"Shut up. That doesn't help me get through this evening."

Usually, Donald had to make himself heard over the loud television noise. This afternoon Margie turned off her show for dramatic effect.

"Well! I'm wondering what you have to say for yourself. It had better be a good excuse. Did you forget you have a mother depending on you?"

"No, I just had some things to take care of. I'm sorry. They took longer than I expected."

"I have a phone, Donnie. It didn't ring. I kept thinking you'd call and tell me when you were coming. I could've had a stroke from the worry!"

He didn't feel like commenting on her exaggerations, so he changed the subject. "I suppose you're hungry."

"I'm starving! I hope you have something substantial in the fridge. My nerves won't quiet down until I have some real food." Then came the accusing tone. "*You* probably ate already."

Donald hadn't eaten. The way his stomach felt, he'd never eat again. "No, Mom. I waited to eat with you."

He was making it hard for Margie to stay angry. "Well, don't take all night to get it ready." And the TV went back on, as loud as ever.

Donald moved in the direction of the kitchen knowing what he was going to fix. Just the other day, he'd picked up four microwave dinners to have around for emergencies. Margie could have those along with some doughnuts. For himself, a lunchmeat sandwich would be more than enough.

Inevitably, her nagging reached him through the wall. "Donnie? Is the food about ready?" She hadn't even asked what she was having. Fortunately for her son, anything edible and filling usually sufficed. He yelled back "Almost!" even though it was going to take a few more minutes to get it to her.

Donald heard no more from the bedroom, and soon the large tray was filled with the dinners. A box of chocolate doughnuts was tucked under his arm. He maneuvered through the door, eager to satisfy his mother. She was turned away from him when he entered, apparently pouting. The food should put a stop to that.

Remembering he hadn't brought a drink, he turned toward the refrigerator on the dresser. It always held chocolate milk along with bottled water and soda. He noticed the refrigerator door was standing open. Apparently, the events of the last few days were making him absent minded. He dreaded to look in the freezing compartment where he kept his mom's stash of ice cream bars. He hadn't been in there since the previous day. The bars would be soup. Something told him he wouldn't get to eat anytime soon. A mess awaited.

Margie hadn't made a peep yet, so he sat the tray on the dresser beside the fridge and opened the freezer door. It was then he received his third shock of the day. The compartment was empty. He was positive there had been at least two boxes of ice cream bars left. Each was a box of eight.

Donald looked at Margie lying still in her bed. He looked at the refrigerator. At her usual pace, even if he'd been holding her, it would take her six agonizing steps to get there from the bed. And six steps back. As a rule, there would be considerable groaning and whimpering while he mostly dragged her, often throwing his back into spasms. The noises on her part were understandable because the weight on her knees caused her considerable pain. This afternoon his mother must have been extremely hungry and very upset when Donald had failed to come home at his regular time. Somehow, in her distress, she'd managed to do something she'd convinced him was impossible.

Donald walked closer to her, praying she wasn't dead. Though such an outcome would solve many of his problems, he was definitely not ready for it. Her heart might have stopped if she had navigated the width of the room by herself. But as he bent over the woman, he could hear her snore. Apparently, Margie had worn herself out while he was in the park. Downing sixteen ice cream bars on top of a little exertion was better than a sleeping pill.

Donald surprised himself by placing a kiss on her forehead. "Nice going, Mom." He grabbed the tray, went back to the kitchen and ate the TV dinners.

❖❖❖❖

He kept expecting his mother to wake up at least in time for their sundaes, but she didn't. Sleeping peacefully, she showed no signs of coming to life even in time for the news. Donald knew she was awake a lot most nights as a matter of routine. Since she received no exercise and ate and drank a sizeable amount of caffeine, she was seldom tired in the way most people are at the end of a busy day. Donald, on the other hand, was exhausted by ten o'clock. Until he signed a contract to commit matricide. Until Margie saw a strange man in her room. Until he jumped at every tiny sound in the night, thinking his mother's time had come.

He toyed with whether to mention to his mom when she awoke that he knew she'd been out of bed. She'd be sure to deny it, and there was bound to be an argument. That she had learned something about her own capabilities was probably enough. Best not to draw attention to the incident.

Donald double checked the locked doors, a futile chore. The only uninvited person who was apt to enter had a key. He looked out the kitchen window toward the McCall house. From his view through the oak tree, he saw no lights. Hopefully, that indicated Amber and her goon were both out of town.

He wished it were possible to see the windows of Amber's basement. Large bushes covered the windows. He thought it would be a good feeling to have confirmation Lauren and Grady were safe nearby. He wondered what they did in the evenings. Grady must be in bed already, sleeping the untroubled sleep of childhood. The boy trusted the adults in his life to protect him, and Donald vowed to do just that.

15
WOMEN WORRIES

Miraculously, Margie hadn't called for her son in the night. Even when he'd served her breakfast, she hadn't mention her twelve-step walk, so neither had Donald.

He was washing the dishes with thoughts of Lauren dancing through his head. He couldn't imagine what was causing that. Maybe it was the pleasant memory of their time in the park. Maybe it was her kind blue eyes. Maybe it was the motherly way she enjoyed all the cute stuff her little boy said and did. He pictured her arm around Grady's shoulders, heard her merry little laugh when he pretended to be an Olympic runner.

"Okay, man. Don't go there. One female on your mind is plenty!"

"I know. I only like Lauren as a friend."

"Sure you do. That's what folks always say when they don't want to admit they care for somebody."

"That isn't fair. Lauren's a nice person, but Amber could be the woman for me. I haven't completely given up on her."

"Too bad the interest isn't mutual."

"She's just got too many things on her plate right now to think about romance."

"What kinds of things?"

Once more, Donald was stumped for an answer. Why did Amber have to keep her activities a secret? The name Red Widow flitted into his consciousness then right back out before he heard a knock on the back door. It was Lauren ready to start her work with Margie. She was carrying a bouquet of assorted flowers. Its smell was sweeter than the cooking odors that still lingered in the kitchen.

"Good morning! I just dropped Grady off at his daycare. Does your mom know I'm coming?"

"Not exactly. She usually copes better if she doesn't get a chance to think about something ahead of time."

"I hope you're right. Today I want to talk about good things without touching on the topics of food or calories. Can you just follow my lead?"

Donald threw up his hands in surrender. "I'm at your mercy. So far nothing I've done for her has helped." The skillet with bacon grease in the bottom could wait until later.

"I have two jobs for you. One is to give me a vase or glass for these flowers. The second is to let me help you get that broken down chair out of Margie's bedroom. Is that too much?"

Donald quickly poured water into a tall drink glass and handed it over. "No, I've been meaning to get rid of the chair. Actually, we have town cleanup day on Thursday so we can just leave it at the curb." In his mind, he was considering the fact that his mother must have used that old piece of furniture as one of the things she grabbed on her way to the refrigerator the night before. An emptier room was going to seem scary to her at first.

"No offense, but it's kind of an eyesore. I'm hoping to brighten Margie's environment. She should feel more in control and like she wants to clean up her life and accomplish something."

"Okay," answered Donald, wondering why he hadn't thought of all that. He never had known what makes women happy. When he was around her, his mom only responded favorably to food. She even looked at flowers as though she were accusing them of not being edible.

"Soon," Lauren continued, "I'd like to purchase an oversized recliner. It'll take up valuable space, but right now there's nowhere for Margie to sit that would support her, except the bed."

"You're right." Again, Donald wished he'd have come up with the idea. However, he'd believed all along that his mother was unable to sit in a chair. She'd convinced him the bed with its hydraulic headboard was her only option. He had to admit Margie had been clinging to the life of least effort. And so had he. It would've meant more lifting and struggling if he'd had to manage additional transfers from bed to chair and back.

Lauren walked into the bedroom with the flowers and a big smile. "Good morning, Margie!"

Margie wasn't used to such cheeriness in the morning. "Hello. Why the flowers?"

"I'm celebrating new beginnings."

And making the room smell better, Donald added to himself.

"They're pretty, but it's going to smell like a funeral parlor in here."

"Not if we pretend we're in a flower garden. What would you like to do today, Margie? If you could do anything you wanted. Just use your imagination."

"You mean if I wasn't too fat to move? Well, I'd maybe go somewhere with a pretty view. And take a picnic lunch of all my favorite foods."

Lauren refrained from amending the food part of the fantasy. "What a good idea! I would definitely want to go along. You can't imagine what a glorious day it is out there." To prove it, Lauren pulled open the dark drapes and raised the window.

"You can't leave that window open, you know. We have air conditioning."

"Sorry." Lauren closed it. "I just hate that you never breathe fresh air. By the way, have you ever been to the park here in town?"

"Not for many years. It used to be my favorite place. I can't go anywhere now. My knees hurt too much."

"That's what we want to change. Grady just loves picnics. Let's make it a goal to get you up and moving so we can go to the park together. Once you're lighter, your knees won't hurt so much."

"It all sounds nice, but look at me. How many years do you have to give to this? Grady will be all grown up by the time I'm presentable enough to be seen outside."

"Not if we set our minds to it. I'm not talking about turning you into a runway model. I just want to get you out of that bed. Not today, but soon."

"You're a nice lady, but you're a dreamer." There was a beat during which she seemed to notice she wasn't eating. "I know I just had breakfast, but I could use a little something more. Donnie, what do we have to offer Laurie?"

"Her name's Lauren, Mom."

Lauren spoke up quickly. "Thanks, but I'm not hungry. I'm too excited about making plans. What are your hobbies, Margie? I mean things you do just for fun."

"Eating," she replied without hesitation. "Maybe that doesn't count, but it takes a lot of my time."

"A lot of Don's, too, I'm sure. Do you know how to crochet or knit?"

"That's for old women who just sit and do noth—" Margie interrupted herself. "No, I don't know how. I used to paint, but I can't do that in bed."

"That's so interesting! What kinds of things did you paint?"

"Landscapes mostly. With oils."

Donald was amazed. She must be making it up. He couldn't remember when she'd painted anything. "She does crossword puzzles." He was sure Lauren was looking for something more active, but he felt like he should contribute something to the conversation, and he was darned if he could think of anything else.

"Do you like card games, like Hearts or Uno?" Lauren asked. Donald wished she'd named Solitaire so as not to suggest one more thing for him to squeeze into his schedule.

The topic brought back memories for Donald of his mom and him playing Pinochle. That was before he was twenty. He'd thought it was her way of connecting with him without going out of the house. The card playing had stopped when she quit sitting in a chair. Games were just too awkward these days, especially when they had to keep stopping so Donald could go find her another snack.

"I used to be excellent at cards. I could beat Donnie." One thing about Margie, she could edit her memories to make herself the star.

"Well, Margie, I think we should bring a few fun things back into your life. You may be in bed, but you aren't dead! You aren't even old. Fifty-two is middle aged."

"I get what you're doing. You're trying to make me feel good before you take away my food. I'll tell you right now, I'm not a nice person when my stomach's growling."

Donald refrained from laughing. When you looked at starving children in Africa, you thought of growling stomachs. When you looked at Margie, that sound was far from your mind. And when he thought of the quantity of food he gave her every day, he wondered how she even knew what hunger felt like.

Lauren ignored Margie's last statement. "Don is going to remove the broken chair from your room. You don't need to look at it. We want you to be surrounded by only positive images."

"That'd be pretty heavy for Donnie. And it doesn't bother me. There are uglier things to look at than that chair."

Donald calculated that lifting his mother out of bed and getting her to the bathroom or commode involved five times the effort of taking a little old rocker to the curb.

"Well, we've already made arrangements. I'm sure you won't miss it." Lauren was good at not letting herself be swayed by her client. "What do you watch on TV at this time of the day?"

"Usually The View. Those women are crazy. They all talk at once, but I like to hear what they have to say."

"Me, too," said Lauren as she moved to turn on the television. "Do you mind if I watch with you?"

Donald hated The View. Loud, opinionated women made him nervous. But he joined the others to watch the show. It was an hour of laughter and deep thought. Lauren and Margie got in a few good digs at the four hosts. Margie, the fashion icon, commented that Whoopi Goldberg shouldn't wear such shapeless outfits.

Donald sat quietly, but he liked hearing his mother enjoying someone's company besides his. A glance at his watch signaled the encouraging news that Lauren had successfully distracted his mother from food for nearly an hour. The only way Donald had ever known to do so was to leave the house.

Lauren followed Donald to the kitchen when he left to fix lunch. Her presence made him very self-conscious. Even though he was constantly preparing meals and snacks for Margie, he never thought of himself as a cook. It had always been something he was forced to do. And his mother didn't seem to notice when he did go to some extra trouble. A stack of frozen dinners was appreciated with the same gusto as a meal he'd made from scratch. In fact, she preferred instant entrees because she didn't have to wait long for them. Kitchen smells wafting into her room while items simmered on the stove or baked in the oven were torture for both Margie and her son. Inevitably, Donald had to listen to, "How much longer, Donnie? I don't care if it's done. Just bring it to me!"

Lauren was a very patient and considerate person. She didn't comment on anything Donald was doing, didn't try to make suggestions. But he would bet she gritted her teeth while he piled mayonnaise onto the six full-size sandwiches each of which held several slices of lunch meat. Instead of a few chips on the plate, he gave his mom an entire sixteen-ounce bag. For vegetables, he put a large jar of green olives on the tray. "It's easier than chopping them up and putting them on the sandwiches. For dessert I'll take her a package of Oreo cookies."

"Do you feel like she needs the whole jar of olives or the whole bag of cookies?"

"Not really, but if I don't give them to her to start with, she'll keep sending me after more until she's eaten the whole thing. It saves time to load her up right away."

"You realize you should be the one in control of portions."

"I know, but she wears me down. I just try to satisfy her so she'll quit begging."

"Believe me, any mother of a small child understands how you feel, but we just have to be strong. When it doesn't bring results, the begging stops."

"I know you're right. But the word *no* would probably mean more coming from somebody besides me. I've been a pushover for too many years. I do try to trick her sometimes though. Like …well…olives are little so I think maybe popping those into her mouth after every couple of bites makes the meal take longer so she feels like she's had even more than she has."

"That's a nice effort, but you have to remember that though things like olives are small, they can have lots of calories. We'll talk about that later. Now what are *you* going to have?"

"I'll fix myself a sandwich and some chips. During the week I don't eat with her at noon. I'm in too big a hurry. After the bathroom stuff and cooking, I usually only have time to throw the dishes into the sink for later. Sometimes I eat something on my way back to the library." Donald gestured to the items on the counter that were left from fixing Margie's sandwiches. "What do you want? Just help yourself to anything."

Lauren looked at her options. "I'm not very hungry. Did I see some fruit in the refrigerator?"

"Yeah. The church ladies dropped off a fruit basket the other day. Somebody ought to get some good out of it. I'll take Mom's food to her, and then you and I can fix ours."

"If you don't mind, I think we should eat with her. Let her know what some people can be satisfied with. I think she has the idea her amount of sustenance is common. Plus, I think a person eats more when there's no one to talk to."

After bringing in an extra chair from the kitchen, Donald and Lauren joined Margie for lunch. If she noticed she had several times more food than they did, it didn't seem to concern her. "Donnie, bring another package of Oreos so you and Lauren can have some."

"No need," said their guest as she helped herself to one of Margie's. "This cookie is perfect for me." Donald followed her example and took one for himself, noting that the one-cookie rule must be one of the reasons Lauren looked so good. Margie watched her dessert disappear without complaint.

His mother dozed while Donald cleaned the kitchen. Lauren pitched in, quickly getting acquainted with what was stored in every cupboard. Fortunately, she didn't look at the highest shelf above the stove where Donald had hidden the contract. When the phone rang, he raised the receiver quickly so it wouldn't wake his mom.

"Hello?"

"It's me." The voice was ominous.

Amber! Finally. Maybe she missed him after all. "It's so good to hear your voice."

"What on earth is going on over there?" She sounded angry.

"Nothing. We just had lunch." What had he done wrong?

"We need to talk, Mr. Meester."

"I thought you didn't want to talk until __"

"This is an exception. When?"

Donald could hear her fury. And she'd called him Mr. Meester. After days of longing to talk to her, he was losing the desire.

"Can you come to the library first thing Monday?" he offered. "I can get there a little early. We can talk in the office."

"Okay. Nine-thirty." She hung up without saying goodbye. He looked over at Lauren wiping off the counter. He'd forgotten she could hear him. Amber would've been furious to know another person was listening.

"Everything alright?" Lauren asked as she continued to wipe.

"No. Things definitely aren't alright," he answered, more to himself than to her

Lauren gave him an inquisitive look but didn't ask him to explain. He wished he could. He desperately needed to talk to someone.

110

16
SEEKING SOLACE

When considering an uninvolved person to use as a confidante, Donald kept running into obstacles. He couldn't even hint at his problems around anyone in his household. He would love to be able to confide in Amber, but she actually *was* his problem. Finally, he went to the only counselor he ever used, his other self.

"I'm the loneliest guy in town. I'm totally miserable and scared, and I can't think of a soul to tell about it."

"Oh, there're folks you could tell, but they'd all see to it you were hauled off to prison. Then what would become of Margie?"

"Yeah. Everybody's always thought I was an odd duck. My admissions would just confirm it. Mom would have to go into a home where they feed people small portions and give them fruit for dessert. All because I couldn't keep my mouth shut."

"Well, Donnie, I don't want to get all praise-the-Lord on you, but where do you think people usually go when they want to be listened to but not judged?"

"You mean church? I've already thought of that and decided against it. That preacher's a kid. What does he know about life?"

"More than you, man. Everybody knows more than you."

That's how Donald found himself hanging around the Church of Hope on a Sunday afternoon wondering if Rev. Guthrie was off visiting relatives after finishing his services. Don got his answer when the young man strode across the church lawn toward him. He was dressed casually in khakis and a plaid shirt. "Donald! Good to see you out and about! Anything I can do for you? Have you thought about the bus idea?"

"No. I've been thinking about other things. I'm having some trouble sleeping."

"Well, that's not good. Do you want to talk about it?"

Suddenly it dawned on Donald that this was the preacher's off-duty time. And he hadn't even called for an appointment. "Yes, but you aren't working this afternoon."

The man looked down at his shirt. "You mean because I'm not dressed for it? Clothes don't mean anything. I'm pretty much always on call for my members. We can go inside or just sit on the church steps."

Donald was immediately frightened by the prospect of talking right out in the open. Their voices might carry. Who knew where his confessions might float off to? "I think I'd rather go inside."

It had been a long time since Donald had entered the church. It was like turning back the clock the minute he was within its walls. He remembered the place making him feel protected and loved. But that was back when he had a clear conscience. Back when he was only trying to make his mother happy by filling her with calories that would come back to ruin his adult life.

"Sorry I can't offer you anything. Wine is about all that's available up here. The church ladies put away the coffee stuff downstairs after services."

"That's okay. I'm not thirsty." Donald's stomach felt funny, and his throat was tightening up. He wasn't sure he was going to be able to have a dialogue with this man.

Pastor Guthrie (Donald wondered if he had a first name) and he were sitting in the lobby in two comfortable chairs. The setting felt like someone's living room. Donald found himself wishing he were Catholic. A confessional with an unseen priest would be far less intimidating than this supposedly casual chat. How was he going to sit here looking into that kind, innocent face and say he had hired a red-haired vixen to kill his mother? Some people would say, "Oh, don't worry. A preacher's heard it all." But Donald was willing to bet that in this guy's thirty-some years no one else had admitted to something so horrific.

"It's tempting to just lay it out there, isn't it Donnie? The little preacher's facial expression would be priceless."
"No I'm not tempted at all. For one minute's amusement, I'd spend the rest of my life locked away. I can't think of a thing I can admit to without causing him to run to the police."
"Then why are you here?"
"Good question."

"Why don't you just start by telling me what you think about when you're lying awake at night? Then we'll know what we need to get to the bottom of."

Get to the bottom of? It would do no good to analyze Donald's reasons for having his mom killed. The *why* was immaterial at this point. How *to stop it* was the only relevant problem now.

"I guess I think about dying." A statement out of nowhere. Partly true.

"Do you have an illness you aren't telling anyone about?"

"No, I'm not exactly sick. I just worry sometimes about going to Hell." *Where did that come from?*

"Lots of people do. You know that's not going to happen if you accept Jesus and his forgiveness." How did he know Donald needed forgiveness? They had gone from him being sick to having done something that needed forgiveness in just two sentences. Donald was going to have to watch what he said.

"I don't want to talk about that."

"About forgiveness?"

"It's not a topic I want to get into right now." That should be vague enough not to give anything away.

"Donald, do you want to tell me about something specific you think you've done? Sometimes just saying it out loud can make it seem less terrible."

This preacher was getting warm. But saying it out loud would make it sound *more* terrible. "I'm not ready to tell anyone."

"If you're worried about confidentiality, I won't share anything you say with anyone else."

"Sometimes maybe you have to."

"The only time would be if you told me something bad was going to happen to someone else. Then I'd be obligated to give out some bits of information. But I don't feel like that's the case here. You can relax in that regard."

Time to be quiet. No relaxing for Donald. "I think I just have to work this out myself."

"Well, Donald, most of us have tried to do that, but it seldom works. We usually find we have to rely on God. He knows it all anyway. He's just waiting to hear it from you."

The conversation was quickly getting into dangerous territory. He didn't like being reminded the Almighty was privy to his dark secrets. That was scary. He might as well try to forget about God and deal with Amber. There was at least a chance he could outsmart *her*.

"Uh . . . I think I've been away from Mom too long. She'll be needing some things. I appreciate you sitting down with me, but I have to go home."

"I'm sure your mom's doing fine, but go ahead if you want to. I'll be glad to talk again when you have more time."

"Sure. Okay. I might be back." He'd have said anything to end the conversation. He'd found himself nearly ready to spill his whole depressing story to this man. Maybe it was because it just felt like time and, ironically, in view of his earlier assessment, because Reverend Guthrie was about his own age. Perhaps the pastor would be able to understand how it would feel to be trapped in a family situation that cut you off from a chance at life.

On his walk back to Fourth Street Donald went over the counseling session he'd just had. How could something so brief be so terrifying?

"Well, that was a waste of time, wouldn't you say?"

"Yes and no. I found out that young preachers aren't really that clueless."

"Careful, Donnie. Getting too comfortable around church folks is dangerous stuff. You know I'm the only one you can trust."

Just the same, it had been good to have somebody willing to listen besides his other self.

17

SERIOUS SCOLDING

Donald slept a few hours Sunday night. He didn't know how he was able to. Mental exhaustion, he supposed. But the minute he awoke, he was besieged by apprehension. On one hand, he longed to see the beautiful Amber. On the other, he kept remembering her nickname and harboring doubts about her true nature. When he first met her he would've said he'd never hear an unkind word from those luscious lips. When they'd spoken on the phone the day before, however, he could almost picture the dripping venom. It had been the voice of a different woman entirely, and he wasn't eager to face this one. He'd gone over and over the possible reasons for her anger. It was difficult to figure out what he could've said or done wrong while she'd been out of town. The one obvious answer was she was not happy about Lauren and Grady being in his house. Perhaps she was jealous. Perhaps she thought he'd taken a lover. It was only fair that he be allowed to explain.

"You really think she cares that much who you see? She hardly knows you."

"Love can happen at first sight."

"Donald, my boy, you aren't that handsome. You'll have to grow on a lady."

"Well, what is it then? Why's she so upset?"

"Complications. Lauren and Grady are complications in her evil business plan."

Donald had the feeling, he'd hit on the real explanation for the phone call, and he didn't want to think that way. No more self-talk.

.

❖ ❖ ❖ ❖

It hadn't been easy, but Donald made it to the library forty-five minutes before his shift. His supervisor looked surprised to see him, but he walked quickly past her as though he didn't have time for even a *good morning*. He was nearly paralyzed by dread over what was to come and didn't have the patience to answer Sadie Harms' questions.

The situation must be serious if Amber was willing to meet with him in a public place after insisting they not be seen together. He didn't know much about committing a crime, but Donald could imagine that allowing oneself to get emotionally distraught could lead a person to be careless. Amber would surely have forced herself to settle down since their last conversation.

At precisely the time agreed upon, the red-haired young woman appeared at the door of the office just as she had the day of the signing. A chill traveled up Donald's spine. It had been two weeks, but she did not look happy to see him. She did not look happy at all.

He sensed it wouldn't be a good time to give the lady a hug. "Hi," he greeted her in a weak voice.

"Don't hi me. I had to go out of town or I'd have talked to you as soon as that woman rented my apartment. What were you thinking, letting two people into your life now? Are you purposely trying to make things difficult?"

"No. I'm just trying to get some help for Mom."

"Duh. Don't you remember the kind of agreement you signed? What's the point?"

"Well. . ." Donald began fidgeting. How was he going to make her understand when he didn't even understand? "I thought it might be awhile, and you told me to go ahead and live like I didn't know the end was coming." That wasn't such a bad answer. And it was true. He was following her orders.

Amber practically spit her words at him. She tried keeping to a whisper, but her irritation was making it hard. "How was I to guess you'd add two people to the mix? I didn't think you knew anybody!"

Donald had a vague feeling he'd just been insulted.

"How am I supposed to find her alone when you've got people hovering around her all the time? You don't know how hard it is to find a way to make this appear to be an accident. If you keep setting up obstacles, we may have to renegotiate the price of the job."

"I didn't think we could change the contract. If we can, I have some—"

"I don't want to hear it. Now get rid of them. I can't worry about Miss Lauren catching on. And I'd rather not have a kid on my casualty list. Forget helping your mother. It's too late. She's a train wreck. Not worth wasting your life on."

Her harsh words were enough to put Donald on the defensive. "You don't really know her. Just because she's fat, doesn't mean she isn't a good person. And it doesn't mean she can't be frightened. Why did your "friend" have to break into our house in the middle of the night? You didn't say anything about him being part of the deal. And you didn't say anyone was going to be creeping around before the … actual time." Donald had almost used the word *murder* but caught himself. Sometimes walls have ears.

"Donald, Donald, you haven't the foggiest idea how I operate. Gavin is my assistant, but we are one and the same as far as the business is concerned. He will do things I don't have time for or things I'm not strong enough to do. Don't worry. He definitely won't tell anyone. He's very professional, and he wants to keep his job. He was just measuring the distance from the back door to your mother's bed in case I have to find my way around in there in the dark. I think he got all the necessary facts in that one visit. Your mother appeared to be asleep. She wasn't meant to know he was there."

"Well, she's a light sleeper. Just so you know."

"I want no more instructions or complaints from you. Just do what I said with your useless guests, and do it soon. Time is getting short." The straight lines of her lips left no doubt she meant what she said. No smile emerged to soften the harsh words.

Donald swallowed hard. He'd been telling himself he still had plenty of time to stop the whole process or to at least make it up to his mother in advance. He'd hoped for a year. "Approximately how long do I have to get them out? If I send them away today, it'll look suspicious." Lauren was a smart lady. And she'd heard him on the phone with Amber. If he all of a sudden told her to leave and then something happened to Margie, she'd start putting it all together.

"I don't know yet. I have to go out of town again at the end of this week. There's a little court thing I have to clear up. It could go a long time or not long at all. After that, I can work Margie into my schedule. You just use the days between now and then to give your friends the boot!" Amber must have noticed doubt in Donald's facial expression, so she kept at him. "This is no time to get a crush on the little mother. You're putting them both in danger. If they aren't out of the picture by the time I get back, I'm not responsible for what happens to them. I can't risk witnesses. I've never had witnesses. Do you understand me?"

Her voice had become snarly again. Donald was fixating on the telling remark, "I've never had witnesses," when Sadie Harms entered the room.

"Thank you," Amber said, not missing a beat. "If you can find those books for me, I'd really appreciate it." She glared at Donald and marched right in front of Sadie on her way to the door.

"Kind of a snippy thing," was Sadie's impression. "Remember, you don't have to take orders from the library customers, Donald."

Oh yes, I do, he thought.

18
POINTLESS PURCHASES

After a whirlwind trip home to take care of his mother, Donald drove to meet Lauren at the grocery store. At the time they'd arranged it, he'd thought the outing was something to look forward to. Shopping had always been a lonely and depressing chore for him. He bought pretty much the same items on every trip to the market, the main criteria being Margie's approval and easy preparation for him. Today might be different. Lauren had a way of making almost any activity fun. He'd have to put his conversation with Amber aside and relax, or Lauren would think he was a pain to work with.

"What good is it going to do to learn to shop properly? Your mom might have only another week or two. Might as well pick up a cart full of desserts!"

"Lauren won't let me do that. I'll be lucky to get to buy one sweet thing."

Unlike his apparently-former girlfriend, Lauren seemed genuinely happy to see Donald. Her smile did a lot to lift the dejection left by Amber.

"Grady's daycare provider let him stay an extra hour today. You don't want to find out what it's like to grocery shop with a child."

Donald laughed. He could still remember what he'd been like, riding in his mother's cart and grabbing the wrong things off the shelves. If Margie had come today, the situation would be reversed.

She'd be riding in a motorized cart and pulling down every box of junk food she saw.

Before they left the entryway to go into the main store, Lauren had a few introductory words. Donald listened closely.

"Your mom doesn't even know for sure I'm going to change her diet, and when she finds out, she definitely won't be a willing subject, so we have to go slow."

Slow. Donald thought of the short time Amber was going to be out of town. If Lauren went too slowly, Margie wouldn't have time to lose a single pound.

She continued. "We should've made a list. It's important to do that and stick to it. No impulse buying. Today, though, we'll just sort of breeze through so you can get an idea of how I'm thinking. Show me where you usually start."

Again, Donald felt self-conscious having her watch his poor habits in motion. There was no rhyme or reason to his path through the store. "Probably the cereal aisle. I try to leave the frozen stuff until last." That was as far as his pattern went.

"Good idea." She gestured at the rows of boxes. "The cereal aisle is a land mine. There are so many sugary ones. What kind does your mom like?"

"The sugariest. I usually give her Fruit Loops."

"Yikes. You need to get used to reading the nutrition listings on the sides of the boxes. Let's find a kind that's high in protein. And no added sugar. That way you'll have a little control."

"I wouldn't, really. She just keeps demanding more sugar if I buy the brands without any."

"The best way to sweeten them is with real fruit. Strawberries or blueberries. It'll be pretty, too."

"I might like that myself. But she'll holler."

The two made their way up and down the aisles. Lauren didn't insist they pass by all his mother's favorites. She just helped Donald make better choices, ones Margie might not notice. Low salt, low fat, low sugar. Fresh fruits instead of canned with syrup. It was shopping Lauren-style. Donald had to remember she had a perfect figure, and his mother didn't. There was no way to argue about whose diet was better.

"Sorry, but no frozen dinners or entrees are allowed. Too much salt and sugar and preservatives. Very little nutrition."

Donald saw his easy answers to meals disappearing. He was going to have a hard time with Margie's menu. Especially when Lauren's time was up, and he was left to handle things alone. He reminded himself there was no need to worry. After all, they weren't talking about a long-range plan.

"Mom doesn't drink much milk," Donald offered as they walked by the cooler. "She prefers soft drinks. But sometimes she'll do milk with cookies."

"That's good. Milk is infinitely better than soda. It gives her calcium and protein. Soda gives her nothing. You just have to try for the lowest fat content. Two percent or lower."

"Mom has to have what she calls the 'real stuff' when it comes to milk. She says she won't drink the watered down kind."

"That's pretty easy for you to control. Just don't let her see the jug. She won't even notice the two-percent and you can gradually get her down to drinking skim."

Donald doubted that. It was hard to fool his mother when it came to food and drink. But he'd try. In the time she had left.

The meat displays were coming up. Donald wasn't very familiar with that aisle. "I don't pick up much meat. I'm not good at cooking it, and it's expensive. Cold cuts are about all I buy."

"I don't eat meat myself. I like edamame, quinoa, and lentils. There are lots of ways to get your protein besides meat."

Donald didn't respond. He hated to reveal his ignorance, but he'd never heard of any of those. And it was a sure thing Margie wouldn't go for something she suspected was a *health food*.

"On second thought, I'm sure from what you've said that your mom would turn her nose up at any of the things I just named. Maybe later."

Later. A word no longer in Donald's vocabulary.

"Red meat should be avoided, but Margie could use some lean protein. I can write up some instructions for you. Meat is filling and will help her muscles."

"She really doesn't need muscles in bed. I figure as long as she has so many McDonald's burgers, and bacon for breakfast, she's good. Once in a while, we have chicken nuggets or fish sticks. They're fast."

"Well, chicken and fish are good for her but not when they're breaded and fried. We need to have a meat talk soon." Maybe Donald was imagining it, but Lauren seemed to be getting a little impatient with him. He didn't like disappointing her, but the truth was the truth. It's easy to tell somebody what to do but harder being the one trying to do it.

Lauren wisely changed the subject. "We haven't gone past the produce aisle yet. That one should be one of your regulars."

"I don't usually even go there. I mean, Mom won't tolerate me serving most vegetables. She thinks they just take up valuable room on her plate. They don't do anything to fill her up, and that's all she cares about. If I say anything about cutting back on her food intake, she always points out that she's doing without vegetables and that should satisfy me."

"I'm afraid your mother has some very uninformed ideas about nutrition. Vegetables should be the source of most of her calories."

"I've tried to give her corn and peas I've doctored up with butter and salt, but she leaves them untouched just to show me she means what she says. Then I have to throw a lot away, and we can't really afford the waste."

"Maybe we can fool her into eating some. Part of what makes people want to consume food that's put in front of them is the color. And vegetables are colorful. They make a meal look so much more inviting than one with none."

"I agree. But mom doesn't take time to notice what the food on the plate looks like. She just dives in."

"We'll just have to slow her down."

Lauren looked at their overflowing cart. "Soon, we'll take away some of these things all together. Then we can slowly add more fresh fruits and vegetables. And you'll gradually give her smaller portions.

"She won't like those changes. You're going to hear a lot of whining. Maybe even some swear words."

"I can take it. Remember, I'm a mother of a five-year-old. I understand the concept of doing things for his own good. If I let him buy the groceries and pick out what he wanted for every meal, it would be mostly junk food. But I love him too much to let him do that."

"I guess I won't be a very good parent. I'll probably let my kids run the house. They'll be spoiled rotten. And maybe fat."

Lauren looked pleased that Donald had understood her analogy so well. "You can practice your parenting skills on your mom. *Tough love* it's called. And you'll be amazed at the difference it makes in your grocery bill. I don't see how you've kept up with the cost of such an enormous amount of food."

"Groceries are all we buy. There's no money for anything else."

"I can't wait until you can afford a real life," she commented as Donald wheeled the cart up to the checkout.

It won't be long. But the thought brought no joy.

19
TROUBLE TRANSFORMING

Following the day of stocking the kitchen, Lauren decided to tackle the rest of the house. Her intention was to bring life to the cottage on Fourth Street, for herself and Donald as much as for the subject of her study. After a fast excursion downtown, she showed up at the Meester's with a carload of items. She'd made stops at Goodwill and other second-hand stores where she'd purchased anything that might cause Margie to perk up. Lauren meant to give the heavy woman a new outlook if it killed them all. She wanted to surround her client with things to think about besides her appetite. So what, if it cost Lauren a few dollars. She couldn't put a price on completing her thesis. Besides that, it had become a personal challenge. She'd grown to think of her time with Margie as a life and death matter. Not only was it essential for Lauren to finish school so she could have a career capable of supporting her son, but she felt a woman who weighed nearly six hundred pounds was courting a loss of life in more ways than one. With a lot of luck and effort, Lauren was sure she could stop it.

She was carrying a large plant and a painting up the front sidewalk when a voice from next door surprised her. She'd never noticed any neighbors outside their houses since she'd been visiting Don.

"I'd help you, but I'm not supposed to lift anything." Lauren saw the remark had come from a tall, scrawny woman with frizzy grey hair who appeared to be seventy-something. She was holding the leash of a small black Pekinese. "I have a serious problem with my back. The chiropractor has given up on me."

"There's no need for you to carry anything. I'll just make a few trips. It's good exercise."

"I'm Amelia Klink. Are you visiting the Meesters or did they move out when I wasn't looking?"

"My name's Lauren Hunt." Lauren stopped and set down her burdens. It seemed the woman wanted to visit. "I'm just a friend of the family helping Donald for a few weeks."

"Good. Those two can use all the help they can get." Lauren wondered whether the neighbor lady had done anything for them herself. *Anything that doesn't require lifting, that is.* "Margie is going to kill off her son if she doesn't hire a companion. She takes advantage of that poor young man as far as I can tell."

"He's a good son," Lauren offered, not willing to encourage the woman's fondness for gossip.

"He is good. I can see that." Amelia had picked up her dog who was now squirming in her arms. "Pretty Boy here sure does like him. Every time Donnie comes home, he barks and wants outside. When we're in the yard, Donnie takes time to pet Pretty Boy and talk to him. You can tell he likes dogs. That's a good trait in a man. It shows he has a big heart. I'd like to see him have some human friends, too, though. It's unnatural for a man his age to live such a solitary life."

Lauren agreed with the woman but didn't want to say so. "He may have friends we don't know about."

Lauren picked up her belongings. While she could understand Amelia's concern, she wasn't comfortable analyzing Donald's social life behind his back.

"Perhaps." But the neighbor woman sounded doubtful. "He needs to get out into the world. He could get a wife if he tried. I told Donnie I'd come over and mother-sit if he wanted to go to a dance or somewhere, but he never did take me up on it. I'm old, but I can talk, and I can cook. Those things are probably all Margie cares about."

"That's a nice offer. I'll remind him you made it. Now I'd better get some work done. I'm glad we met. I'm sure I'll see you again while I'm here." And Lauren continued to the house, before she was made to explain to the neighbor lady the exact purpose of the items she carried. Margie was entitled to some privacy about the self-improvement plan being foisted on her.

Amelia followed Lauren up the walk. "You know, I almost forgot. I baked some chocolate chip cookies this morning. I always give half of them to the Meesters. Goodness knows, I can't eat two dozen."

"Oh, you really don't need to do that," Lauren protested. "We just went grocery shopping yesterday so we're pretty well supplied."

"I'm sure you think so, but I doubt you realize how much it takes to keep Margie satisfied. It's the least I can do. Usually, I put together a few with frosting between them. They seem awful sweet to me, but those two just love them. Tell Marge I'm sorry, but today they're just plain."

"Of course," Laura said, giving in. She could hide the cookies and only mention them to Donald. Amelia was on her way to retrieve the sweet treats.

The neighbor lady might be a nice companion for Margie, but there could be a reason Donald hadn't jumped at the chance to use her. It was possible the woman could get to be too much of a good thing and turn out to be just one more enabler.

In less than an hour, the painting was in place on the bedroom wall at Margie's eye level. The plant was near the window. Lauren had pulled back the drapes, allowing some filtered light to show through the shears. A decorative tray sat poised for snack time. If Lauren had been in Margie's place, the flowered wallpaper would have had to go and be replaced by a neutral paint. That change, however, would involve too much commotion, too many paint smells and too much stress. Besides, Margie might love wallpaper and have the lines of every rose memorized.

Lauren and Margie were awaiting a visit from Kerry, the nurse from the Health Department. If things went well, Lauren would be able to get Don's mother started on a serious exercise regimen.

When Lauren ushered the nurse into the bedroom, the uniform took Margie by surprise. "What's this? I'm not sick. I've been eating more fruit. Doesn't that count for anything?" And she made fists under her enormous bosom in a gesture of defiance.

"You bet it does, Margie," Kerry answered with a smile. "We're very proud of you. But I'm sure Lauren's hoping to get you out of that bed and moving a bit. We just want to be sure your body is up to the exertion."

Margie saw an excuse just waiting for her. "I'm sure I have heart trouble. My mother did. I've always known it would be dangerous for me to walk. That's the only reason I don't."

"We just want to be sure, dear. Most of the time, exercise makes the heart stronger."

Lauren regretted not telling Kerry to avoid the e-word. But, as usual, Margie surprised them both. "Grady tells me exercise is fun. He tries to talk me into doing jumping jacks!" And she giggled at the thought of her little friend.

Her own mention of Grady put Margie into a cooperative mood, and she came through the day's physical exam with flying colors.

Nurse Kerry called the following day with the lab results. Nothing alarming had come to light. Cholesterol and blood sugar were on the high side but still within normal range. "You're free to do what you can to change your client's habits," Kerry said. Lauren detected a smile in her voice. The nurse must have no hope for the success of this endeavor. The impression Lauren got was that the lady was humoring her. The young nurse didn't mean to be discouraging but didn't believe for a minute that Mrs. Meester was going to lose any weight.

Fortunately, Lauren's master's study didn't require that the experiment have a happy ending. The plan was to identify the emotional obstacles to improving the lifestyle of a morbidly obese woman. But Lauren's personal goals were even loftier than her academic ones. She was determined to actually help Don's mom, and now she could get down to business. Kerry would eventually see what determination could do.

To begin the journey, she took out her camera and aimed it at Margie sitting up in bed waiting for the burger that wasn't coming.

"Get that camera out of here!" was the predictable reaction.

"Just ignore it, Margie. I have to document your progress. Someday you'll look at this and won't believe it's a photo of you."

"Fat chance of that. I doubt you can even get all of me in the picture."

Lauren smiled but made no denial. She was finding, sure enough, that it was difficult to fit all of Margie into one frame.

"I doubt if you realize other folks have tried to fix me. They never got anywhere, so there's no reason to think you will. I enjoy good food and always will, so you shouldn't get your hopes up. If it means giving up all my favorites, I'll never be ready for a beauty contest.

"I don't care about that. I only want you able to get out of bed and have a nice life. And I have a favor to ask. Would you try to be a little positive? See if you can come up with some affirmations of the way you wish you were, and maybe they'll eventually become facts. Like, 'I am strong', 'I am flexible', 'I can walk'. Say those kinds of things over and over in a day. Picture yourself that way. Feel it in your mind. And try to believe!"

"I'd just be fooling myself. The good Lord made me pleasantly plump. I can say *I am slim* until I'm blue in the face, but it won't change anything."

"No, but it could help. When you say it, you should visualize it, and then you'll be on your way to making it come true."

"I am hungry! Now that's a sincere affirmation."

Lauren sighed. *I am going to succeed with Margie* she affirmed to herself. But she was having trouble with the visualization.

Donald was getting to the point where he looked forward to going home after work. Assuming he'd have been notified if something bad had happened to his mom while he was gone, he couldn't wait to find out what progress she was making. On Wednesday he arrived at his house to find Lauren in the largely unused front room. She was busy moving the furniture. Donald couldn't imagine why. How would it benefit Margie to have the couch in a different place? She hadn't even seen the thing for at least two years. But Lauren didn't do things without good reason so he was willing to help.

"I don't know what you're doing, but you look like you could use some muscle." Don grinned at his own remark. He thought of himself as a lot of things but never as a male specimen of any kind.

"I do! This sofa is heavier than I expected it to be, and it's hard to scoot it across the carpet."

That piece of furniture had resided against the inside long wall of the room since the days when his mother had some interest in that sort of thing. Donald was almost afraid to find out what all was under it. He knew the coins, crumbs, and other debris would be evidence of his slipshod housekeeping, but he was curious. "Where do you want it? Not out on the porch, I hope."

"I'm thinking it should go right in the middle of the room not far back from the picture window. We'll have to leave room for Margie to maneuver in front of it, but it needs to be close enough for her to get a good view of the outside."

"You know, she can't even get in here. Uncle James widened the bathroom and kitchen doors but not the ones into this room."

"I measured. It's really close, but it can be a fairly short-term goal for her, come sit on the couch, and look out the window. That beautiful elm tree is so pretty to look at, and it's just going to waste.

Margie could also see people walking past on the sidewalk or kids playing. She needs to think about the outside world."

"I don't know. Is it fun to see what you can't have?"

"Not if that was a certainty, like if she were paralyzed or dying. But she can still make changes if she wants them badly enough."

Donald thought a minute before joining her. "Well, I'd love to see if you're right. Let's do it."

The two made quick work of transforming the room. Moving one thing required moving something else, so the result was a whole new atmosphere and a big need for the vacuum cleaner.

Margie, as usual, got in on the act. "Donnie, what are you and the lady doing?"

"Rearranging the furniture," he called out to her.

"Isn't that up to me? It's my house."

"If you want to supervise, you'll have to come in here." Donald knew that was a little cruel, but the truth was the truth.

Her voice became subdued. "You know I can't. I never will."

"Well then, you shouldn't care where the furniture is." Donald was a little annoyed. He and Lauren had been working like crazy, trying to make things better for Margie, and she showed no appreciation. Sometimes he had to ask himself, *Why bother?*

"Would you rather she was excited about the redecorating? Excited about something she'll never get any good out of?"

"Well, no, I guess not. But at least if she were interested, she'd have some happiness today."

"That wouldn't make up for what's going to happen, and you know it."

❖❖❖❖

Later, Donald got tears in his eyes when he took an object from his pocket that he'd found under the couch. His mother's pearls, a reminder of happier times.

Although he must've been only nine at the time, he could remember the night his mom received the pearls. It was his parents' tenth anniversary. His dad had worked late like he usually did, and Margie was growing more upset by the minute. Donald didn't blame her. The boy knew his dad was important enough at the hospital he could've told those people he had to go home for his anniversary. Donald had made her a card, but that didn't seem to be enough to make up for his dad's absence.

Finally Dr. Meester showed up bringing flowers and a box from the jewelers. Those gifts seemed to do the trick. His mom was laughing and giddy, and when his dad fastened the pearls around her neck, Donald could see her reflection in the living room mirror. She was beautiful, like a princess. He remembered being happy that night. When you're nine years old, all it takes for contentment is to have a smiling family. At thirty, that was still all he wanted.

He wondered if showing her the recently recovered pearls would make his mother happy again or just bring back unwanted memories. He decided not to take any chances right away. He took the necklace to his room and placed it into a drawer full of seldom-used trinkets to be saved for a future time.

20
NIGHTTIME NOISES

Midnight arrived and found Donald lying in bed but wide awake. He'd had about an hour of sleep before the quiet woke him with a start. Where was the sound of the radio or the TV? There wasn't even a snore coming from his mom's room. He kept telling himself it was all good. Margie had been so much more active lately that she hadn't had time for all her little cat naps. She was actually sleepy now by eleven or so and didn't need any electronics to entertain her overnight.

He wondered if, after his mother's passing, he would ever sleep again. The silence at night was sure to be a regular reminder, an accusation. He was sure to want the constant radio talk shows on just to make the house sound normal. He doubted a wife would be happy about that habit. If she could just be patient, he'd try to overcome it. Maybe he could gradually turn the volume down to nothing. Or maybe he could wear headphones that would allow him to hear the noise, but his wife wouldn't have to deal with it.

Finally, Donald concluded he might as well get up and check on his mom. It was remotely possible that Amber or Gavin the goon had used his key to come in and complete the job. He couldn't imagine how they could do that without him hearing something, but they were professionals. No doubt they could do horrible things only a few feet away without him even suspecting. He jumped out of bed. He had to know.

The night was cloudy. No light shone in through the windows, so he navigated the rooms by touching objects so familiar he didn't need to see them to know their exact locations. Donald didn't want to turn on a light for fear of disturbing his mom. He made his way slowly across his room and into hers.

When he got to her bed, he gently placed his hand on her enormous stomach. He smiled in the darkness when he felt the rise and fall of his mother's breathing.

Donald was just as careful on his return trip. It would literally frighten the woman to death if she were to wake up and find a man in her room once again. She'd faint away before he'd have a chance to identify himself.

He heard a slow squeak and recognized it as the way the front door usually sounded when it was being opened, like it was begging for an oil can. He tried not to breathe lest the intruder become aware someone was nearby.

The quiet made him feel extremely vulnerable. His mom was, too. If it were Amber coming in, she'd think she had easy access to the big woman who was obviously dead to the world.

Donald tried to locate a weapon of defense. He hated to chance bludgeoning the recent object of his adoration, but he couldn't stand by helplessly as she took out his mother. The only thing he could find in the dark was a bedside lamp. He took position beside Margie's head and held the lamp high, ready to strike.

A loud banging broke the stillness. Then a thud. And a groan, a masculine groan. It must be their brawny neighbor. Donald remembered then that the couch was directly in line with the outside entrance, an area that had always been clear. The intruder was moving according to Donald's diagram so had barreled ahead in the blackness. By the sound of it, the large sofa toppled over when it was hit. It was easy to imagine the goon being disoriented and finding it difficult to determine where he was in relation to the door. If the situation hadn't been such a serious one, Donald would be chuckling. He'd heard of dumb crooks, but this guy won the prize.

Margie was awake, "Donnie!" she screeched at the top of her lungs. That was enough in itself to scare the life out of any normal burglar. "Donnie, is that you in the living room?"

He scooted over next to her bedroom door so his voice would come from the expected direction. "Yeah, just me. I stumbled in the dark. I was trying not to wake you."

"Well, you did! Honestly. It sounded like you dropped the couch!"

The distraction of Margie's screams had given the goon just enough time to get his bearings and find his way back out the door. Donald breathed a sigh of relief. He noticed he was dragging the lamp cord that was still plugged into the wall. The makeshift club wouldn't have done him much good if he'd had to seriously defend his mother.

"You didn't hurt yourself, did you, Donnie?" Margie called through the darkness.

"No, Mom. I'm good. Might have a few bruises." He turned the switch on the lamp and brought light to the scene.

"I knew you'd get in trouble by moving all that furniture around. I don't like to rub it in, but I could've told you somebody was going to run into it. What were you doing in there in the dark anyway?"

"Oh, just my usual. Checking the locks. I couldn't remember doing it earlier."

"Well, next time use a flashlight. That won't wake me."

"Right. I'll remember that."

"Or put the furniture back where it belongs," she added for good measure.

Donald felt he'd covered the situation pretty well, but he was terribly concerned. What had the goon been doing in the house? He hadn't been paying a social call. Maybe the man was planting some apparatus that would later explode. Donald had no clue how many lethal devices hired killers possessed.

"I don't think I can settle back down without a snack, Donnie."

Oh, what the heck. Tonight could easily have been Margie's last on earth. A snack wasn't nearly as harmful as a burly fellow with murderous intentions.

"Donnie, Donnie. How long can you play Superman and come on the scene in the nick of time?"

"Not much longer. I feel like every crisis takes another five years off my life."

"Remember, the guy is only doing what you wanted done. You could just leave him to it."

"No chance. Amber said to go about life in my usual way. My usual would be to protect my mother. He's going to have to get past me to hurt her. I'm not going to help him do his job."

Donald sat on the side of his bed and looked around for something to grab if Gavin came back. Technically, since Don had been the one to hire the killers, the two men were on the same side. Nevertheless, he didn't trust the bungling henchman to be able to pick him out in the dark. Being on the defensive must become his new way of life.

He considered the antiques that sat useless in many parts of the house. Why couldn't one of them be a mace or a poker? A large old-fashioned clothes iron sat on the floor to be used as a door stop if they were ever to leave the front door open. It was the kind that women used to heat on the stove, solid iron and extremely heavy. If Don could lift the iron high enough to hit the goon in the head, he could do damage, or if it were dropped on the guy's foot, it could temporarily cripple him. Donald placed the object on the floor by his bed. That easily-reached weapon in place, he was able to get some sporadic sleep

.

21
MARGIE MEDITATES

Lauren had an activity in mind for Monday morning, and she wasn't expecting it to go well. After seeing Donald off to work, she sat down beside Margie's bed for a heart-to-heart visit. She'd timed the session so it didn't coincide with any of the woman's favorite shows. Lauren grabbed the remote and turned the television off.

"What did you do that for?" Margie was understandably puzzled and thought her new friend must be angry about something.

"I'm just giving us a break from the noise."

"I don't call it noise. It keeps me company." Margie was more in touch with her own feelings than Lauren had expected. "And it won't make me any fatter," she added hopefully.

Lauren laughed. "No, TV doesn't have calories, but it can get in the way of you finding a happier way to live."

"Well, I'll tell you right now, if you take away my Starbucks *and* my TV, I won't be happier. Those are the only things I enjoy." Margie was getting downright frightened.

"Oh, I wouldn't do that. We're only going to take ten minutes of quiet so we can meditate. Do you know what that is?"

"Of course, I do. It's what the Maharishis in Fairfield do. I've heard some of them meditate so hard they rise up into the air. I won't be doing that. This body won't float."

Lauren laughed again. Thankfully, levitation wasn't her goal for Margie. "I just want your mind to float—in a manner of speaking."

"I don't get it."

"For only ten minutes, try clearing your thoughts. You won't think of TV or of food. All you have to do is sit in your most comfortable position and concentrate on breathing. In and out. In and out."

"It sounds like a waste of time. I'm always breathing in and out. Even while I'm eating."

"Just try it. I've been meditating every morning since my husband died, and I couldn't do without it. It's a great way to center yourself and gain control of your worries and your bad habits."

"Oh, that's it. You're saying that thinking of nothing will keep me from overeating."

"It will help, yes. You'll just feel better about yourself and be ready to cope with anything."

"Are you warning me about something awful that's coming?"

"No. But we never know in the morning what the day will bring."

"I think I've heard that meditation stuff is supposed to take the place of prayer. Are you trying to make me into an atheist?"

"Of course not. You can use prayer *as* your meditation. Or you can use a phrase about God. Breathe in saying to yourself, *God is* – breathe out saying *love*. Or you can say something comforting like *All is* and exhale on *well*."

"For ten minutes? I have to keep breathing for ten minutes? Can we turn on the radio?"

"No, that would defeat the whole idea. Let's try now. Pick a phrase or a word, a mantra it's called.

Margie smiled mischievously. "I think I'll say, *Candy is . . . good*."

"Better choose something else," said Lauren, but she was pleased at her new friend's use of humor.

The two managed to keep the meditation going for almost seven minutes with Margie asking twice for a report of the time left. Then just before the end, she piped up with "What if I go to sleep?"

"No problem. But if you're really concentrating on your meditation, you probably won't."

"Do you want to know what phrase I picked?"

"You don't have to say. It's private. And you can use different words on different days."

"Good. Today I used, *Meditation is . . . silly.*"

Lauren sighed. She was glad she'd gotten herself centered before she came to visit Margie.

When Donald came home from the library that afternoon, his mom couldn't wait to tell him she'd meditated just like the Maharishis. "I don't think it worked because I still got upset when Lauren told me we're out of jelly."

Donald was just happy she had something to tell him besides what the women of The View had to say. "Maybe you have to meditate for a few days before you feel more settled."

"If I was any more *settled*, you'd never be able to move me."

She had a point. But again, he trusted Lauren's judgment. If she thought his mother needed to have some quiet time, she was probably right. Goodness knew, the woman tried very hard *not* to have any.

And maybe Donald himself could benefit from meditation. Concentrating on a mantra might blank out the scary thoughts he'd been plagued with lately. His mind, or conscience, just wouldn't let him alone, and he felt anything but centered.

His other self couldn't resist.

"I bet you'd like to blank me out, wouldn't you Donnie?"

"Yes! Some days I would."

22
HOPE FOR A HANGING

The next weeks were routine, if one could apply such a word to a household with as many problems as the Meester's. Because Amber was off taking care of her mysterious duties, Donald was able to periodically relax and enjoy a false sense of well-being. He realized she'd instructed him to use her time away to dispose of his guests, but that was the last thing he wanted to do. And besides, he couldn't imagine any way to do so that wouldn't seem suspicious. He felt it would be like announcing he wanted them gone because he was up to something they couldn't know about. He'd never be able to come up with enough lies to cover his motives.

Each day Donald procrastinated about following Amber's instructions. In the back of his mind, he was hoping she would never return. Maybe she'd find a more lucrative job elsewhere and forget them.

His other self wasn't as hopeful. *"Maybe that will happen. When pigs fly."*

Lauren appeared daily at the house around the time Donald was ready to go out the door to work. He always hated that their contact was so brief. He'd come to appreciate her as a truly fine person. Actually, she was only three years younger than Donald, practically nothing in the adult world. He acknowledged that she was the more mature of the two of them. She'd been married, if only for a year, experienced the death of her husband, and given birth to a son she was raising with no help. Those things made Lauren wise beyond someone who'd lived with his mother his whole life and experienced almost none of the milestones of most thirty-year-old men. He felt he could learn a lot from this second woman in his house. Besides that, she was attractive. Her appearance wasn't as exotic as Amber's, but he was beginning to consider her pretty. Lauren's hair was an indefinite shade of brown, cut in layers to look like most girls he'd seen lately. However, when the air outside was humid, hers insisted on curling around her face, giving her a sweet, girlish look. She had nice features and wore little makeup. For Donald that was a plus. Women with red lips and fake eyelashes made him nervous. Lauren didn't give him the feeling she was expecting him to be something he wasn't. She was independent without being masculine, and Donald thought of Grady as a lucky boy. Even though, like Donald, he didn't have a father, Grady would always be able to look up to his mother as an example of how to be a grownup.

The nicest time of each day was when Donald got home from the library. No more fast food sacks came into the house. Lauren took care of serving a nutritious, low calorie snack after Margie had taken a walk around the bed. By the time her son appeared, the heavy woman was drinking water before taking a well-earned nap.

Lauren tried to get Don to go for a walk with her while Margie slept. He would've loved that but couldn't take a chance leaving his mom unattended and at the mercy of assassins. He wasn't so relaxed he let himself get careless. Instead, he and Lauren went out onto the porch to discuss the day's happenings. Shelving books gave Donald little material for conversation, but Lauren always had things to say. She was eager and upbeat with her accounts of Margie's progress. Sometimes she'd report her client's little comments that made them both laugh. The minutes he spent talking with Lauren were a treat for Donald. If they'd have happened earlier in his life, he never would've agreed to have his mother killed. Sharing the burden did so much to relieve his stress. He wondered if Lauren ever felt that way about being a parent. She adored Grady, but life would surely be easier for her if she had a husband to share the decisions about his upbringing and to laugh with her over his funny little comments.

At four o'clock every day Lauren left to pick up her son from daycare. Surprisingly, the boy preferred to go directly to Margie's instead of to the basement apartment he shared with his mother. An understanding existed between the unlikely friends. Margie experienced with Grady a flashback of maternal feelings she'd largely abandoned. For Grady, since both sets of his grandparents were deceased, Margie served as a very satisfactory substitute.

The easy affection between the overweight lady and the little boy brought thoughts of regret for Lauren. During one of their porch talks, she confessed, "Since Grady was born, I've been so busy earning a living for us and studying to get my degree, I never noticed my little guy's lack of friends and relatives." Lauren explained that she could see Margie was giving as much as she was getting from their arrangement. Donald listened to the glowing praise of his mom with a heavy conscience. What would Lauren think if she knew he had arranged for the murder of this saint? The fires of hell were not going to be hot enough for his punishment.

To keep from becoming suicidal, Donald sometimes patted himself on the back. After all, he was the person who'd seen the benefits of allowing Lauren and her son to enter Margie's life. He could've sent them away, but he'd welcomed them for his mother's sake. Surely, that would be worth a few points on judgment day.

He watched Margie change a little every day. The weight loss (or water loss) was gradual, and he had to pay attention in order to notice. Donald became teary-eyed the day he noticed Margie was wearing a glittering dinner ring on her left hand. She'd flushed the diamond from her husband down the bathroom stool years ago. Looking comfortably loose now was one of her shopping network finds that had been too small when it arrived. Margie had liked it so much she'd kept it in the drawer of her nightstand, a secret sign she hadn't given up hope of regaining her former size.

Just a few more shed pounds and Donald would reward his mom with a real dress. He remembered how vain she used to be. In a nice way, of course. As a young boy he hadn't missed the fact his mom was more put together than many of his friends' mothers. Her hair, nails, and makeup were always just right. One of Don's little buddies said she looked like a movie star. A few years later the same boy said Margie reminded him of Johnny Depp's extremely overweight mother in *What's Eating Gilbert Grape.*

Lauren established small, reachable goals for Margie. Doing ten arm stretches in bed, doing ten repetitions of lifting two-pound weights, walking laps around the bed holding onto the railing. The short-term goal was for Margie to be able to easily travel from her room into the kitchen. It was time she joined the living and came to the table. As long as she was being served in her bed, she wasn't having an active role in her own transformation.

When a big-man recliner was delivered, Margie tried to act upset, but Lauren and Donald could see she was excited. "There isn't room for that thing! And if I get into it, you'll never get me out!" Donald had been thinking pretty much the same things, but he trusted Lauren to have a good motive. As it turned out, the chair was a brilliant idea. Margie couldn't wait to sit there in the evenings. Being in a more upright position allowed her to play catch with Grady if he stood only two feet away. And with a TV tray between them, the two friends could play cards. Twice daily Margie pedaled for ten minutes on a portable set of pedals.

"My days really seem to go fast!" she told Donald. "There's so much to do!"

Such a change of attitude should've thrilled her son. But the happier his mom got, the more stressed he became. It hadn't seemed as tragic to think of taking the life of a miserable woman. To end a life she was enjoying was a much different matter.

A set of oil paints with brushes and easel appeared one day, courtesy of Lauren. At first, Margie refused to look at them, but after a few days she would, with no coaxing, sit in her chair for a few minutes in the afternoons doing her best to revive an old pastime. Donald was no art critic, but he was impressed with her efforts and thankful Lauren had made it happen. Creating landscapes from memory had to be difficult. He wished they could look forward to taking his mom to a place where she could paint real scenery, but he was afraid to let her outside where he couldn't watch her closely. Amber or Gavin could be lurking in the trees.

Days had passed since he'd listened to his inner voice. That part of Donald had been his best friend for as long as he could remember. Lately, he'd talked to Lauren instead. But on a night in July, as he watched TV in his room, his old chum had to be heard again.

"I know what you're hoping Donnie. You're gambling that Amber will be put in jail for some other killing and be out of your life."

"Well, it could happen. She seems to be everybody's prime suspect."

"Oh, they'll catch up to her sooner or later. But she'll take you down with her."

"Thanks a lot for being so negative."

"The facts are negative. You have to face them."

Donald couldn't fool even himself. He was in big trouble. As if to prove that point, an image of Amber McCall appeared on the screen in front of him. Beautiful, innocent-as-a-baby Amber.

". . . Amber McCall has been detained for questioning in the killing of prominent Chicago land owner Herman Foster."

A frightened voice from the next room confirmed his fear that Margie was watching the news. "Donnie! Don't we know that redhead?"

"No, Mom! It's a different redhead." He was aware that seeing Amber's likeness on the screen no longer gave him a thrill. In fact, the sight brought on more of a chill. Hopefully, she wasn't going to outsmart authorities in the Chicago case. And if she were convicted, she couldn't implicate him in that one. Amber would be out of his life. Would such a development be better than he deserved? Absolutely.

23
EXTRA EXCITEMENT

Two days passed with no murder attempts or additional news stories. It was tempting to get comfortable, to think the whole nightmare had evaporated into the summer sky. After all, Markison had to be America's safest small town. Looking out the window over the kitchen sink, Donald could believe he was living in Friendly Village, an idyllic place he remembered from his first grade reader. Friendly houses holding friendly people who weren't a bit interested in killing anything but mosquitoes,

Lauren paused while putting clean dishes in the cupboard. "You know, when I first asked your permission to work with Margie, I said you'd be able to get away and have fun without worrying about your mom. Well, why don't you do that tonight? The temperature has gone down, and it's beautiful outside. We'll be fine here. Just go do your own thing!"

Donald was taken by surprise. He'd never allowed himself to make any personal plans. He often yearned to do what others were doing, but he had only a vague idea of what that was. He didn't have a *thing*. "Well . . . uh . . . I don't know of anything going on in Markison. But thanks." As far as Don was concerned, the matter was closed.

Lauren wasn't ready to drop the subject. "I bet there're lots of things. I saw a poster for The Music Man. It's on at the Community Playhouse this week. Or maybe you could just stop in some place nice and have a cup of tea in peace. Why don't you go ahead and get spiffed up and take off? Do it for me! I'd feel better if you would. Really."

"Well . . . okay, but I don't know why it's such a big deal for me to get away." What was he talking about? He'd wanted to get away badly enough to hire somebody to kill his mother. Now he had the chance, and all he wanted to do was stay in with Lauren and Grady and Margie and watch TV.

Donald's inner self joined him in the shower.

"You're a piece of work, man. You can't think of a reason to go out, and most young single guys can't think of reasons to stay home."

"Most of them have somebody to go out with. They don't just wander the streets alone."

"Some have girlfriends who aren't off murdering people and can go on dates."

"Think I'll just take a walk," Donald said as he opened the front door to leave.

Grady was on board. "Can I go, too? I like to walk!"

Lauren quickly jumped in. "No, this is Donald's grownup time."

The boy seemed confused. "Oh." Then he looked at his mother and reminded her, "You're grown up, and I walk with you."

Margie brought the issue to a close. "I'd be too sad if both my men left. You said you were going to show me how to draw a dinosaur. Oh, and Donnie, if you go past the Dairy Queen or Starbucks, you might think of us."

Donald cringed. Apparently, Margie wasn't cured. He wouldn't even be free when he was out on the town. He'd still be chained to his mom and her cravings.

Lauren put her hand on his arm. "Forget us. We'll fix a snack here."

Donald gave her a grateful smile and left. No sooner was he off the porch than his eyes turned toward Amber's house. There were lights on, but he knew it wasn't her. If she were back from her business trip, her car would be in the drive. Gavin must be the only person in the house. Even so, Donald was nervous about leaving. What if Amber instructed the guy to make the move for her? What if he came over and found more people in the house than he'd expected? He was liable to think he had to kill them all. Donald couldn't imagine how one man could accomplish that, but he didn't want to find out. A short walk was all he'd allow himself before returning to stand watch over his household. He took off down the sidewalk in the opposite direction of Amber's so anyone watching wouldn't see him leave.

The day had been hot and humid, typical of summer in Iowa, but the sun was beginning to set and the air to cool. Lauren was right. It was a perfect evening to be outside, under other circumstances.

Years had passed since Donald had paid attention to the town where he was born and raised. As he walked down the tree-lined streets, he found he couldn't say who lived in any of the houses. He'd walked or driven by them on his way to and from work or to do errands for his mother, but he'd always been preoccupied with getting home as soon as possible. His surroundings had gone by unnoticed.

Markison, he saw now, was quite attractive and well-kept. Most properties out shown his by a mile. He saw many houses he'd like to call home. Donald found himself wondering what Lauren would think of them. He'd have to describe some of the prettier ones when he got back. He doubted she'd had time to explore the town herself.

The people were as interesting as the houses. Families were doing things together besides watching television. They were walking their dogs, barbecuing in the back yard, and playing with their kids. Someday those kinds of activities would be part of his life. If he wasn't wasting away in a jail cell.

Donald had circled back and now found himself near the park. He couldn't resist the laughter of children playing in the pool. Approaching darkness had caused the lights to come on over the water. The whole scene was enticing. For the second time that summer he watched happy people splashing and having fun. The lucky folks sounded like they had nothing heavy on their minds.

Just as when he'd been in the same area with Lauren and Grady, he was startled back to reality by thoughts of his mother. It was time he got back where he could keep an eye on the house.

He hadn't bought anything to eat or drink. Somehow, he felt that was expected on a night out. Donald went to the pool concession stand and purchased a red licorice whip. *Fat Free,* he read on the wrapper. Maybe Lauren would approve. He wondered how foolish he looked as he scooted through the alleys back to Fourth Street with two feet of red hanging from his mouth.

The sun was going down by the time he arrived in his back yard, but a glance at his watch under the street light told him he'd only been gone thirty minutes. Lauren would certainly expect him to entertain himself for longer than that. With the coming darkness to hide him, he decided to sit at the old picnic table in his next door neighbor's yard. Amelia wouldn't care. He hadn't seen her use it much. From there he could see the lights of Amber's kitchen and would have a perfect view if her goon were to come sneaking over.

Stars above, the twinkling of lightning bugs. It was all very peaceful if he could've turned off his internal alarm which was set to warn of hired killers afoot.

A rag rug laid across the table invited him to get more comfortable. He stretched out on his back and gazed at the heavens. Perhaps looking at the stars from that angle, he could drift into some sort of Neverland where he was young and innocent and carefree.

In only a few minutes, he became mesmerized by the evening sounds of birds and owls and, in spite of his best intentions, fell asleep.

"Mercy!" someone screamed in his ear. He jumped to attention, mad at himself for dozing on duty. He had to get over the need for rest if he was going to guard his household. Anything could've happened while he napped.

Amelia Klink was at his side. She'd grabbed the rug and was glaring at him as though he'd tried to steal it. "What in the world are you doing out here in the dark, Donnie? You gave me quite a start."

"I'm sorry. I just wanted some fresh air. It was a little stuffy in the house."

"Well, I guess I can't blame you for that. A pity you don't have a picnic table of your own, but I guess Margie wouldn't be able to sit at one. I brought Pretty Boy's rug out to air this afternoon, and he just now reminded me he didn't have it."

Donald had no response. He looked toward Amber's now dark house. "Do you know the lady who lives over there, Amelia?"

"I can't say I do. It was vacant for a few years after Barry McCall died, but I've seen lights this summer. Maybe it sold. Even though I always thought it was cursed."

"I heard Amber McCall is back. She's Dr. McCall's widow, isn't she?"

"Surely, you haven't forgotten *the murders*?" Amelia was incredulous.

Time for another lie. "Murders?"

"Why, yes!" Amelia was in her element with someone who didn't know about the only truly big scandal she ever remembered in Markison. "That McCall woman had two husbands who died suddenly."

"Both were murdered?" Donald was a natural at acting clueless. "I don't remember that. I guess Mom and I don't keep up on what goes on in town."

"It was before I moved to this house or I'd have filled you in right away. The law never proved the men were killed deliberately, but there was a lot of talk. Amber was what they used to call from *the wrong side of the tracks*. Her name then was Amber Mullins.

She'd have been several years ahead of you in school. Lived with her dad in the trailer court over west of here. She married young, and her husband just up and drowned in the bathtub. They'd only been together a few weeks. He didn't have a bad heart, didn't get electrocuted or anything. Nobody thought much of it until a couple years later when she had another husband drop. Amber was married then to the vet. It was a puzzle why he'd have wanted her. Except if you've seen the woman, you probably understand. She has to be close to forty today, but she's quite a looker. He must have thought she was worth the risk."

Donald sympathized with the good doctor. Amber gave a guy that feeling. "How did he die?"

"He ate some bad fish or something. They'd been married only one month. It wasn't an out and out suspicious situation, but it hadn't been long since she was a widow the first time, so things didn't look right. People sort of assumed she had to be guilty of something even though the police couldn't prove it. Myself, I always try to give folks the benefit of the doubt, but it's hard in her case."

"And then she moved away?"

"Yes, she was gone several years. Around May sometime I saw she was back and had the nerve to move into the McCall place. I'm sure it came to her legally in the will, but you'd think she wouldn't want to come back to where she has such a bad reputation. Probably likes living in a town with a slow-witted police force. I've always thought Markison is a little like Mayberry in that way. Nobody around here will ever marry her, though, I can tell you that. Don't you go near that house, Donnie. You might not come out alive."

Donald swallowed. He realized he should've visited with his neighbor a lot sooner. He managed to say, "Thanks for telling me, Amelia," and hurried across her yard to the safety of his own. Just as he neared the back porch, the screen door opened. He was ready for Lauren to say, "Oh, Donald, I hope you've been having fun! It's such a nice night, I couldn't stay inside any longer." But he didn't hear those words. And the person who stepped onto the porch wasn't his friend. It was Gavin the goon. Donald quickly moved behind the large ash tree that separated his and Amelia's properties. Gavin looked around to be sure he didn't have an audience then ran the distance to his and Amber's house.

Frozen to the spot, Donald knew he should take action. But he wasn't a fast runner and knew the intruder likely carried a gun. He decided to let the man get out of sight, then go inside and find out what had been going on.

Donald hated knowing Gavin had entered his house while he was blissfully sleeping on Pretty Boy's rug. The man must have returned to finish whatever he'd intended when he'd run into the sofa.

"I knew I shouldn't have left them tonight! It was a selfish, dangerous thing to do!"

"No, Donald. You are a free man, not a prisoner. You're entitled to some fresh air."

"No, I'm not. I was kidding myself. I'm not entitled to a thing but maybe a prison sentence."

It hadn't looked like Gavin was carrying anything when he exited the building, so it wasn't likely he was there stealing something. The Meesters' meager physical belongings didn't interest him. He was after higher stakes. Since the man had already been inside to measure and take stock of the layout, Donald feared his purpose tonight was to actually perform the hit.

Donald forced himself to enter the dark kitchen, holding his breath and hoping to hear sounds of laughter from Margie's bedroom. The TV was on, but no one was talking. In all his life, Donald had never dreaded anything so much as opening the door into that room. He did it fast before he could lose his nerve.

"Oh!" Margie squealed in fright. Grady jumped, and a look of terror took over Lauren's face. Donald realized too late they hadn't expected him to come in through the kitchen.

"Donnie! Why didn't you knock or something? You scared me out of a year's growth!"

"Me, too!" added Grady. "We were watching a scary movie, and I thought you were the bad man coming to grab us!"

Lauren couldn't even speak. She just stared, apparently wondering where Donald's head was to cause him to sneak in the way he did.

"I'm so sorry, you guys," he offered lamely. "I was talking to Amelia in her yard, and the back door was the closest one."

Lauren smiled then. "Oh, it's okay. We were just so caught up in the movie, and you came in right before the climax."

"Sorry I made you miss it." Donald was still finding it hard to calm down. What really had been happening in that house before he got there? Gavin hadn't come to the Meesters' to watch the movie.

"Well, Don, I was hoping you'd find something more exciting to do than talk to Miss Klink."

"No need to worry. I had plenty of excitement." His heart was still beating so fast he felt like they could see it through his shirt. "I'm going to get a glass of milk." He went to the kitchen and turned on the light. That room had barely known darkness until Lauren's arrival. Margie had kept Donald going and coming from there so often he'd rarely flipped the lights off. Now he approached the refrigerator and was surprised to see the door standing ajar. A quick look around also showed one cupboard was ever so slightly open. Somebody had been in the room and been in a hurry. It couldn't have been Margie without Lauren knowing. Grady couldn't reach the cupboards. Always meticulous, Lauren wouldn't be so careless as to leave doors open. Amber's henchman must have been doing something in the kitchen and maybe heard a noise and had to get out fast. Donald was desperate to know what he'd tried and if he'd been successful.

His first instinct was to worry about the contract hidden in the cupboard. He wasn't sure what the goon would want with it, but he had to check. Thankfully, his fingers could still feel the document on the top shelf where he'd put it. Was it only a month ago? He wondered if Amber had hidden her copy in a more secure place.

Donald realized he didn't want to drink anything except some water from the tap he ran into his hands and slurped up. The neighbor guy could've put poison into anything edible or drinkable in the room. What better way to kill Margie and make her son and/or Lauren look guilty? The only thing wrong with that thinking was that Donald himself could eat the food, and if he died, Amber and her man would be out of luck. Don had to remain alive to collect Margie's insurance. Surely even muscle man could grasp that fact.

Scanning the room, he noticed the pill bottle on the shelf over the sink. He picked it up. It was a jar of over-the-counter appetite suppressants Donald had bought for Margie some time ago. They hadn't worked, so he'd given up trying to hide them in her food. The bottle didn't have Margie's name on it like a prescription would, but Gavin could have deduced they were hers. The lid had been replaced a little crooked so it didn't seal properly. It was possible that had been Donald's doing, but not likely. The goon must have come in seeking medicine he could tamper with and didn't realize his large victim didn't take any. Donald tossed the suppressants into the trash feeling reasonably confident he was still one step ahead of the killers.

Back in the bedroom, the movie was over, and Lauren was gathering up the dishes from their raisin nut mix. Time now for Donald's report. Margie started the discussion. "Okay, Donnie, tell us what you did and what you ate!"

"Yeah, did you get ice cream or go swimming? That's what I'd do," offered Grady.

"Well . . . I didn't get that wild," admitted Donald. "I had a licorice whip. Otherwise, I just enjoyed the neighborhood and the weather. It was . . . pleasant and relaxing." *Until I saw the devil coming out of our house.*

Pleasant and relaxing sounded boring to Grady. "Next time you should find a dog to play with."

24
FUTURE FANTASIES

Papers were spread over the coffee table in the basement apartment. Lauren had been documenting what she'd learned from Margie thus far and making plans for the short time they had left together. The weight numbers and amounts of food consumed were easy to calculate. Harder, were the intangibles. Had she made strides in understanding the emotional side of Margie's eating obsession? Were any of her efforts planting seeds that would help this family make a future for themselves?

She thought of Don's frightened brown eyes when he'd come back after his night on the town. Poor guy. What she'd meant to be a pleasurable evening for him had apparently been scary. The man, as far as she could determine, knew little of the world except what he experienced in books and television. He seemed to Lauren to be an unfinished portrait just waiting for someone to bring it to life. She was tempted to take on the job but had to remind herself she was in town for academic reasons, and was coming to the end of her stay. Donald would be a long-term project.

I could play matchmaker. I know Don pretty well, I think. There has to be someone who's pretty but not too pretty, smart but not smart enough to scare him, and able to understand a man who's kinder than most but been denied a regular life.

It was a sure thing Donald didn't cross paths with many women his age and wasn't likely to find anyone on his own. *He could definitely use my help.* But Lauren knew no young women in Markison and wasn't apt to run across any in the next month. Her landlady was beautiful and not a lot older than Donald. She lived nearby which should make a relationship easy. But something told Lauren the two would have very little in common. Lauren hadn't sensed any innocence in Amber McCall. Dating the Red Widow would throw Don into no-telling-what kind of dark world. Some things were even worse than caring for Margie.

I feel like I'd like the right to screen Don's love prospects, if he ever finds any. For some reason, his safety and happiness seem to matter to me a little more than they should. Time to refocus and stick to my research. Doctors, nurses, lots of professionals have to guard against getting personally involved with their patients. I just have to stay professional.

Grady had been coloring in his room. Now he brought his masterpiece to show his mom. "It's a pig. I think I'll give it to Margie. Don't you think it'll make her laugh? When she laughs, she jiggles." It was easy to hear in his voice that he'd been paying his friend a compliment, even though his mom thought it a little unfortunate he'd chosen to draw a pig.

"Yes, I think she'd love it. Maybe you can tell her it's a teddy bear. I think she likes those better."

"Ok. A pink teddy bear! Would you write her name on it? I can't spell *Grandma.*"

"Her name's Margie. And she isn't your grandma."

"But I need one. And I bet she'd like to have a little boy. Donald's too big to cuddle."

Lauren was touched by her son's obvious need for more nurturing. She gave him lots of hugs, but she couldn't make up for the absence of a grandmother, especially a big soft one. "You might be right, but why don't you keep calling her Margie for now." And she wrote that name on the picture. He was off then to make his next gift. He knew how to spell MOM.

Grady's wish for a grandma brought back long-ago sadness for Lauren. Her mother, Jane, would've been an excellent grandmother to Grady. And, though not morbidly obese, she had possessed an ample bosom that Lauren had found comforting as a small child. Maybe if she'd given her mother a grandson sooner, Jane would've tried harder to stay healthy. Grady would've made her feel beautiful and loved the way her own children and husband hadn't been able to.

Actually, Lauren's father, Neil, hadn't even seemed to try. Soon after their marriage, Jane had begun to gain weight. That problem increased with the births of Lauren and her brother. Neil, who was a perfectionist and exceptionally trim, had nagged his wife unmercifully it seemed to Lauren. Even in elementary school, she understood her mom ate largely out of frustration. She would hear her father lecturing Jane about how if she didn't push herself away from the table, she wasn't going to be able to get out the door. He told her many times, "You can go to my office parties when you've lost some weight. I don't want you to be embarrassed." As soon as he left without her, Jane would be in tears and headed for the refrigerator to find something to make her feel better. The parties came and went without her, and Jane's weight increased. She didn't approach Margie's size, but was still in the unhealthy zone.

Lauren did learn from her mother's experience and vowed she'd never let herself get overweight. She even had a short bout with anorexia before her brother encouraged her to seek help. By Lauren's twenty-first birthday, she had gained control of her eating extremes, but her mother hadn't been as successful. At forty-four, Jane died of a stroke. Lauren was devastated and blamed herself for not being able to stop her mom's self-destructive habits. They may or may not have contributed to her death, but her daughter would always assume they did.

At the age of twenty-three, Lauren met and married the sweetest man imaginable who gave her a son with the same disposition. She wished every day her mom could've known Grady. His other grandmother was no longer alive either, nor was Neil or her father-in-law. It was a sad state of affairs for a little boy with so much love to give. However, Don's obese mother, who was also likely to have a short life, didn't seem to be a good answer for Grady.

Lauren's career in nutrition may have been the result of seeing how poor eating habits can ruin lives. She was set on a course for helping others which was quite satisfying and left little time for her to miss male companionship. Many of her friends, however, seemed concerned about her singleness and felt obligated to help her find a father for her son. They meant well, of course, but oh, the men they came up with. Lauren had recently concluded that her husband had been the last of the good guys. Those she'd gone out with since his overseas death were self-absorbed, controlling, and/or uninterested in getting to know Grady. Two of them turned out to have wives and children they forgot to mention at the outset. Not one gave her reason to even consider changing her single status. Her son might end up being the only man in her life from here on.

"Mom, you can have this painting!" He laid the masterpiece on her lap. "Now I need a snack. Want me to get you one, too?"

Oh, horrors! Lauren thought. *Is this our future? Am I setting Grady up to be another Donald? Just the two of us in cramped quarters with him bringing me food!* Worse, her son wouldn't have a male role model. *No way am I going to let that happen!*

As she chopped away at apples for the two of them, Lauren continued to analyze her approach to the problem. She wouldn't settle for less than a kind, loving, and loyal person. Someone who was transparent, not hiding grim character flaws. Surprisingly, she did come up with the name of one individual who seemed to fit that description. And, in her eyes at least, he was good looking. She had to smile. Her friends would never believe what young man she was thinking of.

25

COURTING CATASROPHE

When Donald arrived home from work, Lauren came out to the front sidewalk to meet him. In spite of her smile, his first reaction was fear. He was sure she had bad news about his mother. Donald automatically stiffened and prepared for the worst.

"I just had an idea today," she began. Those words didn't sound very frightening, so Donald relaxed and tuned in. "I know you went out on the town the other night just to please me, and I didn't get the impression you had much fun. Am I right?"

"Well, it wasn't actually *fun*, but that was my own fault. I don't know much about entertaining myself."

"That's just it, Don. You shouldn't always have to entertain yourself. You need to be around other people. And I have an idea. You and I should go out to eat and to a movie. My treat."

He didn't know what to say. It sounded like Lauren asked him for a date. Except for the short time at Starbucks with Amber, he'd never been on one. The idea was more than exciting until he remembered his obligations. "But we can't leave Mom and Grady alone."

"I know. But you have to figure something out. A plan that will let you escape every now and then. Do you know anybody who could come in? If not, we'll have to advertise."

Donald didn't need one hand to count the people he knew well enough to ask a favor. Then he recalled Amelia's offer. "A long time ago, our neighbor said she'd be glad to sit with Margie sometime. I think she's wondered why I don't ask."

"Well, there you go! She even mentioned that to me. She must get lonesome in her house with only a dog for company."

It wasn't that Donald couldn't see the logic in Lauren's suggestion. But he didn't fancy setting Amelia Klink up to be an accidental victim. What if Amber or her associate were to come in to do their killing while he was away? How far would either of them go to finish the job? If a person were going to commit murder, would three victims be any more trouble than one? Especially when one was obese, one was elderly, and one was not quite in kindergarten.

"I don't know. I hate to impose on her. I think she goes to bed early."

"You know what? If you don't ask her, I will. She'll be free to make some excuse if she doesn't want to."

"Well . . . okay. I'll just go on over there now." He might as well get it over with. Maybe she was going to be gone or something, and he could feign disappointment. A whole evening out was just asking for trouble.

Donald was self-conscious as he made the trek across the two yards. And it was the first time he'd ever gone up on her porch.

Amelia opened the door as soon as Donald knocked. One would've thought she'd been pressed up against it looking out the window. "Well, hello there. Nothing's wrong with Margie, I hope."

"No, she's doing fine. I'm just here to ask a favor." Pretty Boy was making conversation difficult by yipping and jumping around Donald's legs. Hopefully, Amelia wouldn't want to bring her dog along. He wasn't sure how Margie would respond to an animal in the house.

"Anything, Donnie. You know I can't refuse you. Favors are what neighbors are for."

"Well, Lauren is feeling a little stir crazy so I thought we'd go out to eat and to a movie. That is, we would if you could sit with mom and Grady for a few hours."

Donald's inner self tried to make himself heard. *"A few hours? Bad idea! Bad idea!"*

"Bless my soul," Amelia was saying. "I thought you were going to ask me something hard. It's no trouble to watch TV with Marge. But if she needs to . . . I mean, I have a bad back so I can't lift her."

"You don't have to. I can get her set so you won't need to help her go to the bathroom or anywhere else. All you have to do is visit with her and Grady."

"I haven't talked much to little kids. I'm childless, you know." Amelia offered that item like it was a much-repeated phrase, the shadow over her life.

"Oh, you won't have to think about what to say. Grady will talk to you. He's easy to get to know."

"Well then, you and Lauren go and have a nice time. And I'll be happy to have one night when I won't be alone. Maybe we can even watch America's Got Talent together. What time do you want me?"

Donald hoped he wasn't starting something with Amelia that would be hard to get stopped, but for tonight she was definitely needed.

"It would be great if you can come over by six."

"Don, my boy, are you sure you want to take the risk?"

"No, I'm not sure at all, but I don't want to disappoint Lauren."

"It'll be disappointing if something happens to Grady. Can't he go with you?"

"I think she might want a night on her own."

"Amber and her man probably watch the house and will see you go. They'll think the coast is clear."

"Taking care of three people would be way too hard. I don't think they'll do that if they can help it."

"Well, have fun, Donnie. If you can."

Lauren left supper for Margie and Grady, and she and Don set off to walk downtown. The weather was perfect, not too hot or windy, nothing to keep them from getting a little exercise. Plus, Donald hadn't started the Ford in a while. It might not even have gas.

Markison wasn't overrun with good eating places, but the Pizza Joint seemed a good bet. Margie often ordered from there, but Donald usually let her have it all. He always figured he could fill up on something less costly.

"Want to get pizza?" He thought it would be fairly cheap compared to other places, but was still surprised when Lauren didn't veto his suggestion. Pizza had to qualify as junk food since it was so tasty.

"I love pizza," she admitted. "And it doesn't have to be bad for you." She had a vegetarian personal pan while Donald devoured a four-meat medium. He knew it was more than he should have, but it was such a treat to smell and taste something better than his own cooking that he simply couldn't deny himself. To her credit, Lauren didn't lecture him. After all, it wasn't *his* weight she'd committed to change.

"Have you and Margie ever gotten to go out to eat?" she asked him. It must have been obvious he didn't do this much. His only meal away from the house in recent years had been the disastrous lunch at Amber's.

"No, not for a real long time. My dad used to take us out, and then somebody told mom they'd seen him eating at a restaurant with his nurse. That put an end to that. She told him she didn't want to chance eating somewhere he'd been with his lover."

"Lots of bosses and employees go out for lunch on secretary's day, Boss's Day, and such. It doesn't usually mean anything romantic."

"It was hard to convince Mom of that. I know she'd have been a hard woman to be married to. She was pretty, but kind of excitable."

"So your life hasn't been exactly easy, has it, Don?" Lauren sounded sincerely concerned.

"Oh, I don't know. It hasn't been so bad." He was eager to change the subject. He wasn't going out just to spend the evening complaining. "What do you like to do for fun when you aren't fixing a fat woman's life?" he asked her.

"To tell you the truth, since I lost my husband, I've been so busy with school and taking care of Grady, I don't do much else. My fun is mostly what five-year-olds like to do.

"That's okay. They know more about fun than old folks."

"I do like to run. I've even entered a few races, but this summer I've really gotten out of shape."

"You don't look like it." The compliment slipped out without Donald even noticing.

The two friends chatted easily over pizza and even joked and laughed. Donald felt more himself than he had with Amber. This evening was feeling like he always imagined a date would.

The talk continued after the pizza was consumed. Donald wouldn't have minded visiting with her even longer, but suddenly Lauren put down her water glass. "Oh, look at the time! We'd better get over to the theatre!"

They slid into their seats just in time for the previews of coming attractions. Donald wondered if he'd be able to go to any of those movies. He supposed he could since he'd be free of responsibilities by the time they played. But his next film might be an old one on TV in his jail cell. He was glad they were seeing a comedy tonight and not a murder mystery. He didn't think he could stand any more suspense than he was experiencing already.

Donald was almost ashamed to think how long it had been since he'd been to a movie. In high school while his mom was still at a reasonable weight, he was an easily embarrassed teen, so he always found excuses not to go with her. By the time he'd quit worrying about what his peers would think, Margie was already too large for the theatre seats. And Donald had never worked up the nerve to invite a person his age to go with him.

As soon as the feature started, his thoughts turned to dating traditions. The question was whether this evening qualified as a date. Lauren might think of him as a brother or a buddy. On the other hand, if she meant it to be a date, she'd expect him to hold her hand or put his arm around her. Not that he'd mind, but doing so would be totally inappropriate if she were thinking *brother*. Donald was in a quandary. The only tactic he could think of was to delay. Maybe the answer would come to him on his way to the bathroom. He excused himself and started up the aisle, aware that it was quite early in the feature to be going out.

Halfway to the exit he spotted the last person he expected to see out in public, Amber's man, Gavin. He was sitting on the end of a row, so the two men made easy eye contact. Donald knew his own face must have given away his fear.

In the bathroom, he consulted his other self.

"What do you make of Gavin being at the movie? Is that good or bad?"

"Well, it could just mean Amber is out of town and the guy has a little free time to take in a comedy, but. . ."

"But what?"

"But since he saw you and Lauren here, he now thinks Margie is alone."

Donald desperately hoped the idea hadn't occurred to the goon. With luck, the movie was good enough to keep him from leaving.

His worst fears were realized when, on his way back to Lauren, he saw Gavin's seat was empty. Donald had to convince Lauren to leave right away. He was no actor, but this development was calling for some dramatics.

"Hey, I'm sorry to take so long," he whispered. "I think I might have food poisoning from the pizza. I have to get out of here!"

She looked surprised but sympathetic. "Ok. Let's go!" With many curious eyes on them, the two exited the theatre.

They walked as fast as they could the four blocks to Margie's. Lauren must have thought Donald's lack of speech on the way was because of the nausea. Once, just for realism, he stopped by a tree and pretended to vomit. From there, they ran for the house.

As they came to the front sidewalk, they noticed Amelia outside Margie's bedroom window. She was beating at the ground with a broom.

Lauren ran up to the woman. "Amelia! What in the world are you doing? Why aren't you inside with Margie and Grady?"

Lauren seemed to think the elderly woman was losing her grip, but Donald guessed what was going on.

Amelia was breathless from the exertion. "I'm sorry, but I knew Pretty Boy must be needing to go out so I went home to let him do his business. Then I put him back in his bed and came outside." Her eyes begged to be believed. "I was going right back to Margie's when I saw smoke up close to the house. I was scared the whole thing was going to go up in flames so I grabbed this broom I always keep on the porch to sweep the front walk. I put out the fire, but I think the side of your house got a little scorched."

Donald and Lauren examined the blackened area on the siding and in the grass. It appeared their neighbor had, indeed, saved the day. Donald shuddered at what the outcome could've been had she not left his mom's bedroom. He only wished she'd caught a glimpse of the culprit.

"Thank you so much, Amelia," he managed to say.

"I know you didn't want me to leave Margie for any reason. You don't have to use me again. Unless your mother can stand to have a little dog around. Pretty Boy just can't hold it like a big dog can."

"Oh, don't worry, Amelia," Lauren comforted the woman. "We're just glad it worked out. Do you have any idea what caused the fire?"

"No! Nobody around here smokes that I know of. Maybe it was spontaneous combustion."

Donald was sifting through the grass. He didn't say anything when he found a cigarette butt. "Hard to tell. But please, Amelia, don't say a word to Mom about this. A fire is her worst nightmare."

The front door opened and Grady's head peeked out. "Hi Mom! Me and Margie wondered who Amelia was talking to. I'm glad it wasn't a bugelar."

What's been going on out here is worse than a burglary, Donald thought.

His other self was firm. *"What did you expect, Donnie? No more dates for you."*

Lauren took hold of his arm and asked with concern, "How's your stomach doing, Don? The food poisoning must be better."

"Afraid not," he answered honestly. "My stomach feels worse than it ever has."

Donald regretted his date with Lauren had been cut short. To think that earlier in the evening, his biggest worry was whether to hold her hand. He hoped he'd get another chance at that dilemma.

"Well, if it doesn't get better, we'd better take you to Emergency. Food poisoning can be bad."

"I'll be okay," Donald replied on his way to the bathroom.

His purpose in leaving the others was to see if his other self might have some answers for him.

"Aren't you just an academy award actor? Man in agony. You were very convincing."

"That's because I AM in agony. I wish I knew what really went on here tonight."

"Probably Gavin was looking in Margie's window to see if she was there alone. He may have dropped the cigarette accidentally or he might have tried to burn the place."

"I have to believe it was an accident. I can't face the other."

"Well, Donnie, not facing it won't stop it. Ever think of going to the police?"

"I'm thinking. I just keep hoping I won't have to."

"You're running out of time, my boy."

26
SURPRISE SUITOR

Once Margie got started on the exercise portion of her rehabilitation, she was off and running, figuratively speaking. Compared to her last twenty sedentary years, she was now a virtual wonder woman. She actually requested to move to five pound weights. Lauren had to stop her from pedaling constantly. As soon as she realized she could move around without help, Margie nearly wore out the carpet in her room. Lauren was worried her subject was overdoing a good thing. She didn't want the woman to put too much stress on her knees because at her weight, surgery wouldn't be an option, and most future exercise would be impossible with injured joints.

One milestone was shared with the public. The weather was particularly cool for midsummer, and Margie was acting more chipper than usual, causing Lauren to suggest a walk outside. Don was home from work, so between the two of them, they got their charge dressed in a recently-purchased garment that was not open in the back.

There were the expected protests. She tried the "I'll go walking when I've lost some weight." Of course, her caretakers pointed out that she would lose much more weight if she burned some calories. She also threatened them with the possibility she could fall and break something. Both her son and Lauren assured Margie they wouldn't let that happen.

"But people will stare at me!" was the loudest protest.

"Probably," said Lauren calmly. "But they'll be doing it because they admire you, not because they're making fun."

"Nobody admires somebody who looks like me. But I guess I can do it just this once so you'll be quiet about it from now on."

No promises were made about being quiet, but Donald and Lauren hurried to get started before she could change her mind. With careful manipulation, Margie got through the front door and off the porch. Donald had sworn to himself that if the woman started moaning and groaning, they'd turn around and cancel the whole outing. Margie seemed to sense his intentions, so she kept herself from vocalizing when she was first hit by the sun and the light wind. It helped that Lauren had had the foresight to give her sunglasses.

Several cars slowed down to see the woman who looked like she came straight from the circus. Amelia and her Pekinese came out onto their lawn and watched the progress. Pretty Boy wiggled in the arms of his mistress seeing a grand opportunity to do some jumping and chasing, but Amelia held on tight. No one wanted to see this brave threesome go tumbling to the sidewalk.

Donald got tears in his eyes when he thought how long it'd been since he walked beside his mother. He was also crying because he was probably doing it for the last time.

Lauren recognized part of the significance of the moment for Margie as well as for Donald. She'd brought along her camera and several times caught the fat woman smiling like a movie star for the paparazzi. When they got to the main sidewalk they decided against stopping cars to cross the street. A slow turn-around propelled them back to the house. Margie's only comment was, "I hope Grady will be proud of me."

Donald was standing on the front porch, winding down after the stress of taking Margie outside. He was glad she'd accomplished something that might eventually add years to her life. But then, he had to remember there was no *eventually* for Margie. The fire episode had told him the neighborhood assassins were determined.

Billy, the delivery boy from The Pizza Joint, could be seen coming away from the front door of the house across the street. He spotted Donald on his porch. "Hi, Mr. Meester!"

Donald was slow to answer to that unfamiliar name. "Oh, hello, Billy."

The boy came out onto the street far enough to call, "Is Margie okay?"

"Oh yes, she's better than usual," Donald was happy to report.

"Good. I just wondered since she hasn't ordered pizza lately. Hope I didn't make her mad."

It was understandable that Billy would wonder. Margie'd been one of his regulars as long as he'd had the job. He was one of a handful of people in town who ever saw the woman.

"No, Billy. She's just trying to go on a diet. You didn't do anything wrong." Donald was always ready to blame himself for anything unfortunate that happened. It would be a shame if the nice pizza guy fell into that same habit.

"Well, tell her hi from me!" Billy called as he hopped into his truck.

Normally, Donald would be happy to relay any personal message to his mother, but he thought perhaps a reminder of her favorite snack wouldn't be helpful at this point.

Just as the pizza truck drove away, an ancient Cadillac pulled up in front of the house. An unplanned hello from a delivery boy was one thing, but the car looked like someone deliberately coming to call. These days, Donald was wary of any unusual occurrences on their property, and company arriving at the Meester house was highly unusual. He stood at alert as a teenage boy got out of the driver's side. The boy came around and opened the passenger door to assist an extremely large man out onto the street. The man stood still while the boy dragged a walker out of the trunk of the car and handed it to him. The obese man set off up toward the porch.

The stroll seemed to be a huge effort. Donald watched in amazement. This guy was nearly as big as Margie, and he had a young, fit helper close by, but he was forcing himself to move unassisted. Donald hoped his mom was watching out the window.

"Good evening! Lovely evening, isn't it?" The stranger was breathlessly trying to put Donald at ease. "I'm sorry to intrude, but my grandson and I were out for drive and passed down your street a few minutes ago. We noticed you were out walking with a woman who appeared to be in my weight bracket. I don't know many who are."

"Yes. That was my mother, Margaret Meester. She's resting now."

"That's quite alright. I promised my grandson I'd let him get home in time to go out with his friends. Maybe you could tell Margaret that Jerry Cook stopped by. It just occurred to me when I saw her that she and I might enjoy comparing life problems sometime. Though I'm only in Markison for a week. I'm just down the street."

Donald was speechless. A man was calling on Margie. He'd never imagined such a thing could happen. No male ever came to see her except Billy and the young pastor she'd sent away. Finally, he recovered enough to respond, "I'll tell her. She'd probably like to visit sometime if you happen to catch her outside." He knew his mom wouldn't want to be caught with her hair a mess or without a snack to offer.

Jerry Cook gave a little wave and turned his walker around. Looking at him from behind, Donald noticed that, except for the missing braid, the fellow could have been Margie. Mr. Cook, however, moved much faster than she did. It was a wonder of wonders there was another adult as overweight as his mother. He'd always been sure she was the biggest person in existence.

The grandson waiting by the car opened the door and helped Mr. Cook get back in. Donald wondered if the young man felt trapped, having to haul his grandfather around. Probably not—Jerry had mentioned his grandson had friends. Besides, he was only being asked to endure the duty for a week. A week was nothing.

Inside the house, Donald saw Margie's bedroom curtains were pulled back. She must have witnessed the scene with Jerry Cook.

"He was hoping to meet you." That must've sounded like a lie. It even sounded that way to Donald.

"Why would he want to meet me? Because I'm fat like him?"

"He just thought you might have things in common." *Like being fat.*

"Well, I doubt that. I don't generally like overweight people. They irritate me."

"This one seemed very polite and intelligent. You might want to give him a chance."

"A chance to what? Steal my money? Any man who wants to get acquainted with me is only interested in my life insurance."

"Well, if you think like that, you'll miss out on all the honest guys, too. Jerry Cook seems like he might be one of those, and he has no way to know how much insurance you have."

"Cook doesn't sound like anybody I've ever heard of. I'd remember that name." And the woman smiled slyly as though she was actually making a joke about her own obsession with food.

"Well, Mom, you don't get around to see who lives in Markison this millennium. Maybe that's going to change now that you're on the move."

"Don't get your hopes up, Donnie. I just walked a few feet. That doesn't mean I'm ready for an affair."

It was Donald's turn to smile. Margie having an affair or even using that word was incomprehensible. She was full of surprises. And as frustrating as their crazy conversations were, Don knew he was going to miss them.

27

MARGIE'S MAKEOVER

Lauren was faced with a risky task. Margie had gotten the idea she wanted a *short, sexy* haircut. What prompted that decision was a mystery the woman wouldn't share. She made the case for clipping off her long braid by convincing Lauren she would be able to take charge of her own hair if it were short. Plus, it seemed important to her to look *more modern.*

Realizing Don was used to dealing with his mom's long tresses, Lauren insisted on calling him at work before she attempted anything drastic.

"I'm so sorry to bother you, but Margie wants a haircut. Today. And she wants it short. I used to cut my mom's, so I know how. I was just afraid the change might shock you."

"Oh, that's okay." How could he deny his mother a new hairstyle at this point? "The braiding isn't hard to do, but it's hard to wash the long stuff and get a comb through it. I dread the job every week. Anyway, do what you want. Just make her happy."

The worry for Lauren was that, except for food, what made Margie happy varied from day to day. Tomorrow she might want her braid back. But the woman insisted. She'd heard someone say on The View that if you have a round face, it helps to have hair framing it. Lauren couldn't help wondering who Margie was hoping to impress. She held her breath as she handed over a mirror at the end of the operation. "What do you think?"

Margie was silent for a few seconds and then came out with, "It's cute!"

Lauren wasn't sure *cute* would ever describe her subject, but she was very struck by the quality of Margie's hair. With all the weight gone, it fell in big ringlets, displaying the kind of body Lauren always wished her own hair had. "You're going to love taking care of this," she assured Margie. "And you look like a whole new person."

"Well, good. It's high time I looked different. How about lipstick? With my hair gone, I don't want to be taken for a man."

Again, Lauren wondered who was going to be judging Margie. She and Don and Amelia were the only people around, and they certainly knew she was a woman, braid or not. But Lauren obliged and put a little pink on Margie's lips. It was unlikely with all the eating she did that it would last long, but for the moment, the big lady's face appeared a lot more attractive than usual.

It seemed a shame to let the new look go to waste so Lauren suggested they go into the back yard and see if Amelia was around. "I'm sure she'll be interested to see your new hairdo. I don't think that woman has had one in the last thirty years. You could inspire her."

Margie seemed to like the thought of showing off to her neighbor, so she agreed to venture outside again. Luckily, Amelia was lining up tomatoes to ripen on her picnic table. She looked up, her face showing disbelief. "Is that you, Marge? My goodness." She straightened up and ran her hands through her own grown-out perm. "My goodness. You sure do look different. Younger."

That seemed to be the correct response because Margie smiled in delight. "I just felt like a change," she said modestly.

"Well, bless you. You make me feel like an old frump. Maybe you should go out on the town tonight."

"Oh, I don't need to do that. I just like to look my best for the family."

Lauren was surprised to be referred to that way. She felt a stab of regret that half of Margie's "family" would soon be leaving her. Before she guided her friend back into the house, she glanced toward her own apartment and saw Amber's partner standing by his van. It looked like he'd been watching her, Margie and Amelia. When he saw he was being noticed, he walked slowly to his back door. *I didn't think men were as interested in their neighbors' lives as women are. This guy seems very interested.*

As soon as Margie got back inside, she checked her reflection in the hand mirror to be sure her hair hadn't gotten mussed in the wind. Lauren smiled and smoothed down a few stray strands for her, happy the woman was obsessing over something besides food.

The doorbell interrupted the beauty concerns. Lauren made her way to the front door expecting to see a delivery man. Instead, there stood a middle-aged obese gentleman leaning on a walker. He was holding a box that looked suspiciously like chocolates. "I was wondering if I might speak with Margaret Meester." Though she'd never seen him before, Lauren sensed the gentleman might be the real reason for Margie's makeover.

Margie put down the mirror and smiled sweetly. "I'm Margaret. You must be Jerry. Come on in." Lauren realized she'd never seen such a bright-eyed expression on the woman's face except at the sight of a cheeseburger.

"I'm usually not so forward, but when I saw you in front of your house the other day, I felt compelled to meet you. Life can be lonely for people our size, so we should probably seek each other out."

Lauren was impressed the man seemed so in touch with reality, so honest. If she'd had the idea of a love interest to lift Margie's spirits, she'd have told herself there was no possibility. But Jerry seemed to be just what the doctor ordered. Except for the chocolates. How would Lauren's fruit snacks ever compete with candy from a sweetheart?

Jerry held the box out to Margie. "I confess somebody gave me these for my birthday. People always think big people love chocolate. I'm allergic, however. I'd love for you to enjoy them."

Margie shocked Lauren by demurely refusing. "That's awfully nice of you, but I'm on a diet. Trying to keep my girlish figure."

You'd think she had a sense of humor, thought Lauren, and she took the box into the kitchen. Chances were good Margie would want them as soon as Jerry left. She reentered the room to find the two heavy friends laughing like old acquaintances. It struck her they could be siblings. Not only were they the same size, but the man had hair the same color and length as her client. Lauren wished she could snap a picture but hated to interrupt the party.

Margie tried to catch her up on the conversation. "Jerry was telling me about his little dog, Tiny. I was picturing them together. They always say on The View that people choose pets who look like them. I guess Jerry isn't like most people." The new friends laughed some more.

Margie was getting comfortable so came right out with the question on the tip of her tongue. "You said your wife died. Do you have a girlfriend?" She was getting personal awfully early in the relationship, in Lauren's opinion, but Jerry didn't seem to mind.

"No, not yet. I'm looking, but I haven't found Miss Right yet."

Lauren was curious. "How will you know when you find her?"

"Oh, I'll know. She'll have a good personality, and she'll be beautiful. By *beautiful,* I mean slim. I could never be attracted to someone who's overweight."

Margie's face fell and her voice quivered. "Well, why did you come here then? Do you want to ask Lauren out?"

"Oh, I'm sorry, Margaret. I didn't mean to hurt your feelings. I thought . . . well, that is, I assumed you knew I wasn't thinking romantically about you. I only meant us to be friends. I was sure you'd welcome that."

Lauren's heart ached for Margie. The woman had been so thrilled by Jerry's visit, and now she'd been shot down and made to feel like a misfit. By a man who looked just like her. "You may go now, Mr. Cook. Margaret has lots of friends already, so you don't have to do her any favors." The man appeared genuinely shocked and puzzled. He seemed to have no idea what he'd said wrong. Margie switched on the TV to shut him out. Jerry Cook was just another disappointment she would probably never speak of again. Lauren showed him to the door.

"My grandson isn't supposed to pick me up for another half hour, but I suppose I can walk back to my daughter's place. It's only a block away."

"I'm sure you'll manage. Thanks for stopping by," said Lauren, ignoring his hint for a ride but knowing she'd watch him from a distance to be sure he made it okay. By the time she saw the fat man make the turn onto a sidewalk down the street, the distasteful visit was history, and Margie was ready for some sugar.

"Let's have a look at that box of candy."

Lauren didn't have the heart to say no, but vowed it would be only one piece. Jerry Cook wasn't going to sabotage all their progress.

While retrieving the candy from the kitchen, Lauren heard Margie's shaky voice. Since no one else was in her bedroom, she must be talking to herself. "I am beautiful. I am fascinating. I am beautiful. I am fascinating."

Later, Margie dozed off watching Ellen. Lauren was amused to see the woman was trying to take her nap sitting up. It seemed she didn't want to lean back for fear of flattening her new hairdo. *Vanity can be a great motivator,* Lauren was thinking. *I'm going to have to try to capitalize on that.* Her cell phone went off, and she was glad she'd forgotten to take it off vibrate earlier. She went into the kitchen to answer.

"Lauren, this is Kerry. The nurse who came to examine Margie at her house?"

"It's so nice to hear from you. Unless you're calling to say some test came back with a problem."

"Oh, no. Nothing like that. We were just talking in the office, wondering how your work with Margie is coming. I heard someone say they saw her walking outside her house!"

"Yes. She didn't go far, but it was a big milestone for her. I think we're actually getting somewhere."

"Wow. I can't tell you how happy we all are to hear that. I have to admit, I expected you to be scared off the same way everyone else has been. But congratulations on hanging in there."

"Thanks. That means a lot. You'll have to stop in sometime. It would give Margie a reason to show off what she's learned about a healthy lifestyle. And you can see her new haircut!"

Kerry laughed. "Amazing! I hope I can make it over soon. Though I guess the longer it takes me, the more weight she'll have lost."

"Yes, time is our friend when it comes to her fitness. It's all baby steps, but I'm sure in a year or so, Margie's going to shock everybody with her transformation. If you wait that long to come by, the old Margie won't even be living here anymore."

28
ACCIDENTS ABOUND

Satisfied that Margie was none the worse from her discouraging afternoon, Lauren left Donald in charge of serving her a healthy dinner of salmon, broccoli and baked potato. She picked up her son from daycare and looked forward to an uneventful evening with him.

Grady's hands were full of papers and crafts from his day. As soon as his mother turned the key in the lock of the door to the basement apartment, the boy started his flight down the stairs. That feat had become Grady's favorite way to wind down after a day of organized activity. His short legs barely reached from one step to the other, but he took them so fast, he managed to sail to the bottom. Lauren held her breath every time. She was sure she'd be the one to take a tumble, since her attention was always focused on her son.

On this particular day, Grady disappeared after the third step. Lauren screamed and looked down. Papers lay strewn down the stairs. Her boy's small hands were gripping the board below a wide hole where another step was obviously missing. "Hang on, baby, I'll catch you!" Lauren carefully stretched her leg over the hole and hurried down the stairs. She went under the staircase and held up her arms. "Jump, honey! You're a paratrooper!" Grady let go then because his grip gave out. They both tumbled to the floor. Grady had a soft landing on his mother. Lauren hurt from the impact, but luckily, her head had avoided contact with the cement.

Grady scrambled to stand up and then helped his mom. "I'm sorry! I'm sorry!" he kept saying. He knew his mother had saved him but believed it was from his own recklessness. "I didn't mean to run! I'll go slow next time!" He was sobbing, thinking he may have injured his mother.

"It's okay," Lauren assured him, even though she didn't feel okay. Every part of her body ached, but worse than that, she was terrified. When they'd climbed them earlier in the day, the steps had been solid. There'd been no sign of a weakness. She'd have immediately reported a broken one to her landlady. Looking from beneath the staircase, she could see now the board was completely missing, leaving a hole big enough for a small child to slide through. An area of unpainted wood revealed the step had been sawed away and apparently discarded. She could think of no good reason for something like that. At least no reasons she wanted to think about.

Lauren lay on the couch for a few minutes to let her muscles relax. Grady fetched water and a carrot to make her feel better. "It's the last one, but you have to eat it. It'll make you healthy."

Mother's little caretaker, she thought. *I could easily be taking my son to the hospital right now. What on earth just happened?* Amber and her friend had no cause to want her or Grady injured or dead. Maybe they were simply a pair of psychopaths.

As soon as she'd determined that neither she nor her son had any physical damage, Lauren's main concern was to get them out of the house. They'd go out through the cellar door and visit the Meesters as they'd previously planned to do. Lauren wondered how she was going to explain the accident without stirring up Margie. There was no chance she could convince Grady to keep mum.

"I fell through the stairs, and Mom saved my life!" he announced before he was completely in the door to Margie's bedroom.

As expected, Margie's eyes grew wide. "What happened?"

178

Donald, too, looked alarmed. In fact, he looked *too* alarmed in view of the fact that both his friends were obviously unhurt.

Lauren slowly and calmly related the details of the incident. She emphasized the superman strength Grady had shown by hanging on so long. "He was actually the hero of the day. And he took care of me after it happened. I'm starting to get a little bit sore now, but nothing's broken."

She could tell Donald saw nothing positive about her story. He stood quietly contemplating what had just taken place and why. He knew he was going to have to take some action. Setting a booby trap for Lauren and/or her son was outside the boundaries of the contract. Not generally a tough guy, he was devising a way to make somebody pay.

Margie looked ready to cry. Her little friend had had a close call, and it had touched her deeply. As for Grady, he now had an opportunity to comfort another woman in his life.

"Margie, don't be sad. I'm okay. We can play Hearts if you want."

Margie had to smile at that. "Sure. Let's do. And, Lauren, you two have to stay here tonight. I don't know if you're safe in that redhead's house. Donnie locks all our doors and windows, so nothing else bad will happen to you if you're with us. And we don't have any stairs to worry about."

Lauren accepted the invitation though she wasn't comforted. *We might be safe for a few hours, but what about tomorrow?*

A scuffling noise from the porch drew Grady's attention. "I hear ghosts!" he announced. No one else had noticed, so his words were ignored as being products of a child's imagination. It had grown dark outside, and while they played cards, Grady and Margie had been discussing the chances of a scary movie being on TV later.

"I did hear them. I'll show you!" And Grady left the game to exit the room and fling open the front door. His eyes grew wide. "Margie!" he proclaimed in horror.

Lauren and Donald rushed to see what the boy was talking about. Margie, after all, was safely in her chair behind the card table in her bedroom.

Lauren was the first to understand whom they were looking at. Lying on the floor of the porch, face down, was the obese gentleman from earlier. Lauren could imagine how Grady mistook the man for Margie.

The fellow tried to look up at them but was having the difficulties of a beached whale. He seemed to be having trouble breathing and was unable to do anything but roll back and forth on his stomach. Lauren switched on the porch light exposing the big man's predicament.

After much effort, Lauren and Donald got Jerry on his feet. No one asked for an explanation.

Lauren still held bad feelings about the guy who had been so rude to Margie, but she couldn't let him stay where he was. She feared he might have a bad heart, and the fall must've been a dangerously traumatic experience for him. She could only imagine how Margie would've reacted if she'd had such an accident.

"What is it?" Margie was more than curious and a little frightened about the activity she was missing.

"Nothing, Mom. A visitor has had a fall on our porch."

"Land! Everybody's falling today. I hope I'm not next!"

Hardly likely tonight, thought Donald. *Unless she falls out of bed. Heaven forbid.*

"Come inside, sir," invited Donald, and he assisted the red-faced gentleman into the front room, switching on the overhead light so there'd be no more tumbles.

Margie was feeling left out. "Whoever it is, bring them in here where I can see!"

"Coming, Mom. Can't go very fast."

Donald and Lauren weren't getting much help maneuvering the obese man through the front room. He seemed dazed and confused and was pretty much dead weight. Once they got to Margie's door, they were faced with the question of where to put their reluctant guest. The only place big enough and accessible was Margie's bed. They lowered Jerry onto it.

"Well, I don't believe it." Margie was astounded to see her would-be sweetheart. "I bet you didn't ever think you'd be in my big ugly bed! You fit though." *One point for Margie.*

Jerry couldn't have looked more humiliated. "I don't know what to say. I'm not really sure what happened."

"I think you slipped and fell flat, but you didn't go through the floor. And you didn't tear your pants." Grady knew those were positives.

"Well, I do have a few aches and pains, but I don't think anything's broken."

Donald was relieved the man wasn't making noises about a lawsuit. That was the last thing their household needed.

"It doesn't hurt so much when you're fat. I don't get hurt when I fall down in my snowsuit." Grady had made a good comparison, but Lauren feared Jerry wouldn't like it.

"You're right. I'm pretty well padded," was his good-natured answer.

Lauren actually felt sorry for the gentleman. He had tried earlier to be so dapper and dignified. Now he was definitely neither. "What brought you back tonight?" she asked him.

Jerry was quiet for a few seconds as though trying to remember. "I felt so badly about the mean things I said to you." He was looking at Margie. "My daughter made me see I was being a typical fat man. Trying to pretend I was too good for a lady who is twice as attractive as I am. It was thoughtless and bad-mannered. There are no excuses."

Donald didn't have the faintest idea what the man was talking about. Lauren couldn't imagine what Margie's response should be. She almost hoped for one of the woman's signature rude remarks.

Instead, her friend smoothed the waters with, "Do you want a sundae?"

"Actually, that sounds very refreshing," responded Jerry.

Lauren was disappointed her program for healthy snacks was being challenged, but she coped by fixing yogurt sundaes with fresh fruit topping. No one complained, and an agreeable evening was had by all.

When he felt sure their visitor was uninjured and getting his strength back, Donald offered Jerry a ride home. In the car, he fished for a clearer explanation of what had occurred on the porch. "Did you stumble on a bad board?" That was certainly possible. Donald knew he should replace them all.

"No, I didn't trip over a thing. Actually . . . I didn't want to talk about it in front of the boy, but somebody attacked me."

"Really? Who?"

"Somebody I'd never seen. A man. He looked very angry, like he wanted to kill. He lunged for me, and then when he got a good look at my face, he dropped his hands and ran. That's when I lost my balance. Now I'd rather not think any more about it. I'm going back to Des Moines soon, and I don't want to worry my daughter."

Watching the obese man as he spoke, Donald was struck by his resemblance to Margie, especially the size and haircut. It didn't take much to realize what had happened. The crazed killer next door had been skulking around the place and thought Jerry was Donald's mother. Donald could easily have had another death on his conscience.

"I think it will be best if Margaret doesn't go out alone at night," advised Jerry Cook.

"Don't worry. She never does. And I'll find out who the man was. You can be sure of that."

"I don't want to be questioned by the police or anything."

"You won't have to be. I'm going to take care of it." Donald sounded very strong and in charge. He wished he felt that way.

29
ACTING THE AVENGER

Immediately after delivering Jerry, Donald parked the car and hurried across his back yard. He was about to step onto Amber's property when he came to a halt. He'd rushed off without forming a plan. *I'd better take a minute to figure out my attack strategy.*

Donald was not used to confrontation and knew his limitations if it came to anything physical. It was a good thing he didn't have a weapon or he'd have tried using it. Somebody wasn't playing fair. Since Amber's car had not returned, he knew she was still out of town. Even if she'd been at home, she probably wouldn't have been able to saw through the sturdy basement step, and she wasn't big enough to attack a morbidly obese man, so it left only Gavin. Gavin the goon. Or Gavin the lover. It no longer mattered. That man was threatening the most important people in Donald's life.

"Amber has no right to get someone else to do her dirty work! She told me I had until she came back to get Lauren and Grady out of town. What harm are they doing anyway? She's getting rent from them. And why not supervise her employee better so he doesn't attack the wrong people?"

"Oh, man, you have no common sense. You trusted the word of a hired killer. If she eliminates innocent, helpless folks for money why would you expect her to play fair?"

Even though he'd just told himself he had none, Donald decided to trust his instincts. A light was on in the kitchen of the McCall residence. He could see Gavin at the sink. Like nothing had happened. Like the man hadn't recently sabotaged a woman and a child and tried to choke a stranger. The figure at the window was a perfect target if only Donald had a gun.

"Who are you kidding, Barney Fife? You don't even know which end the bullet comes out of."

Donald ignored his inner voice. He felt empowered by his fury. He wouldn't worry about a gun he didn't have. He was ready to try out his fists.

"Right. And if it comes down to your fists against his gun, what then?"

He'd think of something. He'd have to rely on luck.

"You have so much of that."

Donald was saved from finding a response. He was close now to the kitchen window of Amber's house. The goon must have needed some fresh air because it was open. Donald could see the shirtless man was talking on his cell phone.

Inching his way along the side of the house, Donald stood with his ear against the window frame. From there he was able to hear one half of a disturbing conversation.

"I think I put that woman and her son out of commission . . . Trust me. The setup was simple but effective . . . How should I know? I wasn't here at the time, and I didn't go down there to find out. It's dark downstairs though. Don't know what that means."

Donald thought it curious that Gavin seemed to be keeping his methods to himself. He'd never once mentioned the stairs. Amber apparently didn't require him to report his activities in any detail. They must have been together a long time to have established so much trust. He shuddered to think how many people they'd "put out of commission" together.

"No, the police would've been here by now if she'd called them. She was probably just thinking about the boy. They must not have gone to the hospital 'cause her car's still in the drive, and I didn't hear an ambulance. I'm sure they're scared and ready to move out. They'll be out of town by tomorrow . . . Can't the rest wait 'til you get back? I'm kinda losing my taste for this thing. I didn't know it was going to mean hurting a kid. I've got one of those somewhere, so it doesn't seem right to me."

Like any of this business was right. But the goon had a flicker of conscience. And he and Amber weren't involved in anything more than a business relationship. The bad part was that Donald got the idea from what he was hearing that Amber had told her assistant to get rid of Lauren and Grady and didn't particularly care how he did it. What kind of female could be that cold?

Gavin continued to complain to his partner in crime. "Oh. Well, I'll see. These things aren't so easy, you know. Donald keeps pretty close guard on her. . . . Yeah, yeah. I know you can't help it. I'll do my best. . . . Okay. I'll let you know. It might take a while, but it'll be clean. And I won't leave here until I get my cut of the insurance." There was a pause. "Why *wouldn't* the money be important to me? I'm not doing this crappy stuff for fun!" And he ended the call.

Gavin had sounded like he didn't like Amber very much, or respect her. Donald wondered if the goon realized his life was probably not worth a dime to his boss. When he finished his assignment, he would probably be finished himself. His would be another fatherless child in the world.

The half of the phone conversation Donald listened to made it clear Amber was issuing orders for Gavin to do more. It wasn't hard to figure out what he'd been talking about when he'd asked, "Can't the rest wait?"

Gavin had chosen not to tell Amber about his fiasco on the front porch with Jerry Cook. He was probably confident he'd get things right before she returned. He didn't plan to confess he almost killed the wrong person. The goon was very motivated to complete the contract and get into Amber's good graces before the payout.

Anger welled up inside Donald. If his mother were to see who was attacking her, that big fierce-looking man would look so much more frightening than the petite redhead. Margie might even have had a chance against her. Amber, he knew now, must be an executive who didn't get her hands soiled if she could help it. He

185

replayed Gavin's words about getting his cut of the insurance. His mother's insurance. His inheritance. The thought was enough to make Donald feel faint.

Knowing Gavin was likely armed, his earlier courage waned. Donald saw nothing to do but go back home. He felt inadequate not being able to tell the people there he'd settled the score. And he couldn't tell them what he'd overheard. All he could do was try to act like all the mishaps were accidents and then prepare to spend another sleepless night.

❖❖❖❖

"Well, Jerry is safely at his son's. I think he's pretty embarrassed about what happened." He looked at Lauren. "Maybe you've already talked about it, but you should stay here tonight."

"I told Margie we would, but I've changed my mind. You don't have room, and I have to make lots of notes about the day. If I wait, I'm sure to forget something important."

"I've got a computer and printer. You're welcome to use those. I'd feel a lot better with you here. Tomorrow maybe we can figure out what's going on." What a phony he was. He knew what was going on. He just didn't know how to stop it.

"But all you have for sleeping is your own twin bed and the sofa in the living room."

"You can take my bed. I have a sleeping bag that hasn't been used since I was a little boy. We can put it on the floor for Grady. I'll sleep on the sofa. I'm a little too long, but I always curl up anyway." He left the room to make the sleeping arrangements. It was good to have a definite action he could take.

Grady had heard the plan but had a better idea. "Margie, can I sleep with you?"

Margie rose up to see Grady's eyes peering over the foot of her bed. She was speechless for a few seconds.

"You don't have to do that," Lauren assured the woman. "The sleeping bag beside me will work just great." Margie's bed obviously had no space for another sleeper, even a very small one.

"No, I'd like to have him join me. I'm fluffy enough he won't even need a pillow." Margie was getting better all the time at making light of her size.

"She says I can, Mom!" And Grady lost no time taking off his shoes and socks and climbing in with his friend. Instead of lying beside her whole body, he sat tucked under her left arm. It was the equivalent of having his own arm chair. "Me and Margie are going to watch monster movies!"

"Says who?" Margie teased him. "I'll get scared, and then I won't be able to get to sleep."

"Don't worry," Grady comforted. "I'm pretty brave, so if you have to close your eyes at the scary parts, I'll tell you when to open them."

"In that case, we'll do it. What are we going to eat? Popcorn?" She looked hopefully at Lauren.

"I'll fix some in the air popper. No butter and only a tiny bit of salt. Small bowl. Can you handle that?"

"Should we say yes?" Margie asked Grady.

"Yep. That sounds supercalifragilisticexpialidocious!"

Margie laughed. "Okay! But you'll have to hold the bowl. I can't move my arm!"

While Lauren was in the kitchen, Grady started a whole dialogue inspired by thoughts of monsters. "Do you know what I love most?"

"Ice cream?" Margie was probably answering for herself.

"I LOVE Halloween! Do you love Halloween?"

"I used to. I used to love handing out treats. Not many children come here now. When they do, Donnie has to go to the door. He doesn't talk to the kids like I did."

"I'll come this Halloween, and I'll walk all the way inside so you can talk to me! You can give me an orange. It's healthy, and it looks like a little pumpkin!"

"Good idea! I can't wait until Halloween! I hope I recognize you in your costume."

Donald walked past the bedroom door on his way to make up his bed on the couch. He glanced in just in time to hear Margie's last statement and to see the way his mother's face lit up at the idea of something to look forward to. Tears filled his eyes when he remembered Gavin's words on the phone to Amber. Donald's mom wasn't going to see Grady on Halloween.

With the deadline upon him, Donald realized he had to confide in someone, and the absolute only person he knew who had any understanding of the circumstances was Lauren. What would she think of him? If she were smart, she would gather up Grady and all their belongings and get out of Markison before sunup. He would do that if he were her.

"Lauren's not going to think you're much of a person when you admit you hired a hit woman to take care of your mother."

"And she'll be right. I have no defense except that my mind was clouded at the time."

"The only thing you can do to redeem yourself as a human being is to let Lauren detest you so much she'll leave. Fast."

"I know that's what I should do, but I hate for her and Grady to go. I can't imagine not having them here."

"Too late, sucker. You shouldn't have gotten infatuated with the first female who talked to you. You should've waited for the real thing. It would've been so worth it."

"Right. But I have to forget all that now and concentrate on keeping Lauren and her son away from here. At least until Amber is finished with Mom."

"That whole mom thing is going to be harder on you than you think, and you won't even have Lauren to help you through it. This situation is going to go from bad to worse."

30
COMING CLEAN

When Donald had finished his nighttime preparations, he entered Margie's bedroom to find she and Grady had both dozed off, the popcorn sitting between them barely touched. Lauren was writing in her notebook. She looked up and smiled, giving a nod toward the pair in the bed. Donald motioned for her to come with him. Lauren obeyed after taking away the bowl and switching off the television.

Donald led her to the front porch. Though the evening had grown dark, he didn't turn on the overhead light. He didn't dare. It would be easier to confess his sins if he didn't have to see her eyes.

Lauren started the conversation. "I'm so thrilled your mom and Grady are friends. It seems to give her a new outlook on life. She'll do anything he says, and he's turning out to be my best helper."

"I know. When I give Mom a snack she'd have refused a few months ago, she actually takes it. I think her biggest criteria for choosing food is WWGD. What would Grady do?"

"He's becoming a little health nut. Not because of what I tell him, but because he understands it's good for Margie. He's determined he's going to get her outside to play ball."

"Wow. That's a big ambition." Donald nearly choked on his words. Thoughts of disappointing Grady were adding to his already enormous shame. "Lauren, I-I'm afraid I have something to tell you."

At his tone, she instinctively sat down. "I get the feeling it isn't a happy something. Are you sick of my interference? I can back off a little if you think I should. Don't be afraid to tell me."

"That's not it. Actually, I can't thank you enough. You can't imagine how much you've done for Mom and me in the short time you've been with us. But it's important that you leave town. Tonight, if possible."

"What?" He couldn't see her facial expression, but it was obvious from the way she leaned forward in her chair that she didn't believe her ears. "Was it something I said?"

"Of course not. But I'm serious. A stupid thing I did before I met you is putting your and Grady's lives in danger, so you shouldn't stay. There isn't any more you can do here." He might as well be blunt. It was best to just cut her heart out in one big swoop.

"Don! Have you been drinking?"

Donald didn't answer. He wished his problem was something solvable like alcoholism.

"Of course, I have more to do here," Lauren continued. "And Grady does, too!" When Donald didn't reply, she softly added, "I thought you liked having us around."

"I do! But that isn't the point. You have to go."

"You're being evasive, man. This isn't what you planned to say. You were going to tell the truth. Remember what that is?"

"Okay. Here goes. I have to be honest if I'm going to convince you. Before I got your letter, I was getting pretty desperate about my life. I felt like I was mom's prisoner, and I was afraid I'd never be free to get married and have a career and a family. Right when I was at the lowest point, I met a pretty red haired lady at the library."

Lauren immediately guessed the identity of the redhead. "Amber?" She probably thought Donald's sad story was going to be an ordinary tale of unrequited love.

"I fell hard for her. I know now it wasn't real. I didn't even know her. She saw me for what I was, a lonely desperate guy who had no one close to him to get suspicious." His voice became barely audible. "She made me a deal."

Neither of them spoke for several seconds. Donald couldn't go on, and Lauren didn't encourage him to. She just waited. He saw no movement and heard no breathing. No cars went by on the street. Amelia's house was dark. The night belonged to the two people on the porch. Two people who'd soon be saying goodbye. If Donald judged her right, Lauren would first get her son to safety and then call the police. He could expect nothing else.

"I signed a contract with Amber. In exchange for killing my mother, she'd get half of Mom's life insurance."

"Oh, Don," Lauren breathed. "How could you?"

"I can't answer that. I got caught up in it, like it was inevitable or something. It didn't take me long to regret it. Right now, it doesn't seem like I could ever have been at that place in my mind. But I have a contract to prove I was."

"You sound like such a creep. Somebody with no heart, no spine and no morals."

"I know. I hate myself more than she does."

"When and how?" Lauren sounded cold, horrified, like she was talking to Satan.

"She didn't say. That was part of the agreement. I was supposed to forget it was coming. Which, of course, I can't do." Then came the hardest part to tell Lauren. "If you're here when she's ready to make a move on Mom, I think she's going to . . . get rid of you, too. I should've made you leave sooner. I'm sorry." How lame was that?

"What do you mean, *get rid of me*?" She spit the words. He hadn't known Lauren was capable of so much bitterness. It wouldn't be surprising if she killed Don before Amber murdered Margie.

"Get rid the way Amber gets rid of people, I guess. I don't want to find out."

"This is a nightmare! I don't know what to do. I can't let anything happen to me because of Grady, but I also can't leave Margie in the hands of a couple of killers!" Donald wished she'd keep her voice down. It wasn't the sort of thing they should be broadcasting throughout the neighborhood.

"She thinks of you as a killer now. How does that feel?"

"It sucks."

Lauren got up from her chair. Her voice quivered with emotion. "I'm leaving now. I'm going to get my son and try to explain why I have to drag him away in the middle of the night and go to a motel. The minute he's safe, I'm going to call 911 and report a potential homicide. Hopefully, the police can get here in time. May God have mercy on your soul, Don."

Just as she opened the screen door to go inside, they both heard a child's voice from the back yard. "Mom! Mom! Where are you?" Donald forgot his own predicament and ran to see why Grady was outdoors.

Lauren followed. "I'm here, honey. I thought you were asleep!" The streetlight shone on her small son in his bare feet. When she reached him, she saw he was shaking violently even though the night was warm.

"What's wrong?" Lauren asked, trying to keep Grady from hearing the fear in her voice. She hugged the boy close, trying to still his shivering body.

His words were soft and halting but too easy to interpret. "A man put a pillow over Margie's face and ran away! I … I … tried to catch him, but I couldn't. If I had my shoes . . ."

Donald couldn't believe Gavin had tried something with Grady in the bed. He must not have seen him in the dark. Margie could be dead, or at the very least, frightened out of her mind. He knew he had to go check on her, but he couldn't make himself go inside.

"Donnie? Grady? Somebody help me!" It was Margie calling from the back door. Donald ran toward her voice, glad she could speak, but terrified she was injured. He found the woman stuck in the door frame, unable to go forward or backward. Maybe she could've pushed herself all the way through the opening if she hadn't been so winded from the exertion of walking across two rooms.

"Mom! Where were you trying to go?" Donald asked as he took hold of her and gently got her turned around. Her sudden mobility was a bright spot in this frightful evening.

"Oh, Donnie! Somebody tried to put a pillow over my face! I woke up and couldn't breathe. I guess Grady scared the person, and he stopped. Grady went after him, and I was so worried my boy was going to get hurt." Margie was crying. Donald couldn't remember her ever being so concerned about somebody besides herself.

Lauren and Grady helped Donald get his mother back to her bed. After the adrenaline wore off, Margie was like a rag. She was limp but surprisingly calm, considering she'd almost been suffocated. As soon as she was comfortable, Donald offered to fix sundaes. "No, thanks, Don," Lauren said in a voice devoid of kindness. "Dessert is not the answer. This is much too serious to be fixed with food."

Donald knew she was right. All his life, he and Margie had used treats as tranquilizers. If he couldn't do that, what could he do?

"This is a matter for the police. We have to call them. Grady and I can't stay here, and we can't leave Margie unguarded unless Amber McCall and her friend have been arrested."

"Amber?" Margie was astonished the intruder was somebody she'd actually met. "You mean the woman with the red hair? Why would she want to kill me? I tried to be nice that day she was here!"

Lauren and Donald were baffled as to how to finish the conversation without upsetting Margie even more. Donald decided to tell a white lie. "Mom, I think Lauren is mixed up. We don't know who it was. Now I think you should try to sleep. It's way past your bedtime. Lauren and I are going to visit in the kitchen where we can see both doors. No one can get into your bedroom unless they come past us."

"What about this window? It's right over my bed. I could be dead before you know it."

"That window is locked. I check it every night." To prove it, he gave the handle a tug. Donald assured himself Amber didn't have a way to open it.

"Is Grady okay?" Margie asked when she noticed the boy was no longer in her room.

"He's fine but worn out. Lauren's taking care of him. He needs his mom right now." Grady had followed his mother to the kitchen. He was still groggy and confused by all the late-night scariness.

Donald left the bedroom, but knew without looking back that Margie's eyes were stuck in their awake position. He and Lauren would have to talk quietly.

❖❖❖

Grady immediately curled up on his mom's lap and closed his eyes. After making sure he was asleep, she got right to the point. "Do you want me to make the call?"

Donald knew there was no way to escape his guilt for what had happened. "What will you tell them?"

Lauren was an honest person. Of course, she'd tell the truth as she knew it. At last, she whispered, "I'll tell them what happened and that Amber McCall and her friend are the likely suspects. And, Don, if I'm pressed, I'll tell them about your part in it. If I don't, Amber will."

She was right of course.

"Well, this is it, big guy. You're up a creek. To prove Amber is guilty of attempted murder and get them to arrest her, you'll probably have to produce the contract. And you know who else will be implicated by that."

"I might as well turn myself in. The only good thing about this is Mom is still alive. I won't have her death on my conscience while I'm sitting in prison."

"You will have if you don't see that Amber gets locked up. She's going to try again. I doubt if she's ever failed to fulfill a contract. Even if she knows she won't get the insurance money, she'll want to maintain her perfect record."

Not only had Donald been gravely gullible, but he'd thrown away his life before it really got started. "I guess it's just as well I didn't put the contract in a safety-deposit box like Amber told me to." He opened the cupboard above the stove and reached as far back as he could, dragging forward a sheet of paper. He'd never planned to look at it again, but it had waited for him. Instead of being Margie's death warrant, the contract had proven to be his. Handling it like a hot coal, he passed it to Lauren. She read every word. He never had. He'd only skimmed the document. He was no lawyer so probably wouldn't have spotted anything wrong even if he'd gone over it with a fine-toothed comb. A knock on the back door prevented Lauren from commenting.

"Oh, God," gasped Donald. "Somebody must have heard us and reported suspicious activity."

"Well, go to the door and find out." Lauren must've been hoping he was right.

Looking through the screen, Donald saw the terrified gaze of Amelia Klink. His first fear was that she'd been standing there a while and had heard more than she should have.

"Is something wrong, Amelia?" he asked in what he hoped was an everyday tone.

"That's what I'm wondering!" Ms. Klink, in her flowered robe, didn't budge from her spot near the opening in the door, as if demanding to be invited in. She was holding her Pekinese. "I let Pretty Boy out to go potty, and I heard the child screaming. I told myself to stay out of it because whatever was going on isn't my business. But I just couldn't stop worrying about Grady."

"I appreciate your concern," Donald told her. He was hoping to cut the dialogue short. "He heard a noise behind the house, probably an owl or a cat, so he went outside and then got scared."

"Poor little guy," she said. "When I heard you adults were out there, too, I almost went back to bed, but then I got to wondering if you needed my help." She continued to stand in place, waiting for an invitation. When it didn't come, she approached the subject that was actually on her mind. "I had no idea that Lauren and Grady spent their nights here. I mean, I don't care, but—"

"They don't. Now, you should get back to bed and stop worrying about us. Everybody's fine. I'm sorry we disturbed you." Donald couldn't think clearly during all the woman's chatter.

"Oh, it's no problem," she said, a hint of reluctance in her voice. She turned to go. "You know Pretty Boy and I don't get much excitement, so we're always happy for a change of pace. As long as no one gets injured. I remember how scary it was the night of the fire!"

"Nothing like that going on this time." It took a gentle push and "Good night, Amelia. Thanks for your concern," to force the woman off the back porch.

Lauren was looking extremely irritated. "That's all you need. More people involved. More people for Amber to get rid of."

"Well, in a way, it's nice to know someone notices what goes on here. I thought nobody did. But you're right. I don't want to make Amber any madder, and we don't want any rumors to draw attention to us. Amelia is very good at getting those started. I'm sure my boring life has been a disappointment to her all these years."

"She isn't the only person you've disappointed." Lauren sounded so sad that Donald had to change the subject. He could stand her anger easier than her hurt feelings.

Lauren continued to speak, this time in her mad-mother voice. "Better make that call or the police are going to wonder what you were waiting for."

Donald started for the phone, but was interrupted by a shout from the bedroom. "Donnie! Who was at the door? Don't let anybody in!"

"It was just Amelia, Mom. She heard us outside. She's gone now. Go back to sleep."

"I can't sleep! I'm scared you're going to call the police. I don't want them here, Donnie. Promise they won't come and ask me questions. I'm not strong enough for questions. You can go down to the police station tomorrow."

"Okay, Mom. Don't worry. I'll take care of it." He had to stop making promises like that, promises he couldn't keep.

There was only quiet from the bedroom. Donald knew his mother was still waiting for the police.

"Well, Donnie, how do you plan to take care of it? I can't wait to hear." The sarcasm was actually coming from Lauren. And Donald didn't have an answer for her.

"I know a way," she continued. "You can go to the police and tell them Amber's assistant attacked your mother and explain to them how you know that. Your little contract should make it all clear."

He had to admit, her solution sounded sensible. It also sounded like a recipe for a prison sentence. Decision making had never come easy to Donald, and this particular decision was way too much for him to deal with. "I don't know what to do."

"Well, I do," Lauren said firmly, not looking at him. "I'm calling. She was still holding her sleeping son but managed to retrieve her cell phone from the pocket of her sweater. She started to dial, then seemed to think better of it. "Margie's right. They'd want to come here and get a statement from her and figure out how the intruder entered the house. It would set Margie back a mile."

Still in her room, Margie made herself known. She had a sixth sense where her son was concerned. "Donnie! I want to hear what you're talking about. I feel like you're keeping secrets."

Lauren called out a response. "Grady and I are going home now, Margie. Try to get some sleep."

Knowing his mother would be upset at their departure, Donald exited the room to try reassuring her. Keeping the women in his life at peace had become his fulltime job.

Lauren seemed eager to get herself and her son away from the house. Since Grady was too heavy for her to carry, it was necessary to wake him. She slipped shoes on his feet with no help from him. "Come on, honey, we have to go stay in the motel tonight." Her son was groggy and disoriented and didn't want to go.

"I'm staying all night with Margie," he protested.

"Not anymore." Lauren was about at the end of her rope after Donald's admission, the attempt on Margie's life, and Grady's proximity to professional killers.

"We have to go. It's too late to tell ghost stories now anyway."

"What if the bad man comes back to get her?" Grady hadn't forgotten the pillow scare.

"Donald will take care of it. Don't worry." And Lauren practically pushed her son through the house and to the front door. Donald came to his mom's bedroom door to see them off. "Tell Margie we're sorry," she snapped at him in a hushed tone.

He hated to see them go, afraid they'd never be back. He didn't try to stop them because he knew it was for the best. Still, it was hard to hear Grady's words as he followed Lauren outside. "I don't like this night, Mom."

"I don't either, baby," was her tearful reply. "I don't either." It looked to Donald like she practically made the boy run to their car.

And so it went. The Markison police didn't learn about the midnight incident on the corner of Fourth and McKinley. By morning, life had returned to what passed for normal at the Meester's.

The contract had gone back into the cupboard. Lauren couldn't bring herself to break Margie's heart by letting her learn the truth about her son. Margie was still extremely shaken after her traumatic night, and Amelia Klink had the feeling she'd missed out on something important.

Donald convinced himself that if Lauren and Grady stayed safely away from the house after dark, he could find a way to thwart the plans of the two neighbors who were intent on acquiring the insurance money. He might never sleep again, but none of Don's loved ones were going to be killed on his watch. All his nights would be spent listening for the opening of a locked door.

31
PERILOUS PACKAGE

Donald lingered in the fiction section of the Public Library. With a burning desire to stop the killer-for-hire fiasco, he decided to play detective, to try thinking like Amber. He was browsing through the books his former love interest had shown such a preference for. Murder and more murder. Perhaps the volumes should come with a warning, *Possibly dangerous to the reader's mental health.* It seemed to him, Amber's hobby had morphed into an obsession and then into a career. He vowed never to allow his future children to read such stories.

He scanned the titles wondering which one might have served as inspiration for killing an obese woman. In addition to the Mystery of the Tainted Chips, there were names like The Cupcake Murders, Poison in the Pancakes, and Deli of Death. Corny as they sounded, all the books were about killing human beings, and that was a serious theme. He imposed on his colleague Charles to tell him which of the paperbacks Amber had checked out in the past month. Without taking too much time from his work routine, Donald checked out a few of the books to scan for clues as to what could be in store for his mom.

Back in the office, he looked at the stack of mysteries. He dreaded the stories they would tell, but he felt good about taking some action to stay ahead of the Red Widow. Absently, he picked up the morning paper. Amber's face looked at him from the front page. It was a close up, unsmiling image that made his heart stop.

He almost expected the photo to talk to him. "Have you sent that woman and boy away yet? I'm coming home soon!"

The photo remained mute, but the text had a lot to say. The heading *WOOTEN GUILTY* was followed by an article which Donald read with horror.

In Chicago, the trial of 25-year-old Edwin Wooten has concluded with a guilty verdict. Accused of the murder of his mother, Wooten had been tearfully adamant on the stand that the actual killing was committed by Amber McCall, who coerced him into signing a murder-for-hire agreement. He indicated the contract was in his briefcase at home. No such document was found. In the absence of conspiracy evidence, Edwin Wooten was declared the sole killer of his mother Emily. He has begun serving a life sentence at the Statesville Correctional Center in Crest Hill, Illinois.

Edwin's photo accompanied the news release. Donald empathized with the poor man. He'd probably had a crush on the lovely Amber, and, like Donald, let her convince him to do something he wouldn't have done otherwise. At first, Donald was surprised Edwin had admitted to signing a contract. That piece of paper would have implicated him as much as it would have Amber. However, Edwin, already on the road to jail, wouldn't want to go without being sure his hired woman would serve equal time. Donald vowed, then and there, if he were ever to be in such a position, he would tell the police about the contract in the cupboard. Maybe he could exact a little revenge for Edwin, as well as for himself. Amber needed to be stopped. He shuddered to think how many Edwins and Donalds were sitting in cells, perhaps on death row.

One point of justice was that Amber must not have scored financially in the Wooten case. She escaped persecution, but she couldn't have made any money since, as Donald remembered reading somewhere, a convict (Edwin) wouldn't be able to inherit his mother's life insurance since he played a part in her death. Therefore, Amber wouldn't collect anything. On the dark side, she must be feeling desperate to recoup some of the lost income. Even her assistant must be worried about where his next paycheck was coming from. The pair were, no doubt, eager to speed up access to the Meester money.

Donald wondered if Lauren would ever return to finish her work with his mother. He'd been tempted to call her the night before, but he knew she needed time. Understandably, she must be having second thoughts about bringing Grady back into such a dangerous situation. On his way home for lunch on Friday, he worried Margie would force him to explain Lauren's absence. He hated lying to his mom, but it was going to be necessary.

"I'm home," he warned as he opened the door.

"Come over here, Donnie," said his mother. Her voice revealed no hint of trouble, but something had definitely distracted her from the questions he was expecting. "I just had a package delivered. From Chicago! It says it's perishable."

Alarms went off in Donald's head. *Chicago. Food. Titles of paperback mysteries.* He definitely smelled a rat. "Don't open it!"

"Why not, Donnie? Are you jealous your name isn't on it, too? You've probably forgotten I have a birthday coming up next week. I bet that's it. Some old friend remembered and is sending me a cake. I can have at least one piece, can't I?" She looked pleadingly at her son.

Donald grabbed the box which actually did look the size of a bakery cake. "I'll open it. You can't be too careful about mysterious packages, and a couple of strange things have happened lately."

"Donnie, you are no fun these days," his mother whined. "But go ahead and open it if you have to. I'm sure it's nothing for you to get all worked up over."

He took out his pocket knife, a long ago gift from his father, and carefully opened the box. Inside were a dozen cupcakes. They looked delicious and harmless. There was no card. He remembered *The Cupcake Murders* and knew in his heart Amber had taken a cue from that book. The Margie she'd met would've had half of the cakes eaten before Donnie even got home from work. Not a bad idea on Amber's part, but it wasn't going to work. He promptly took the box into the kitchen and could be heard sending each cupcake down the garbage disposal. He sealed the wrappers in a plastic baggie so no animal was apt to smell them in the trash. When he returned to Margie's room, she was staring at him as though trying to make sense of what had just happened.

All Donald could feel was relief he'd gotten home in time to intercept Amber's poison parcel. No longer could he feel safe from the woman just because she was out of town. Her homicidal activities knew no geographical boundaries. And how did Amber know his mom wouldn't share the cupcakes with him?

"Donnie, I'm worried about your mind," was all Margie could offer. But on the positive side, she seemed more concerned about her son's mental health than about the treat she'd been denied.

The afternoon hours at the library passed in a haze. Lauren and Grady were safe at the hotel, but it was a temporary solution. Amber must have learned by now that her assistant had messed up every attempt to complete his assignment. She was sure to be back in town as quickly as possible to find out if the package was successful and if not, resort to an alternate, and likely more extreme, method. He was sure she had many lethal possibilities in reserve.

As he went through the motions of shelving books, Donald debated with himself.

"That was a close one with the cupcakes, man."

"Too close. I don't think I can dodge bullets much longer."

"You're going to have to do something drastic. You have to go on the offensive. Even if you die doing it."

"I'm willing, but I don't know what to do. I should at least buy a weapon. What criminal is put off by an unarmed man? Knowing I had a gun might slow him down."

"We've already eliminated that idea. You'd probably shoot yourself in the foot before you got a chance to shoot Gavin. You have to think of a better way."

❖❖❖❖

When he returned home from work, he saw any opportunity he might have had to kill the killer was temporarily being removed. Gavin's white van sat in Amber's driveway. Donald watched the muscleman carry two large boxes from the house and load them into the vehicle. The guy proceeded to make what seemed to be a final trip to pick up his jacket and boots which he threw into the passenger side before he got behind the wheel and backed noisily onto the street. It appeared Gavin had had enough or that he'd been fired. He was getting out of Dodge. Hopefully, he'd meet Amber, and they would ride off into the sunset.

After a few hours, Donald's hands quit shaking, and he was able to give his mother an occasional smile. He knew the reprieve from tension wouldn't last, but it had come in the nick of time. Another night of near tragedies, and Donald might have been a case for the psych ward.

With the immediate danger alert at a low level, he remembered his mom's earlier remark about her coming birthday. With the ominous goings on in the house, Donald had completely let that date slip his mind. There was no way he could pass up the chance to help Margie celebrate what was probably her last big day.

She'd never seemed to mind her advancing age, but instead looked upon the parties as chances for more cake and ice cream. For Donald's last birthday, his mother had called Hy-Vee bakery and ordered the biggest two-layer the store's pans would allow them to bake. And the two Meesters ate it all. Donald was certain he'd never buy chocolate cake again. But since he'd thrown away the cupcakes Margie received in the mail, he felt himself weakening.

He was sure Lauren would disapprove if he did give in, but for the life of him, he couldn't think of a good substitute. It would be cruel, it seemed to him, to give her a relish tray with a candle in the middle.

He knew it wouldn't be welcome, but he made a call to Lauren.

"Hi, this is Donald."

"Is Margie okay?" Her voice was cool, like a stranger's.

"She's fine, but I just remembered her 53rd birthday is Tuesday. I can't think of a nutritious treat to get her."

"Don't worry about it. I'll think of something." And she hung up. He couldn't believe she'd hung up. She was probably thinking he had no right to make any birthday preparations after arranging to end Margie's life. She was right, of course, but his mother wouldn't understand his reasons and would miss him fussing over her.

He should at least buy her a gift. Lauren couldn't forbid that. He'd given his mom something every year since he was five, and he wouldn't stop now. But all things considered, it was hard to come up with a gift for a woman in Margie's circumstances.

Donald sat on the top step outside during the time of day he and Lauren had been regularly having their talks. Since he'd told her his secret, he'd had no one to visit with except his oldest buddy, himself.

"Donald, my man, you take the cake – no pun intended. You think getting a birthday present for Margie is even appropriate this year?"

"Sure, it is. I just hope she's still around by Tuesday."

32
BIRTHDAY BASH

"I guess somebody will remember my birthday tomorrow," Margie said to no one in particular at the commercial break of *Keeping Up with the Kardashians*. She'd been throwing out such remarks for the past few days. Donald largely ignored them since he had no idea what, if anything, was being planned. Lauren had said she'd take care of it, so he was confident his mother wouldn't be forgotten.

For his share of the festivities, Donald had gone shopping at Shopko and picked up baseball equipment for Margie and for Grady. He purchased a plastic bat, a ball, and two Cardinals caps. With luck, the friends would get in some play before one of them disappeared. But his mom hadn't yet arrived at the stage where she could participate in such games, and he was very afraid Lauren was planning to take her son back to Iowa City before that milestone was reached. Oh the promising side, maybe the hope of Grady getting to finally play ball with Margie would keep them around longer.

❖❖❖❖

Tuesday started out like any other morning with bath, toilet, and breakfast rituals. Donald's distaste for those chores had lessened since Lauren had been around to share the work and since Margie's attitude had improved.

Grady patiently watched TV while holding two large rolls of yellow and green crepe paper. At the first lull in the activity around him, he would get busy with the decorations. Everyone was in a good mood, and a party atmosphere was ensured when the birthday lady announced, "I think I should wear my pink dress."

"Funny you should say that," Lauren responded. "You might as well open my gift now."

"Oh, really! I was sure you'd make me wait until later." And Margie happily took the festive-looking box Lauren offered her. Grady moved in close just in case his friend needed help.

Donald liked to see his mother excited about receiving something besides food. Sadly, he didn't remember her ever getting much else from him or anyone else. He probably should have brought her non-edible gifts once in a while even if she didn't need them. *Too late to think of it now.*

"A new pink dress!" Lauren had found, or had someone make, a lovely garment of a different fabric and shade than the much-worn one that tied in back. This was a real dress with a scooped neckline to prove it wasn't a nightgown.

All three of the adults struggled to get it on the heavy woman who did her best to assist with the operation. The result was a near-glamorous, semi-elegant, and totally beaming Margie. "I wonder what Jerry Cook would think of me now!"

"He'd see that you're too classy for him," answered Lauren. She was fussing with the woman's hair and makeup, making her pretty for the photos she intended to take. Donald had slipped into his room, returning with something in a sack. His wrapping skills were nonexistent. The most he'd tried for was to cover the surprise with the only paper available.

The gift he held now was a spontaneous decision. "This is something I wanted to see you wear again." And he revealed the double strand of pearls he'd found under the couch. Somehow, this birthday party seemed the right time for them.

Lauren gave Donald a questioning look. She must have been wondering where he got the money and why the pearls were in a wrinkled Shopko sack. But Margie didn't worry about those things. Her voice held wonder. "My pearls. You found my pearls. Thank you, Donnie." And her eyes glistened with tears as her son fastened them around her neck. He prayed they'd reach, and they did. The result was a choker rather than their intended length, but no one cared.

"Margie, you look beautiful!" The declaration from her favorite child was as good as a present. They were almost the same words Donald had uttered years ago on his parents' wedding anniversary. Looking at herself in the hand mirror Lauren held in front of her, Margie was likely picturing her old self, the raven-haired beauty who only needed pearls to make her look like a star.

Grady was ready for some action so he began his offering by unwinding the crepe paper. With help from his mother and Donald he quickly wound and hung the streamers until they were all used. Soon the bedroom looked like junior prom, the day after. The decorations hung low within Grady's reach, and he topped off the scene with a large original crayon drawing of Margie and him playing baseball. The caption was somewhat difficult to make out, but it seemed to say, GO MARGIE. Donald suspected he'd had help with the spelling.

Margie was, of course, delighted with anything that came from Grady. He was rewarded with a bear hug that threatened to squash him.

The drawing served as Donald's cue to bring out another Shopko sack and announce it was something for both his mother and her small friend. He added a statement to the effect that its contents were to be used *at a later time*. Lauren didn't smile at that part. She was probably thinking there'd be no later time, and he was mean for saying there would be.

The lady in pink laughed when she opened the sack of baseball caps and equipment. She promptly put on her cap and promised Grady it wouldn't be long until they could play some ball. Lauren seemed pleased with her positive attitude, warranted or not.

What was left of the morning was taken up by card games. Margie occupied her chair like a throne. The red cap served as her crown, the necklace sparkled like jewels, and her court sat around a card table in front of her. Lauren was subdued throughout the competitions. At 11:00, she excused herself to prepare their lunch.

Huge chef's salads with rolls were tasty but everyone seemed to be eating them half-heartedly, waiting for the cake. Donald knew it wouldn't be their usual two-layered Death-by-Chocolate, but he was interested to find out what Lauren would consider a healthy compromise.

When she entered with a tall red and white cake, her family burst into an off-key *Happy Birthday* and waited for their honored guest to use what they imagined would be her large supply of air to blow out the candles. Margie huffed and puffed and blew out five of the fifty-three. She seemed shocked at her failure.

"Don't worry about it, Margie," Lauren quickly interjected. "Your breathing is improving all the time. Next year you'll get them all on the first try." Donald wasn't the only one present who was pretending Margie had a future.

The still-fat woman kept blowing until all the flames were out. Donald made his own wish. He tried pinning his hopes on the words *next year*.

The relatively harmless angel food topped with fresh strawberries was tasty, but everyone prudently stopped after one piece. There would be another chance to have some at dinner. If no homicidal neighbors came to call before then.

❖❖❖

Since Lauren and Grady had done the cooking and decorating, Donald cleaned up when the party had wound down. By the time he finished, Margie and Grady were both starting to doze off so Lauren and Donald went onto the porch and left them to an undisturbed nap.

"I think her day has been really nice so far, don't you?" Lauren was trying to make conversation.

"Yes. Thanks to you. I've never been good at throwing parties. All I ever could think of was making sure she had all her favorite foods and movies. Not very original."

"Well, her options are limited. We were lucky Grady was around. And the pearls. Where did they come from?"

"I found them. They were a gift from my dad that had been lost for twenty years." That statement sounded more magical than "I found them in a pile of twenty-year-old dirt under the couch where she threw them after he left to live with his nurse."

"They were an anniversary present," he continued. I remember they made her really happy when she received them."

"That's lovely. And your timing couldn't have been better."

They stood in silence then, wondering where to go from there. Talk of the recent past was off-limits, and they had no future in common. "It's a nice day," Donald finally observed.

"Yes. What is Margie's favorite DVD?"

"Well . . . probably Sleepless in Seattle. It's an old one but she never gets tired of it."

"I don't have anything planned for this afternoon. Guess we can pull the drapes and watch that when everybody's awake."

"Grady won't like it."

"It isn't his birthday. He'll have to think of something else to do."

And Grady did. He planned to play out in the sun while the adults were hunkered down to watch a romance. He notified Margie he was going to try out the new bat and ball.

She didn't mind him using those gifts from Donald but had to offer her advice. "It's hard to be pitcher and batter at the same time."

"A bat can be a golf club, too," his tone of impatience said she should have known such a fact. "A bat can be lots of things."

"Have some fun, but whatever you do, don't talk to anyone unless it's Amelia. And don't go out of the yard." Lauren wasn't really worried. Grady was usually very obedient.

Lauren and Donald were pulled up close to the bed on either side of Margie. They were watching TV but also protecting the birthday lady. Nothing harmful would get close to her on this special occasion.

The miniature golfer had confiscated a spoon before he left for the course. That tool was useful for digging a hole in the front yard. It wasn't any bigger than it had to be, but his ball was, after all, baseball size. Then he began practicing his putting. Grady sometimes watched the golf channel and knew Tiger Woods started at around his age. He concentrated on improving his game.

"Hello," came a voice to his right. On the sidewalk was a lady dressed in white. Even her hair was almost white. But she carried a black purse. Grady remembered his mother's instructions and didn't respond.

"I know you're not deaf. It's okay to talk to me. I'm a nurse."

Grady had never been told that nurses were an exception to a mom's rules so he didn't say anything.

"Your mother said you go to preschool every day."

The lady knew his mother. Maybe she wasn't stranger-danger, after all. "I stayed home today."

"I see. I came to see Margie. She needs a flu shot."

Grady got flu shots but not in the summer. "It's not time yet."

"It is for those who're shut-in and who are at high risk. We like to get them taken care of before the fall rush of other people."

While she was talking, Grady was watching her. The white hair looked fake. If she were wearing a wig, she couldn't be trusted. That was one of his own rules. "Margie doesn't want a shot today. It's her birthday." He knew if the woman stuck her with a needle it would ruin their celebration. Margie might even cry.

"I'm sorry, but I don't take orders from kids. I'm going to do what I came here to do. You stay outside or you'll get a shot, too."

"Where's your needle? Maybe you aren't really a nurse." Grady had watched enough Scooby Doo to know that bad people sometimes wore disguises.

"I don't have to listen to your questions, but just so you'll leave me alone, here." She opened what he'd thought was a purse and showed him needles and vials. They looked very real. Nobody but a nurse would carry those things around.

"Come back tomorrow," was his suggestion.

"Donald will be home on Saturday. It has to be now. And I don't want you coming inside." She glared at him as she said it, and he peered at her eyes through her glasses. He could see they were green and cold. The evil eyes of the woman from their apartment.

"I know you! You're the lady that hates me."

She knew she'd been recognized, and she couldn't risk letting the child tell anyone. She made a grab for him. "Come home with me, and I'll give you some candy to bring back to Margie for her birthday."

Grady was too smart for her. He knew nice people didn't offer kids candy. He picked up his bat and started whacking her. "Go away, or I'll tell Don! And my mom!"

The nurse apparently saw she'd made a bad choice by challenging a child and turned to flee before some other neighbor witnessed the scene. Grady's continual bashing caused her to drop her equipment, but she kept on running toward her car in the driveway next door.

When Grady showed off the black case containing a full syringe, Lauren was aghast, and Donald's heart stopped. They listened with horror to the boy's description of the lady in white with the mean green eyes. Amber was still free and still trying. If she'd have come by on a day when Margie was alone in the house, Amber might have pulled off the masquerade. No telling what she'd intended to inject into his mom's veins. If she could have found them. Shots were never very successful in her fleshy arms. But maybe in her neck? And Margie probably wouldn't have fought a nurse. She'd have accepted the effort to prevent her from getting the flu. She'd have given permission for her own murder.

Amber was getting more aggressive and more careless. She was behaving like a hit woman in a hurry.

He stared at the black case that held the lethal needle. How did one dispose of a full hypodermic?

"Listen, fella, you have a potential weapon in your hands. That's evidence. You should probably hang on to it."

"Yes, it's evidence—of a crime I'm involved in. Who am I going to show it to?"

"I don't know. But if Amber someday tries to pin the whole thing on you, you could turn it over to the police. She probably left her fingerprints on it."

"I touched it, too."

"Just the same . . ."

Donald gave in and put the black case on the high cupboard shelf beside the contract. At least it was out of Grady's reach.

As usual, thoughts of the boy made Donald desperate. The assassins had twice directly endangered him. Amber and her goon were low-lifes even when compared to other killers.

He wondered if he could qualify for a large loan. Or talk his mom into borrowing on her life insurance policy. Somehow, he needed to acquire fifty-thousand dollars so he could pay Amber to abort the job.

33
MISERY MULTIPLIED

"Hello." Donald knew his phone-answering voice must sound frightened and apologetic. That was because every time he answered, he was anticipating the police or the outraged female voice of either Amber or Lauren.

This time the caller was male. "Hello, Donald. This is Pastor Guthrie. I've been thinking about you."

Uh-oh. What was the preacher thinking? He could be worried about some unknown person being in danger. Donald had hinted at that when they last talked. For the fiftieth time, he regretted ever going to the church.

"You don't have to worry. I think I've pretty well figured out answers to my problems. I'm actually back to sleeping all night. I don't even dream."

"I'm glad to hear it. But when we were talking the other day, I got the feeling you don't get a chance to let your feelings out very often. I understand how that is. Ministers confide in God, but not to many earthly people. Do you want to have another go at chatting? I'm pretty sure we could help each other."

"Donnie!" Margie called from her room. "Who's on the phone? Is it the telemarketer I talked to this morning?"

He put his hand over the receiver. "No, Mom. This call's for me. Somebody selling house siding."

"Don't buy any," was her quick response

Donald's mind was spinning. This felt like a trap. No preacher was going to "confide" in him, the most muddled man in town. There was an ulterior motive at work. He didn't know how to answer. "Uh . . ."

"Maybe I'm wrong, but keep in mind that I'm interested in your situation and not in judging or punishing you for anything you carry on your heart."

Whoa. Again, this guy sounded like he was reading Donald's thoughts.

"Maybe. If I don't change my mind, I'll stop by after work at three thirty." That was his tongue speaking without his permission. He really didn't want to go back to that place.

"Three thirty would be great. Oh, and Donald, why don't you come to the parsonage next door to the church. I think we might be more comfortable talking there."

Yikes. Was the guy a molester, inviting him into his lair? Donald had heard grim stories on the news about ministers, teachers, and so forth who preyed on unsuspecting young males. But he was sure he was physically stronger than Rev. Guthrie. And he guessed he wouldn't have to go all the way inside the house. "Okay. I'll be there."

In spite of his fleeting suspicions, it was nice to think perhaps he'd found an uninvolved person who wanted to help. He'd gotten the impression that maybe Pastor Guthrie was lonely himself. If the man had any choices, why would he call Donald Meester?

"Don't go spilling your guts to this man. It'd be just like you, Donnie."

"Why do you think that?"

"Because you've got so much built up inside you, and because you don't have much of a filter. You just plunge ahead and regret it later."

"Well, I think I've learned a few lessons this summer. The hard way. I don't trust everybody now."

"Good. Almost nobody deserves it. Go easy."

****

Donald had to call up all his nerve to walk onto the porch of the parsonage. He'd always held those houses somewhat in awe. Like the White House or the Hermitage. He never imagined that a guy from the neighborhood could just show up there. On the three-block walk, Donald had gone over instructions to himself.

"I won't mention red-haired women, hired killers or troublesome mothers. I'll just let the man keep guessing what's on my mind, but I won't actually contribute anything."

"Do you want help or don't you?"

"Getting arrested won't help."

He knocked timidly on the parsonage door. Sure enough, it was opened by the reverend. Today he was dressed in jeans and a t-shirt.

"Hi there, Donald. I was afraid you might decide not to come."

"Well, I probably shouldn't have, but . . ."

"Don't worry. I'm not going to grill you. Come on in. We have some lemonade—or tea."

"Lemonade sounds good." Guthrie had said *we*. For some reason Donald had thought he was single. He wondered if the missus was going to take part in the intervention. He currently had to answer to enough women. One more sounded like one too many.

Guthrie went into the kitchen, and Donald expected him to return with his wife, but he only brought back two full glasses.

"By the way, my first name is Bruce. Most of the people at church call me that, except for the older ones."

Donald realized his thinking was along the lines of the *older ones*. He didn't feel like he could ever refer to a preacher as Bruce. "Okay."

Bruce motioned for him to sit in an armchair. "How are things going for you and your mom? I want to visit her soon, but I'll call and let her know when I'm coming. She must miss getting out like she used to. I understand she was a regular attender and very active at Church of Hope."

Donald couldn't believe anyone had told him that. "It was a lifetime ago. I hardly remember it. She isn't the same person she was then." There it was. He was babbling, just like he swore he wouldn't.

Bruce smiled with supposed understanding. "Just because she's heavy, doesn't mean the old Margie isn't still in there."

"Being so fat changes you. It changes how you think." Now there was an idea Donald didn't recall coming up with before.

"I'm sure the weight has changed her life. And yours, too."

The pastor hadn't asked a question, but Donald felt compelled to comment. "Yes. I don't really *have* much of a life." He had to get out of that house. It was only a matter of time before he did just what his other self warned him about, spilled his guts. If he admitted how he felt about his mother's condition, Bruce Guthrie would remember those words when he heard Margaret Meester died suddenly. No more complaints.

"Donald, I know you think I don't understand how being your mom's caretaker affects your life, but I might have a clearer idea than you give me credit for."

Everybody always thought they knew. *Let them spend a week with her and her demands. Let them give up any dreams they might have had. Let mister "I know what it's like" find out how it would be to care for somebody who can do nothing for herself and will always need him in order to stay alive.*

Bruce stood up then and excused himself. Donald considered slipping out onto the porch. It was obvious the visit had been a mistake.

He was inching his way toward the front door when Bruce came back. This time he was pushing a wheelchair. In it was a woman who appeared very young, twenties maybe. She had the unnaturally still look of someone who was paralyzed. Her face had the waxy finish and fixed stare Donald had seen somewhere before. Then there was the breathing tube which told him with certainty the woman was not functioning on her own power. He was speechless.

216

"Donald, I'd like you to meet my wife Lana. She's the love of my life, and we've been together ten years. They haven't all been easy, especially for her. Lana, this is my new friend Donald Meester. He lives with his mother Margie. They have their share of problems, too."

The reverend probably talked a lot to make up for the fact his wife couldn't. Donald looked around the room, searching for the right words, words he'd had no chance to prepare ahead of time. Finally, he found his voice.

"I'm pleased to meet you, Lana." He held out his hand, but she could only give him a crooked smile. He put the hand down and shakily smiled back. He made himself look over at Bruce Guthrie. "I'm sorry."

"Nothing for you to be sorry about, Don. We had eight wonderful years. Then an accident changed our lives. I guess lots of people have burdens we don't know about."

Donald could just imagine how helpless the lady must be. Her husband obviously had to do everything for her, everything. At least Margie could feed herself and talk to people. "Er . . . uh ...does she have a nurse?"

"Not yet. We haven't been in Markison very long, and so far, I haven't run across any in-home help. Lana just has to be patient while I'm at the church."

"I can understand how that goes." Now who was presuming to understand something he couldn't? Donald was definitely ashamed for his earlier thoughts.

"I did run across a little encouragement the other day though. A woman saw Lana and me in line at the grocery store and struck up a conversation. She was very understanding, and said she would do her best to come up with a solution for us. She didn't say what kind of solution, but I'm willing to listen if she calls."

Alarms were going off in Donald's head. He tried to sound calm. "What was the woman's name? I've lived here all my life. Maybe I know her."

"To tell you the truth, I don't remember her first name. Amy or something like that. Her last name was McCall, I think. Long red hair."

Donald almost dropped his lemonade.

He didn't remember how he got out the door and away from the parsonage. Following the news about his former love, he was in a state of shock. Amber was subtly soliciting more business even while she was in the midst of fulfilling a contract on Margie. The whole situation spoke of greed and overconfidence. How did she expect to get by with creating so much mayhem in the little town of Markison? He knew the answer. She was counting on pitiful, good guys like himself and Bruce.

His first instinct had been to be silent regarding any knowledge of Amber. But that would make him almost an accessory if she made the same arrangements with Pastor Guthrie as she had with him. Donald was reasonably sure the reverend would never succumb to such a plan for his dear wife, but people would've said the same about Donald Meester whom they knew as a devoted son.

He stopped on the sidewalk in front of his house. His choice was clear. He called Bruce Guthrie. "This is Donald. I just got to thinking about the lady in the grocery store who offered to help you. I know all about her, and I know you can never talk to her. She's criminally insane and will ruin your life."

"Well, thanks for the heads up, Don, but she seemed perfectly normal to me. Are you sure we're talking about the same Ms. McCall?"

"Oh, I'm sure. There's only one like her. You just have to trust me on this." He prayed Rev. Guthrie wouldn't ask for any further explanation.

"Okay. I won't fall for anything she has to tell me. I doubt I'll ever hear from her anyway. I guess I'm just a little desperate at this point."

"That's what she's hoping."

34
STARTLED AT STARBUCKS

From an easy chair in her motel room, Lauren contemplated leaving town. She'd done what she'd come to do, even though recent revelations told her it would all be for nothing. She'd accumulated enough hours and enough data that she should be able to complete her paper on her own in the safety of an apartment in Iowa City. Soon it would be time for Grady to start kindergarten where he'd be occupied enough to forget the friends he left in Markison. Lauren knew that was wishful thinking, but whatever disappointment and heartache her son experienced, he'd be alive. Nothing was worth the risk of letting Grady suffer from Donald's disastrous plan. Even if he didn't get injured, her son might have to see what happened to his friend. They couldn't stay around for that.

"Mom, can we go see Margie? I want her to help me read *The Cat in the Hat.*"

"Maybe after the weekend, baby."

Grady persisted. "I don't think she's busy tonight. She's always at home."

"Yes, but we agreed I'd only visit her during the week. We'll go over Monday morning." In spite of the suffocation and hypodermic attempts, Lauren had the irrational belief that most murderers waited until dark to do their evil deeds, and tonight she just wanted to be safe with Grady in the motel. Donald could defend his own mother. After all, he'd caused the whole horrible situation in the first place.

Grady grinned knowingly. "You scared of the dark? You afraid of monsters, Mom?"

"Yes, honey. I guess I *am* afraid of some of them."

One of the monsters she feared most lived in her heart. Lauren was ashamed to admit to herself that she'd fallen in love. With Margie and with her son. Her awkward, unworldly son. The guy who'd appeared to have such a pure and unselfish affection for his mother he'd given up his own ambitions to take care of her. It wasn't a smart thing for him to do, but it was endearing. So different from other men she'd met in the last five years, Lauren had seen Don as being the most sincere person she'd known since Grady's father. How her judgment had deteriorated over the summer.

The plan for Monday was to go back to the Meester's to wind things up. She'd park her car in Amber's driveway and walk with Grady over to Margie's. After spending some quality goodbye time with her client, she'd go back to the Victorian house to get their things and load them into the trunk of the car. Hopefully, she wouldn't run into Amber or her companion. Even if she did, that wouldn't stop her from moving out. Her rent was paid ahead so no one should mind if she left the apartment vacant for them to rent to someone else. Hopefully, they would fix the broken step first. Amber should consider herself lucky Lauren was leaving town without suing for the apparent neglect that had caused Grady's accident on the stairs. That would call for an investigation, and she was quite sure Amber didn't want one of those.

Knowing Lauren and Grady were not going to be in town much longer, Donald would've loved to take the day or the rest of the week off, but his at-will employment didn't allow those kinds of perks. He was stuck at the library trying to work but finding he was mostly wandering around the reading room, already missing Lauren.

Sadie Harms must have noticed he was distracted and decided to give him a new task. "Donald, we're going to need some refreshments for the staff meeting this afternoon. Would you be kind enough to go to Starbucks and pick up some bakery items before they're all gone? Oh, and take your time."

Donald was relieved for the excuse to leave the building. The reading room had become a place of horror for him. All he could think of when he was there was the day he'd signed the contract. He desperately wished he could turn back the clock. If he had it to do over, he would never have approached Amber McCall. He'd never have asked Charles who she was. And Lauren and Grady wouldn't be leaving.

"Oh, and go ahead and add a coffee to the tab," Sadie added. "You look like you could use one."

He knew lack of sleep was going to be a permanent condition. There wouldn't be enough coffee in the world to repair the dark circles under his eyes when his mother was gone forever.

Starbucks didn't make him feel as miserable as when he was in the library, but it did bring back its own share of depressing memories. Donald got to go so few places, and now at least two of those had been tainted by the redheaded contract killer. Besides the library, he used to enjoy the coffee shop, and now its aromas spoke to him of coming disaster.

Without much interest, he selected an assortment of scones and other random pastries. Sometimes after past meetings, Sadie had sent leftovers with him for his mother. There'd be no need for that today so his order was small. Lauren wouldn't be around to protest, but he still didn't intend to return to old habits. He ordered a skinny latte for himself and looked for a small table where he could take a break in his usual solitude.

As he pulled out a chair, he glanced at the corner where he'd sat just a short month ago with the woman he'd adored. He blinked to be sure his eyes weren't playing tricks. But sure enough, there she was, Amber McCall, looking slightly bedraggled and talking intently to Rev. Bruce Guthrie.

Donald stood rigidly in the center of the shop, trying to decide whether to sit as he'd intended, to leave before Amber saw him, or to rush to the corner table and break up what he knew must be a murder-for-hire proposal. A mental picture of the lovely but helpless Lana Guthrie made the decision for him. He had to interrupt the plot to kill her.

As he walked toward them, the couple spotted him in unison. The green eyes were wide and fearful. Bruce Guthrie wore a guilty smile.

"Donald, good to see you!"

Amber said nothing. She was, no doubt, surprised her victims knew each other. Almost instantly, she switched her expression to indifference. She was looking at Donald as though he were someone she'd just met.

"Come sit," Bruce went on. "Ms. McCall and I just happened to run into each other here." He must feel the need to explain why he was doing just what Donald had begged him not to do. "She was just about to tell me her answer to my home care problem. Amber, why don't you explain it to Donald as well? He's dealing with similar circumstances."

Donald was speechless but hated to leave before he heard how Amber was going to handle this development. She looked distressed and trapped. It was good to be on the other end of those feelings.

The Red Widow, however, was accustomed to talking her way out of uncomfortable situations so didn't hesitate to explain.

"My solutions are unique for every case. And always a private matter."

"That's okay," Donald answered. "I need to be going anyway." He could've insisted on staying, and it might have kept her from approaching Bruce, but it had occurred to him he should get on home. If Amber was lining up more work, it probably meant she intended to finish the Margie job right away. *I'd better stay close to home. Every time I've taken a chance and left, there's been an attempt on Mom's life.*

"You have a good day, Donald. And don't worry." The pastor was probably just going to listen, out of curiosity, to what Amber had to say and would tell Donald later what he thought of it.

Sadie was in the meeting room when he returned. He delivered the requested pastries and asked if he could go to lunch right away.

"Sure. Go ahead, Don. Tell Margie hi from me. That isn't quite as fun as donuts, but I'm assuming you haven't gone back to giving her those."

"No, I haven't. And it's been awhile since she asked. It seems like her tastes are changing a little. At least I hope so."

"Well, good for her. Maybe I need to hire that woman to help *me* resist donuts. What'd you say her name is?"

"Lauren Hunt. But she's about ready to leave Markison. We'll be on our own soon."

"Hmm. That idea must be a little scary, huh?"

"Yes. It is, actually." *A lot of things in my life are scary.*

Donald had driven to work, so now he could make a quick getaway to go home. On the way, his other self insisted on telling him what to do.

"Well, Donnie, you know why Amber is back. Her man Gavin hasn't done his job, and she's going to get things moving herself."

"You don't know that. She looks tired. She might just need a rest after fighting her legal battles."

"She'll rest better when Margie is gone. You have to have a showdown with that woman."

"Right. Showdowns are just what I'm good at."

"Not a duel or anything. You have to stand up to her with words. Call her bluff."

"But she isn't bluffing. She's killed before."

"She can't stop you from warning the police."

Donald was afraid his other self was becoming less valuable as a confidante. The guy didn't really get it. Amber had her copy of the contract. The one he had signed.

"Sure she has the contract, but what did it actually say you were agreeing to? Not a killing. It specified only **services***. You might have thought you were signing an agreement for her to mow the yard for Margie. Or clean her house."*

Donald almost brought the car to a dead stop. Where did that revelation come from? It was correct! The contract hadn't spelled out anything. Amber had been so careful not to reveal too much, she hadn't revealed anything. So it was her word against his concerning the services.

"So?? Are you going to confront her?"

"She told me not to talk to her. She's probably furious already because I showed up at Starbucks and said a few words."

"Listen chum, Amber doesn't rule the world. What will she do if you talk to her? You could make an announcement on the radio, and she couldn't do a thing. With her reputation . . ."

"You mean I've been running scared all summer for nothing?"

"Well . . . Gavin was a very real threat, but I think he's out of the picture. The ball's in your court, my man."

Donald had never blindly believed his alter ego, but he desperately hoped the advice was right this time. It all seemed to make sense, but he might be missing something.

35

SILENT SPIDER

Lauren's car was in directly in front of Amber's house. She must have left it there so she could come do some packing after she finished at Margie's. He was eager to talk to her but not until he tried to put a scare into the Red Widow. If ever he needed to call on his inner Incredible Hulk, it was now.

As he approached the Victorian, he gave it an objective look. It was a very inviting house in spite of its owner. Lately, he'd dreamed of living there someday, but not with Amber. With Lauren and Grady. An impossible dream maybe, but one worth fighting for. Maybe even worth dying for.

A car turned in front of him and entered the driveway, pulling up close to the back door. It was Amber. She must have finished convincing Bruce to sign away his wife's life. Or maybe she had only primed him for later and left with an invitation to have lunch at her house. Complete with violin music and peach pie.

Still at the wheel of the Galaxy, Donald pulled ahead and parked in front of the entrance to Amber's drive so she couldn't get away. That action alone made him feel like an aggressor. He jumped out and slammed the car door to get her attention. Amber ignored him. She was struggling to get a large grocery sack out of her trunk, one hand still holding her Starbucks cup.

Donald was annoyed by her indifference. And you don't annoy the Hulk. He rushed up the drive ready to ambush the woman. "I need to talk to you. Now!"

She finally looked his way, her features showing a little shock, it seemed to Donald. She must be questioning the identity of the forceful man behind her. He looked like Donald Meester but didn't sound like him. For a moment, she was unable to respond. She set the grocery sack back inside the open trunk. Her green eyes shot daggers, daring him to come closer. Finally, she spoke, her voice revealing the strain and irritation brought on by a life of crime. "You want something?"

Before he lost his nerve, Donald blurted out his demands. "I can't take any more of this! I want out of the contract. I made a mistake. I don't want to kill my mother. I don't want to get rid of Lauren and Grady. And I don't want anything more to do with you."

He had given the speech with all the gusto he could manage. However, her sardonic smile told him Amber was not intimidated. She reached into the front seat of the car and took out her briefcase. "It's too late, sweetie. You signed your name." She patted the briefcase to emphasize the contract was still alive. "*You* signed her death warrant. And it's nonnegotiable." You're just tense because it's taking so long. Your mom is a difficult case because she's always in her bed. That doesn't leave many options that won't be blamed on you. But don't worry. I've been working on a foolproof plan. It will never be traced to us."

"You always think your plans are foolproof. And don't say *us*. I'm not part of this anymore. I'd rather go to jail than let you kill Mom. Anyway, that bogus contract would never hold up in court."

"Listen, Donald my clueless client, you know nothing about the law. I've had experience with these things. I know what works. You'll thank me someday."

Donald was on a roll. Almost hysterical with the thought of how naive he'd been, he vowed to keep at her. He took time to note that she'd aged since their last encounter. There were creases around her eyes he hadn't noticed before, and dark circles revealed recent events may not have gone well. Donald's courage increased when he saw how vulnerable she looked.

"You might want to know I was wrong about the insurance policy. My dad cancelled it before he died and didn't tell me." It was an idea that had come to him on his way from the library. Since money was Amber's motivation, all he had to do was remove that guarantee.

She managed to maintain her grasp on the groceries and still hold on to the briefcase and coffee. She was trying to appear unconcerned, like Donald was hardly worth a pause in her action. She made her way toward the back of the house, talking as she went. "Oh, Donnie, Donnie. You think I don't do my research, that I just took your word about the insurance? I looked into her policy before I made up the contract." She stopped, opened the screen door, and fumbled for the key in her purse. "Nice try, though. Now, enough of your crazy complaints. It's been a long day."

But Donald wasn't ready to end the conversation. It could be his last chance. Once he'd gotten up his nerve, there was no stopping him. "And you'd better stay away from Pastor Guthrie. I didn't sign anything that says I can't report I saw you in a deep conversation with him."

She hesitated just inside the door. "If you say anything, if you breathe one word to the police, you'll be sorry you were ever born!"

"I'm stronger than you are. And now you don't have your goon. He left. I suppose you know that. He must not be as dumb as he looks."

"Gavin goes on scouting trips. He'll be back." But her fingers holding the coffee cup began to quiver.

It was then Donald became sure Gavin was an important part of the killing duo. He might appear slow, but he was the muscle she needed. She'd be very limited on her own.

Donald was growing braver by the minute. "I saw him throw things into his van and slam the door. I don't think he meant to come back. He looked as fed up as I am."

"You're lying!" But he saw her realize there was still no sign of her friend, that the house was deserted. Donald had planted some uncertainty. Her eyes took in the presence of Lauren's car out front. "Your slut is here. He might have told her how long he'll be gone."

Before Donald could warn her, Amber scrambled through the basement entry to the stairs. He heard a high-pitched cry. And then silence. He stood still, knowing what must have happened. His uncharacteristic bravado deserted him. Much as he hated the threat posed by Amber, he'd have to help if she'd injured herself on the missing step. He doubted Gavin had taken time to replace it.

Donald cautiously stuck his head in the basement door and listened. Nothing. Holding his breath, he stepped forward on the landing and looked down. Amber lay at the bottom of the stairs, her fiery locks fanned around her head, which was bent at an odd angle. Groceries and papers were strewn around the area. Apparently, she'd fallen head first into the cement wall at the bottom. Donald had the presence of mind not to go racing to her aid. He went back outside and tried the cellar door meant to be a fire escape. It was unlocked, so he went down its six steps into the basement. From that direction, Amber's hair hid her face, but her stillness left no doubt in his mind he was looking at a dead body.

Donald became aware of someone behind him. He was going to be found standing over a deceased Amber McCall. He'd be blamed for the accident her own partner had caused.

"Don! Why are you here?" It was Lauren. Then she saw the body. "You didn't . . . did you?"

When his heartbeat slowed, Donald replied. "Amber must have stumbled over the missing step. I heard her scream."

Lauren gave him a skeptical look. He was sure she questioned his story. After all, why would he be here if he wasn't up to something?

Before he could explain further, he spotted a lone piece of paper that had fallen from Amber's open briefcase. He recognized the bold word **CONTRACT** and his own signature. Donald shot a quick glance at Lauren. She was staring at the same piece of paper. What would she think of him if he took it? Though he'd already judged it to be worthless, he certainly didn't want the police—or his mom—to know of its existence.

Lauren saw the question in his eyes. Her answer was to stoop down and pick up the contract. She folded it and put it in her tote.

"Are you going to call 911 this time?" she asked him. But Donald was already dialing.

"You'll have to explain why you were breaking and entering. And why you were visiting Amber McCall. Better get your alibi ready. Make it good."

"I shouldn't have to invent a story. I didn't hurt her."

"Tell it to the cops. Are you going to admit you knew about the missing step and who sawed it off?"

"I don't know. I need time to think."

The sirens coming down the street brought Donald undeserved feelings of guilt. He wisely held his tongue while the paramedics checked for signs of life in the victim. There were none. It was hard to know whether to feel sad or relieved. At first, he felt both, but then realized it was premature to be relieved.

The policeman who seemed to be in charge instructed Donald to come with him down to the station to give a statement. Lauren offered to come along since she'd also been on the scene early. Donald wondered if she was worried about him bungling his story. Even if he did, even if they arrested him, Amber was out of his life and everybody else was safe. He'd be the only casualty. "Why don't you go ahead and pick up Grady," he instructed her. "The police can let you know if they need any information from you." Donald knew his mother must be frantic hearing the sirens and not knowing where he was.

"I'll shred the contract," Lauren told him. Then she briefly laid a hand on his arm and walked toward her apartment.

36
TRUTH TELLING

During the short ride to the police station Donald had time to consult his inner voice.

"I don't know how much I should tell these guys. I'm sure to mess up and incriminate myself."

"You won't. Why should you? Just answer their questions. Don't offer any extra information. The simple truth is always safest. And in this case, the truth is that you did nothing to Amber."

"Right. I can't forget that. I just hope they don't ask me any trick questions."

"At this point, they don't care about tricking you. You're a witness, not a suspect."

His little pep talk buoyed Donald's spirits. Telling the truth should be reasonably easy. In a few minutes, he could be free.

Matters at the station moved more slowly than he'd have liked because, try as he might, he couldn't shake the feeling he'd been arrested. The scene matched the one in his mental picture of what would happen when his mother died in an unexplainable fashion. Except in the vision, he was wearing handcuffs.

Finally, a receptionist showed him to the detective's office for an "interview". Donald reminded himself they were in a small town precinct, and the people who worked there had very little experience with violent crime. Vandalism was as bad as things usually got in Markison.

Detective Barnes smiled and greeted him. "Hello, Donald. I'm sorry you had such a disturbing afternoon."

Donald simply nodded. That it was *disturbing* was a gross understatement not calling for a comment.

"We just have a few questions to give us a better idea of what happened to your neighbor, Amber McCall." Donald braced himself. The first one was a doozy. "How well did you know Miss McCall?'"

"Not real well. We'd talked a couple of times." It was the truth. Amelia Klink knew more about her than he did.

"How did you happen to be at her house today?"

"I was driving by and saw her trying to unload some stuff out of her car. I stopped to see if I could help carry anything. She said she didn't need help." *Not exactly true.*

"Did you talk about anything before she went inside?"

"Not really. She seemed tired and in a hurry."

Miraculously, the officer didn't pursue that line of questioning. "Why did Amber go in the basement door instead of the one into the kitchen?"

"I didn't ask her." *The truth. Incomplete, but not a lie.*

"Did you see her fall?"

"No, I was outside, starting to walk to my car."

"What made you go back and find her?"

"I heard her scream."

"What did you think could've caused her to do that?"

"I guess I thought first of a mouse." He had, actually.

"You went inside to help?"

"That's right." No extra information.

"Where was Amber when you first saw her?"

"At the bottom of the stairs, just like she was when the ambulance came."

"Did you check to see if she was breathing?"

"I didn't touch her, but I looked to see if her chest was moving. I had the impression she was . . . gone."

"The officers at the scene said a step had been sawed off. Were you aware of that?"

"No!" Donald managed to sound surprised. *A big lie.*

"There's no telling how long it had been that way. Maybe Amber had known but forgotten. She'd never mentioned any repairs she needed done on the house?"

"No."

"How was it you didn't stumble on the step like Amber did?" That sounded like an accusation.

"I figured something had tripped her, so I looked down and noticed the big space between the steps. I managed to get past it." He'd thought about trying that.

"The lady at the scene, was she with you?"

"No. She came right after the accident."

"Why was she there? And how did she know to come in the other basement entrance?"

Donald had to be careful. "She's been renting an apartment there. She usually uses the cellar door. Fewer steps, I guess."

"Well, I think that will do for now, Donald. I appreciate your help, and we'll let you know if we think of anything else. The detective didn't look like he was insincere when he said, "Hope the rest of your day is better.

The patrolman who drove him back to McKinley Street asked, "Do you want to be let off at your vehicle, or shall I take you home?"

"I'd better move my car. Anyway, my mom might have a coronary if she saw me getting out of a police car." He tried to smile.

"I hear ya! I know how that is. Mothers and wives." And the two men seemed to have become buddies.

Donald was grateful to live in Markison where the police expected a young man who cared for his mother to be innocent of any wrongdoing. Especially when the victim is known as the Red Widow. The law was probably not especially upset about her demise. They knew killers have enemies who sometimes give them what they deserve.

37
POIGNANT PARTINGS

To be on the safe side, Donald asked Lauren to meet him on the porch after supper before she and Grady left for the motel. He wanted to tell her what he'd said to the officer who asked about her part in the accident. They would need to keep their stories straight if the police decided to pursue an investigation.

Before he could give her the information, Lauren began talking. "Donald, I think you got lucky this afternoon. Amber saved you. Thanks to her evil schemes, she brought on her own punishment. 'If you live by the sword, you die by the sword.' Isn't that how it goes? Now nobody needs to know you and she were partners in crime."

If the lady with him on the porch had been anyone besides Lauren, he'd have been nervous. Being the only person who knew the truth, she was in a position to blackmail him. He knew she didn't think along those lines, but she probably should.

"That's fine for Amber," said Donald. "If she hadn't ordered you and Grady harmed, she'd probably be alive now. It's justice for sure. But what about me? Where's my punishment? I feel like I have some coming. I was worse than her. My own mother."

"I probably should tell Margie what you almost did. Living with your mom after she learned you'd hired a hit woman would be all the punishment you could stand. But I don't want to hurt her. Such news would be like stabbing her in the heart." Donald shuddered inwardly at her words.

"Thanks. I mean, I know it's Mom you're protecting, but thanks from me. I owe you so much."

There was silence for a minute while Lauren gave him the chance to say more. When nothing came, she said. "Grady and I are leaving town right away. I think you know how to handle Margie now if you'll just do it. Before too long, you'll get to find your own place. Then you'll only need to visit her, do some errands, and keep cheering her on."

"But there's no danger anymore. I was hoping you might change your mind and ..." Donald was struggling to express his feelings. He'd been so worried about his own skin he hadn't had a chance to go over the words he wanted to say to Lauren. "Uh...won't Grady be disappointed?"

"Oh, sure. But he'll get over it. I've told him we have to get him back for school. He's looking forward to that."

"I guess. As he gets older, he won't even remember mom and me." Donald could hardly speak. He'd been thinking of Grady as his future son, Margie's grandson.

"You have to understand. He's my whole world, and the things I've learned about you ... well, they aren't what I want for him."

Donald's voice cracked on, "I don't blame you."

A car pulling up out front saved the deteriorating conversation. It was Rev. Bruce Guthrie. He hopped out of the car and hurried up to the porch. Donald didn't know whether to be glad or frightened to see the preacher. Bruce may have guessed his secret after talking to Amber.

"I just have a minute, but felt like I had to tell you," he was speaking to Donald, "that I understand why the name Amber McCall makes you so upset."

"Did she . . . try to get you to do anything?"

"Oh, yes. I heard all I needed to. She could've saved her breath. I'm a man of God. I don't look at her solution as a solution at all. I can see why some people are tempted by the idea, though, if they're desperate and looking for a way out. And if they let her charms get to them, they could make an impulsive decision. One I'm sure they'd regret, probably even before the deed was done."

"Tell me about it." It was Donald, wondering how the young preacher was so much wiser than he was.

"No matter how helpless Lana gets, I love having her near me. I can talk to her, and she can hear. We always had such wonderful conversations. Now they're one-sided, but there're good moments when I see in her eyes she understands. She loves and trusts me. God will decide when she's had enough. Not me."

"I'm glad you didn't give in."

"Things'll turn out well for you, too, Don. I know it. And you're forgiven, you know, for anything you might have been ready to do. Now you need to forgive yourself." And Bruce shook Donald's hand. "If you ever need to talk, just stop by. I'm never far from home." He smiled sadly and walked back toward his car.

Lauren had been listening thoughtfully to the conversation she could only partially make sense of. "Don, I'm sorry. I should've been more –"

Suddenly a small voice from inside the front door shouted, "Batters up!" Grady was holding his fat plastic bat, and Margie was right behind with their small rubber ball. "We're tired of catch. We're gonna play baseball!"

Lauren and Donald cleared a path, and the heavy woman made her way to the edge of the porch. Grady, on the ground, was the pitcher. A natural lobber, he threw the ball to Margie, and she swung away, missing. Donald picked up the ball and threw it to Grady who hurled another one right down the pike. This time Margie hit it all the way to the front sidewalk. Everyone squealed. Then all eyes fell on a patrol car that had pulled up right beside the ball. The squealing stopped. Detective Barnes got out, picked up the ball, and strolled toward the porch.

Donald didn't see any handcuffs, but this visit couldn't be good. His first concern was whether Amelia next door would take care of his mom after they took him away.

The officer tossed the ball to Grady and grinned. "I was just on my way home. Thought I'd check on you folks and see if everybody's doing alright after the turmoil this afternoon."

Donald felt obliged to respond. "We're pretty good. I mean, we feel bad about Ms. McCall, but it's our last night together, so we're trying to have some fun."

"Good!" said Detective Barnes. "I was hoping you weren't worried about more questioning. The officers met just a little while ago and decided to rule the death an accident."

Margie and Grady were as puzzled as Donald by that announcement but recognized it to be good news, so they joined in the smiles and handshakes.

Amelia came scurrying over with Pretty Boy in her arms. "Is something wrong over here?" she asked eagerly.

"Don't worry, Ma'am. Everything's under control," answered Barnes on his way to the car.

❖❖❖❖

The baseball game was a short one. Margie was tired, and it was starting to get dark. Everybody adjourned to her bedroom where she voluntarily grabbed a bottle of water from the refrigerator and maneuvered into her chair, leaving the bed for later.

Donald was trying to digest the information that he was in the clear. Amber wouldn't be causing him any more anxiety, and he wouldn't be spending the rest of his life in prison. If only the situation with Lauren were to have such a happy ending.

Lauren and Grady stood in the middle of the room. With tears in her eyes, Lauren addressed the woman she'd spent the summer coaching. "Margie, Grady and I both love you and are so proud of you." At that, Grady walked over and stood by the recliner with his arm around his friend's neck. Lauren, too, gave Margie a hug. "I have a lot of work to do now compiling all you and I have learned these past weeks. And my big boy has to get back home because kindergarten starts for him on Monday." Margie smiled. Grady had been talking about school for weeks.

Lauren continued, "Iowa City isn't far away. I know you and Donald can handle things, and we'll pay you a visit next month. If you're resolved to keep doing what we've started, you'll be ready for a trip to the park by then! You can even get in the water."

Margie must have felt tricked. She'd known they'd be leaving, but this departure seemed quite abrupt. "I thought you wouldn't leave until I was on my feet more. What if I forget some of the things you've told me? What if I can't remember how many repetitions?"

"No fear, my dear. I am leaving two pages of reminders for you and Don along with my cell phone number. I'll answer day or night. She handed the sheets of notes to Margie, emphasizing that the responsibility for carrying out the program was in her hands rather than Don's.

"I hope I don't let you down. I'm kind of weak when it comes to things like New Year's resolutions and such." Margie was already losing her confidence.

"Oh, come on! You're the strongest person we know. Right, Grady?" Grady gave Margie a high five. Lauren continued firmly, "You can do anything you set your mind to. Do you remember some of your affirmations?"

Margie looked Lauren in the eyes and uttered in a soft shaky voice, "I am slim and quick."

Lauren giggled at the large lady's faltering belief in herself. "Louder now. I want to be able to hear you in Iowa City."

"I am slim and quick!" and Lauren was favored with a big smile. "I see it!" the fat woman continued, her dark eyes shining. "I see myself rushing out to greet you when you come here."

"Me, too, Margie. Me, too!"

"I'll need a smaller dress."

"When you do, just say the word."

"Maybe not pink."

"It can be purple horizontal stripes if you want, my dear lady. Now, remember, you won't be losing weight to please me or Grady. You have to do it for yourself and for Don. You'll have to cooperate with him because he's a busy guy and could get burned out. And we need to work on him to go out more!" The tears were starting again, so Lauren took Grady by the hand and went out of the house.

Margie got up and slowly made her way to the front door. Donald followed. Lauren hadn't told him a personal good-bye or given him a hug. She hadn't even met his eyes. As he watched her go down the sidewalk, his heart screamed at him to follow her.

"Man, you're a doofus!" his inner self was shouting. *"You think you've changed, but you don't act it. The old Donald would've done just what you're doing now. Nothing."*

Grady's mom had opened the car door for him and was helping with his seat belt. Donald made his way past Margie and, in four long steps, reached Lauren beside the Tempo. There was an awkward moment while they stood looking at each other. Then Donald decided to go for broke. He threw his arms around her, and she embraced him back.

In the front doorway, Margie was clapping. Inside the car, Grady was clapping. Next door, Amelia Klink was clapping. So just to make everybody happy, Donald gave his friend a very quick kiss on the lips. You had to be paying attention to catch it, but his closest observers did. And Lauren didn't seem to mind. She looked straight into his eyes when she said, "Take care of yourself, Don. See you soon." Donald took that to mean he mattered to her again. That could refer to something romantic – or not. But he suddenly had hope. It felt to him like more of a beginning than an end. And he refused to discuss it with his negative self.

If anyone had been in the back yard at that moment, they'd have seen a white van pulling into the drive of the nearby Victorian. A strongly-built man got out and put a hand up to shade his eyes. He was smoking a cigarette and looking across the yard at the Meester house. Further observation would've revealed the story wasn't over. Gavin got into the back of his van and pulled out what appeared to be a wire.

38
WORTH THE WEIGHT

Satisfied her son and Lauren were having an important conversation out by the street, Margie shut the front door on the August heat and lumbered back inside her air conditioned house. Standing in place had been hard for her, and she could tell no one in the front yard needed her just then. Amelia Klink was, no doubt, quizzing her son about his relationship with Lauren. Whatever his answers, Margie was finding herself agreeable. *If Donnie thinks he has to kiss some woman, then I'm glad he picked Lauren.*

The recent emotional activity had drained the large woman's energy and, in fact, brought on a ravenous bout of hunger. She walked into the kitchen and looked around for something to renew her strength. The refrigerator loomed to her left. She hated to face it these days since Lauren had plastered on the door a photo she'd taken of her notorious trek down the front sidewalk. Margie had been so proud that day, but seeing the reality of her size captured for everyone to remember was the best deterrent Lauren could've found for keeping her away from the fridge. *That girl knows me so well.*

Much as she already missed her friends, Margie did feel a certain amount of freedom. With them gone she wouldn't be found out if she were to cheat just a little. No one would know if she helped herself to something forbidden just this once. After all, she'd been good for a long time. But there were no candy bars or chips in sight, and she had to admit she wasn't even craving those things. A bunch of bananas on the counter appeared to be at just the right stage of ripeness, so she helped herself to the biggest one. After peeling the whole thing, she stood gazing out the window, peel in one hand, fruit in the other. Margie was as content as she once had been holding an ice cream bar.

When she started to take a bite, she heard footsteps on the back porch. *Grady must be coming to see me one more time!* She moved as quickly as she was able, but the door opened before she got to it. In front of her stood a tall man with a scowl on his face and a piece of wire in his hands. Margie had the feeling she'd seen him before, but couldn't remember when.

"Move it, lady," he growled and tried to force her backward into the room. She struggled to stay standing.

"D-Donnie is outside," she stammered, sure this rude man wasn't there to see her.

"Are you alone in here?" he asked in a harsh whisper.

For some reason, Margie chose to tell the truth. "Yes," she squeaked. She silently cursed her weight. Because of it, she couldn't run, even though her instincts were ordering her to get away from the uninvited visitor. Her family and friends were in the front yard, but they might as well have been in the next town when it came to her chances for rescue.

"Get your fat butt outta the way so I can get in and finish what I started."

What did he want to *finish* inside her house? Donald hadn't hired anyone for repair work in a long time. One thing she did know was that any man who'd talk to a lady that way wasn't a person she wanted around. She stood her ground hoping to use her body as a barricade.

"You should be dead by now. Didn't you take any of those diet pills on the window sill? I fixed them good. Just one should've done the job."

"I . . . I don't take medicine." Margie said timidly. She didn't even recall having such pills and was a little insulted the man thought she did.

"Whatever. I've fooled around long enough. Your idiot son thinks that because my boss is dead, the deal must be off. I think different." And he muscled his way past her, his eyes sweeping the room.

"W-what deal?" Margie grabbed onto the counter for support. She was sure now. The man thought she was somebody else.

"I've got money coming to me, at least for all my time. I ain't going to walk away with nothing. I'll deliver the service all by myself, and that fool Donnie will fork over the money or be sorry. Your time is up now, lard ass!"

Margie tried to call for help, but no sound came out of her mouth. If only she'd picked up a knife along with the banana.

"It'll be easier if you don't fight it." He stepped closer, facing her and held up the length of thin wire. Even Margie could figure out his intention. She backed against the sink. She'd watched crime shows and knew the man needed to be behind her to use the wire. Let him try to move her five-hundred-pound body.

The woman's firm stance angered the goon, and he let out a string of expletives that made her more determined than ever to hold him off until help showed up. He apparently decided to approach her head on, putting sufficient pressure on her fleshy chin to cut off her air supply. He wasn't strong enough to move her away from the sink, but he could shove a wire into her throat with force. *What will Donnie do without me? He'll be all alone, and he'll blame himself. This man might even kill him.* Concern for her son was enough to bring out the fight in Margie.

Still unconsciously holding onto the banana, she batted at him causing enough confusion that the wire fell from his hands, and he had to bend down to pick it up.

Margie used the spare second before he stood to grab her own neck for protection and, in the process, dropped both the skin and the fruit of the banana. The intruder lunged at her and promptly slipped on the peel. His legs went out from under him, and he hit the floor hard. The instant he went down, Margie saw her chance. She intended to escape to her room. The man's arm was in the way, so she attempted to dodge it. Her size did not allow Margie to dodge. The instant she tried, she lost her balance and went down, her huge bottom landing squarely on her attacker's head and shoulders.

Sitting with her legs stretched out in front of her, the fat woman was happy to be alive. It had been a close call, but she had come out on top. She could feel squirming and hear noises from beneath her but, even if she'd wanted to, she couldn't have gotten up.

"Donnie!" she meant to scream, but trauma had closed off her vocal chords. She tried again and again. Eventually, the noises under her stopped, and Margie gave up her attempts to be heard. She remained where she was and waited. After a while she was able to convince herself the lumpy thing she sat on was a bunched up rug.

Refusing to panic, Margie passed the remaining minutes breathing in and . . . out. *All is . . . well. All is . . . well.*

She was close to dozing off when Donald came bursting through the front door. "Did you see, Mom?" he hollered from the front room. "Lauren let me kiss her!"

Knowing her son had arrived gave Margie back her power of speech. "Donnie! Get me up!" she shouted.

Donald made a quick dash for the kitchen and was aghast at the sight of his mother looking up at him. He could see what appeared to be a male torso and legs protruding from under her back side.

"Mom! Are you alright?" Donald dropped to the floor and gave her a big hug before he called 911 for the second time in a week. He specified they send their strongest officers.

When the police and paramedics arrived, they managed to pull Margie to her feet and make her comfortable before doing any questioning. They had little trouble piecing together the scene. After listening to the woman's disjointed description of the incident, the officers reported that an intruder with a crude weapon had had the misfortune to be suffocated by the weighty Mrs. Meester. Evidence showed the man had inadvertently brought about his own death. Donald had nothing to add. He still subscribed to the practice of not offering unsolicited information. And he was busy kicking himself for not anticipating the goon's return.

When asked if she had any idea who the man was or what he was after, Margie replied in all honesty, "I don't know his name. Somebody must have told him I was rich. He said something about wanting money, but I didn't even have any cash to give him."

"The guy must have been pretty desperate to try to rob you in the middle of the afternoon. Probably needed drug money and thought you'd be an easy target. You're a lucky lady."

Margie gave the officer a knowing smile. "Oh, yes. I'm lucky I'm still pleasantly plump."

ACKNOWLEDGMENTS

Thanks so much to those who encouraged me while I was writing Worth the Weight. My daughter Heather Wiges was first to know and critique the plot. Greg Holt, Jayne McKinley, Roseanne Foster, Sandy Fulcher, Lee Wiges, and Jayne Draper offered further feedback. Kristi Paxton and Robyn Mulder did proof reading. Those good folks confirmed what I've always believed. Two eyes and one brain are not enough to bring a story to life.

ABOUT THE AUTHOR

WORTH THE WEIGHT is Linda Wiges's second novel. Her debut was the successful HAPPY DREAMS, currently available on Amazon.com and Goodreads.com, plus at area libraries.

Previous creative writing experience includes full-length stage plays such as *Stressed to Kill* and *Best Seats in the House*. She's directed both locally.

Linda lives in Traer, Iowa with her husband. After careers as a high school English teacher and as an office professional at the University of Northern Iowa, she's been enjoying this new way of using her writing skills.

You may contact her at linda.wiges@hotmail.com or on Facebook: Linda Wiges Author.